CATASTROPHE THEORY

A NOVEL

REBECCA LOWRY WARCHUT

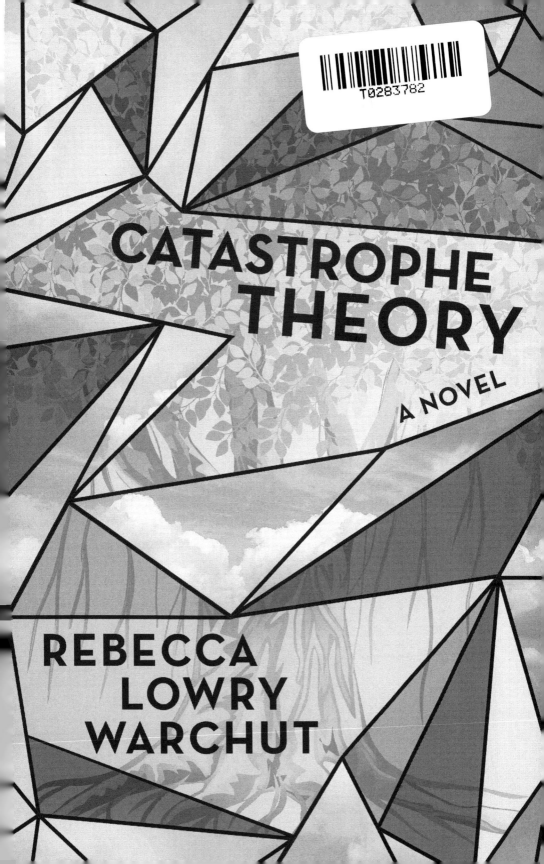

CATASTROPHE THEORY

REBECCA
LOWRY
WARCHUT

woodhall press
Woodhall Press
Norwalk, CT

woodhall press

Woodhall Press, 81 Old Saugatuck Road, Norwalk, CT 06855
WoodhallPress.com

Cover design: Jessica Dionne Wright
Layout artist: Amie McCracken

Library of Congress Cataloging-in-Publication Data available

ISBN 978-1-954907-40-9 (paper: alk paper)
ISBN 978-1-954907-41-6 (electronic)

First Edition
Distributed by Independent Publishers Group
(800) 888-4741

Printed in the United States of America

To Lowry and Athena,
may you never be afraid to rewrite your stories,
reinvent yourself, and rise anew

PART I: RAIN BANDS
OCTOBER 10TH

CHAPTER 1

VERA

Vera clung to her mom's hand to the left and the armrest to the right. Vera hated the descent. Her ears kept popping, her head dizzying. Since she'd been diagnosed, trying to stand on flat ground, much less hurtling through space in a metal tube, was disorienting. Her mom made them whisper three Hail Marys when the flight took off, a travel tradition Nana and Pops had insisted upon, but it didn't make Vera feel any better. She even doubted her mom believed it. At least she couldn't see if anyone was giving them strange looks. There was an upside to going blind.

They repeated this ritual not once, but twice. Eliza didn't talk about money much, at least not to Vera, but Vera had overheard her telling a friend that flying direct was too expensive. Her mom had said that even though she hated connecting flights, with the medical expenses piling up and no clear end in sight, they'd have to sacrifice when they could. So, Vera didn't complain.

Even though flying was quicker than driving, if Vera had stopped to consider what was actually happening, she would have a full-on panic attack. She was much more comfortable on the ground, cleats digging into freshly mowed grass as she raced to intercept a pass and charge toward the goal. She'd never flown before today, at least not that she remembered, not since she was a baby. Just when she was sure they were all going to die, the plane skidded to a stop. A small crowd let out a collective cheer speckled with a few amens, while Vera relaxed her vice-grips. I'm not dead yet, she thought.

A scratchy voice over the intercom announced: "Welcome to Tampa/St. Pete. The local time is 9:43 p.m. We should be taxiing to the gate soon."

"Hungry?" Eliza asked. Nowadays, her mother was always checking on her, worried she'd eaten too much, too little, or the wrong things. Vera shook her head no, but she lied. More than anything, she was ready to be out of this plane, standing on firm ground—or, even better, asleep in her own bed. Sleeping had been difficult. Her mom kept finding new ideas online, from melatonin to white noise to a bedtime routine—whatever that meant—for Vera to try, but Vera's restlessness continued. She would never admit that even at 17, most nights, she'd pull out Senyor Conill, her beloved stuffed rabbit she'd had as long as she could remember, to help her fall asleep. What would she do when she finally left for college? What would her future roommate think?

"We'll explore St. Pete tomorrow… I'm beat," Eliza said.

"Have you been here before, Mom?" Vera asked.

"No. I've been dying to check out the Dalí museum here. I've only been to the one in Figueres."

Her mother had studied abroad in Spain, savoring the architecture of Gaudi and embracing the Catalan culture. Vera only knew that because of the pictures in their bathroom, one of the gravity-defying human tower and another of the plans for Gaudi's still not-yet-finished Sagrada Familia. As far as Vera knew, those pictures were the only souvenirs her mother brought back from Barcelona. Besides Senyor Conill. And her, of course.

"They're opening a new exhibit, the Dalítorium," the man sitting next to them offered.

How long had he been listening to them, Vera wondered?

"I live in downtown St. Pete, and my phone is blowing up with posts about it. Cutting edge, they say."

"Thanks for letting us know. We'll have to check it out." Sensing Vera's uneasiness, her mother ended the conversation in a decidedly southern way: "Take care, now."

The plane must have finished taxiing, as Vera's body jolted forward and then back. She heard the rustling frenzy of passengers shuffling and gathering of belongings. Her mother patted her shoulder, signaling it was their time to move. Vera stood and reached towards where she thought the next chair back would be, grabbing something soft and lumpy instead.

"Excuse you!" a voice ahead of her crackled.

Vera said nothing. Her normally dynamic, toned limbs betrayed her.

"After practically assaulting me, the least you can do is get my bag."

"Your bag?" Vera asked, in the general direction she was heading.

"If you took off those silly sunglasses, you could see it."

Vera froze, uncomfortable in the body she usually trusted, unsure of what to do next. None of her instincts on the soccer field could help her now. This was not her game.

"Well?" the woman snapped. "Teens today… Sunglasses inside… No respect," she muttered under her breath.

As Vera stood paralyzed, Eliza went into mother-bear mode. "She's lost her vision. She can't help you."

"Oh, I'm so sorry," the woman was quick to apologize. "Bless her heart."

What Vera hated the most was the pity. Her mother grabbed Vera's arm and practically dragged her off the plane. Even though they couldn't move as fast as they used to, Vera couldn't get to fresh air and firm ground fast enough.

CHAPTER 2
LUCIA

Lucia grasped the cool metal railing and looked out through triangular prisms of light across Tampa Bay and then down at the growing crowds outside the entrance. Soon, the doors would open: one to patrons flooding to see the new exhibit at the Dalítorium and the other to her promotion.

"Ready?"

Shaken out of her reverie, Lucia spun around to see Nick standing there, his square jawline and broad shoulders so much like his father's.

"Everything set?" she asked him.

"We've checked. Three times," Nick said.

"Security in place?"

"Of course."

"The cellist?"

"Warm."

She originally hired a string quartet, but changed her mind. Hearing him mattered too much. But she couldn't cancel the cellist. Something about the cello's F-Holes, so prominent in Dalí's final works. "The sparkling?"

"Being popped as we speak..." Nick confirmed.

"The bathrooms. They have toilet paper?"

"Lucia..."

She took a deep breath. She reached toward him, grabbing his tie by the knot, tightening it. "There." Nick had been at her side for the past two years. If anyone knew how important tonight was, it was Nick. "Open the doors. Let Lazarus rise."

With her command, Nick turned, radioed security, and headed down the spiral double helix staircase—the life-giving force of the building—towards the lobby.

Instead of standing at the entrance, as she did for other events, she followed Nick, stopping halfway down the staircase to observe from afar. This was Director Harold Dodding's night. He would greet the masses and schmooze with donors. When people gushed—if they gushed—the director would take credit.

It might not be her resurrection, but it was her professional rebirth. She'd not only thought of the idea and pitched it, but also worked closely with the media tech company throughout the process, combing through countless hours of footage and weighing in on expressions of authenticity.

The swarm, swathed in their most eccentric and surreal, procured just for today, descended upon the Dalítorium, fanning out to be the first to talk to their collective muse. A familiar face, with bulging eyes, bushy brows, a formal suit outfitted with paisley accouterments, announced to the masses, "*Greetings, I am Salvador Domingo Felipe Jacinto Dalí i Domènech, and I am back.*"

Through the power of Artificial Intelligence and deepfake technology, they had brought Dalí to life again. *The Lazarus Project,* she aptly named it. Now, fans clamored to meet him first. Lucia silently judged those who stopped in the gift shop, vying to be the first to snap and post a selfie with the artist, even though she was glad the publicity stunt was working. The limelight-seeking Dalí would have approved. She approved of those who moved deeper into the museum's bowels, likely toward their favorite exhibits, hoping to find him and his insight there.

From her perch, she could see not only the lobby Dalí, but also two other virtual Dalís. With thirty-three Deepfake Dalís in total, thanks to *The Lazarus Project*, Dalí lived—if not breathed—again. As the Dalí selfie line grew longer, Lucia took pleasure in overhearing a closer Dalí.

He stroked his gravity-defying, pencil-thin mustache sticking up in perfect handle-bar curves and mused, "*I have a long-standing relationship with death, almost thirty years. I have always believed the desire to survive and the fear of death were…*"

"Lucia, there you are!" Andre interrupted, handing her a flute of something bubbly, "You should be so proud. I haven't seen energy like this here since the museum was first built! How could you not get the job?"

Taking the crystal glass, she countered, "They're vetting external candidates from Spain, New York, the MOMA."

Andre raised a bristly eyebrow. "I'm on your team, babe. You did this. And only you know the proposed expansion inside and out."

She'd told him not to call her babe, but she let it slide. "I know. But I can't think about it tonight." It was all she thought about. "Go mingle. You've got an election in November." Even though they had been together for a few years now, she wanted to be alone. This was her moment, not theirs, and she didn't want silly chatter to distract her from her first priority, seeing her audiences' delight. Their praise and reviews would be her professional litmus test. She did not watch Andre go, but waited before wandering, seeing her future in a new light.

She paused when hearing Dalí, "*I do not believe in my death. Do you?*" There had been times in her life when she felt like dying, like she could have died, but today, this overcast evening in early October, was not that day. She checked her phone. The social media likes for The Dalítorium had hit an all-time high, and the number of people who posted and shared Salvador selfies continued to climb. Harold had also texted: The board wanted to see her Monday afternoon.

CHAPTER 3

ELIZA

When Eliza and Vera finally got to the Ronald McDonald House, they were both exhausted. They'd agreed to call it their hotel to have less stigma, to feel more normal, but Eliza slipped up from time to time. When she did, Vera was quick to correct her. After Eliza checked them in, she led Vera to their room.

"Where am I sleeping?" Vera asked, stifling a yawn.

"Here," her mother said, leading her to the king. "They were out of doubles."

"Like old times... when Nana and Pops were around, and we slept in your old room." Mentioning Nana and Pops took them both back to happier memories; warm kitchens filled with baking gingersnaps or simmering tomato sauce. The little bungalow Eliza grew up in was overflowing with both stuff and love. When Eliza had brought Vera home from Spain, ending her college career early, her parents had not judged or asked questions. Instead, they'd fully embraced Vera, and she'd given them a new lease on life.

After they both died, Vera got her own room and a little more privacy. Eliza had slowly changed some things, like replacing the ivy wallpaper in the kitchen with bright yellow paint and donating her parents' clothes to their church, but other things she couldn't part with. After so much change, if keeping the eclectic Wade miniature collection from Pops' beloved Red Rose tea on the windowsill made them smile, the better for them both. Unbeknownst to her daughter, Eliza had brought one—a turquoise seagull—along with her. A talisman to protect her through what was to come.

Eliza found Vera's pajamas and Senyor Conill and handed both to her.

As Vera changed, Eliza asked her, "Big spoon or little?"

"Little," Vera said, rolling to her side and pressing herself into her mom's warm embrace. Eliza found it funny when they had to share a bed and Vera wanted to be the little spoon, since she was four inches taller. When Vera had asked her about it, Eliza just said Vera's dad had been tall. Eliza's parents were even shorter than Eliza, and Nana shrank a centimeter or two each year before she died. Nana used to joke she would be too short to go on the carney rides with Vera anymore and would instead have to watch Vera have all the fun, especially on the Flying Swings ride, their favorite. Even though Nana hadn't been on the Flying Swings since Vera was seven, Vera and Eliza both laughed instead of correcting Nana. Until the day she died, no one corrected Nana.

"Besides, Mom, I'll only be here for a night or two. Then, you can have the whole bed to yourself. I'll be stuck in the hospital."

"Don't say that, Vera." Eliza was hoping for a few moments when they could be together like they were before. Before the tumor.

"Why not, Mom? It's the truth..."

Eliza sighed. There was no going back to before. There was only this moment, and the next, and whatever came after that. "You'll only be there as long as you need to, and I'll be there every day, as much as they'll let me. And then we'll go home."

"Mom?"

"Yes?"

Vera paused.

"What is it, Vera?" Eliza asked her, stroking her cheek, gently pulling a strand of Vera's maple hair out of her mouth, tucking it behind her ear. "Try not to chew on your hair, honey." Vera had quit that bad habit years ago, and it troubled Eliza to see her doing it again. At least they wouldn't need to shave Vera's head and could operate endoscopically. Vera loved her cascading hair almost as much as her mother did. They'd made a pact years ago that as long as Vera let her mom brush it, and later as long as Vera kept it brushed, Vera could keep it long. Double French braids for games. Vera could do them herself now, as that was one of the few things that didn't require eyesight, but who needed braids when Vera couldn't see the ball?

They hadn't really talked about how Vera was feeling about the surgery. She must be terrified. Eliza was. Eliza didn't talk about it because then she'd have to face her own fears. What if Vera didn't make it?

"I… It's just… I love you." Vera shrugged away from Eliza.

"You too, pumpkin…" Eliza tried to hold her close, and at first, Vera resisted, but then she relaxed, drifting off to sleep.

Eliza had thought those first few months had been hard, pacing the floors, searching for some elusive key to calm and soothe her colicky babe. She could eventually get Vera to sleep, but only when Eliza curled up in a protective C around baby Vera. Dishes and dirt piled up. Even when Vera finally started sleeping in her own bed, she would eventually end up back in Eliza's.

Hearing Vera's heavy, rhythmic breathing but unable to go to sleep herself, Eliza turned on the TV. The words "Hurricane Phoenix, Category 1…" flashed across the screen. She tried to change the channel, but the remote control wasn't working. The weatherman pointed to the map. "This major hurricane in the Caribbean is three and a half to four days out and that's bad news." It cross-faded to an ominous projection: "This could be the big one." Eliza turned it off. They had enough to worry about.

Still unable to sleep, Eliza escaped to a future fantasy, imagining all the whimsical creations the new Dalí exhibit might hold. Of course, she wanted to see the exhibits, but more than that, she wanted to see the building itself. Ever since she'd read about I. M. Pei's protegee, Yann Weymouth, winning the design competition with his tessellations of glass hugging a concrete cube, she had to see it. She couldn't think about this Dalí museum without being transported back to the museum in Figueres, adorned with golden eggs.

So much, including Vera, had started in Figueres. If Eliza knew how much studying abroad would have changed her life, would she have gone? That was a foolish question. She'd worked so hard to get out of her small town, refusing to date anyone from home, working two jobs to save up for college, making sure she was at the top of her class, acing the SATs, just so she could get a scholarship. Wake Forest was not as far away as she'd hoped to go, but they gave her the most money, and it made her feel closer to her brother. She dreamed of ambling through the center of town, searching for a kalimotxo and tapas, Jamon Iberico, if she was lucky, with Vera's father on her arm.

CHAPTER 4

LUCIA

"The gala couldn't have gone any better," Andre praised, as he and Lucia clinked glasses of Gran Reserva he bought for this occasion.

"Did you see Nick work the crowd? He was such a help, Andre."

"Glad you could put that boy to some use. I'm ready to get him off my sofa and back to school."

"He'll be ready soon." Not too soon, I hope, she thought. "The buzz has been great," she said, changing the subject.

"People gushed, and I passed out over a hundred fliers."

Lucia raised an eyebrow but stopped herself from saying something, lest it ruin her night. This was not another campaign opportunity but her piece de resistance. Up for re-election as Deputy Mayor, he might have been included in the reception list without her, but he'd been there as her plus one.

"It's not like that, Lu. It's just. We're doing it. Remember when I told you I wanted enough going on downtown that anyone could just show up and know they'd find something great? You're doing that. You're making things happen."

Dagny protectively curled in a figure eight around her legs. "Oh Dags, I've been ignoring you," Lucia apologized, picking up the tabby she rescued when she moved to St. Pete. Getting a pet hadn't been her idea, but she came to love the company, especially before she met Andre.

As she cradled and caressed her cat, Andre turned on the TV. The Weather Channel. Practically the only thing she ever watched. The words

"Hurricane Phoenix, Category 1 . . ." flashed across the screen. The possible projected paths, marked by a bright yellow, curved funnel, covered almost all of Florida's Gulf Coast. Andre flipped to Sports Center.

"I was watching that," Lucia protested.

"It's October in Florida. Tropical storms are always brewing. But the Rays possibly blowing their postseason chances? That's the real catastrophe."

Her phone buzzed, interrupting them and spooking Dagny. Lucia looked at the caller. Harold. "I need to take this," she told Andre, balancing her wine and the phone, heading out to the balcony overlooking the gulf. Lucia knew what she wanted. She'd created her own algorithm before shopping for apartments: a balcony overlooking the gulf on the third floor or higher—above the flood zone—topped her list. The breeze cut through the humidity, and from here, she could see the glittering lights of both St. Pete and Tampa, across the bay. She held her breath, letting it ring one more time before answering.

"Lucia," Harold said, "Tonight will turn us around. The board is raving."

"Everything went as planned," Lucia agreed. "Better, even."

"Dalí would have loved every minute of it: the publicity, the technology, the immortality. And you brought him to life."

Her heart raced with excitement, but since 'Collaborative visionary' topped the list of descriptors the board was looking for in the next director, she deflected. "My team did."

"You did." Because he usually took credit for any success the museum had, this surprised her. Perhaps he was getting nostalgic with retirement around the corner. Perhaps he wanted to see her as the museum's next mantle-bearer.

"Thank you." She took the praise. She'd worked hard enough to make this happen. She'd almost lost her last promotion for not being likable enough. That's what she'd overheard the head of HR saying after he thought she was out of earshot. "But is she likable enough?" She broke half a dozen different china plates that night, using the fragments to create a Gaudi-inspired mosaic for her patio.

"And the next director? The person to oversee the expansion? The board basically counted you out already, but after tonight, I told them to add you to the shortlist. You'll have to prove it to them, though."

She exhaled, relieved.

"It's still a long shot, Lucia. Prep the pitch of your life," he said.

Before she could say, "Goodnight," he hung up. She knew her sacrifices, the days inventorying in the city, the after-hour events, the life she had given up, could still be worth it. She chose not to linger on knowing she'd almost been passed over again and instead tilted the glass back, salty air pricking her face, born anew. Andre came outside to find her.

"Good news?" Andre asked, setting his now-empty glass on her table, wrapping his arms around her waist, and kissing the back of her neck. When she wore heels, which was almost always, she towered over him.

"No news yet," she lied, "but the turnout was better than expected and this week's ticket sales have doubled." While he talked about a shift in campaign strategy, her mind drifted to everything she wanted to do tomorrow to prepare for the final round of interviews, conceiving other ways technology could enhance the Dalítorium's profile in the art world, strengthening their expansion plans for the city. When he mentioned St. Pete Rising, his revitalization campaign to drive both tourists and locals downtown, her ears perked up. She liked to be able to weave his language about revitalization into her expansion plans.

When the proposed Dalítorium expansion was approved, they could do even more special exhibits like the miniatures—collection of tiny, little-known paintings by Dalí himself. Shit. They were supposed to have shipped out yesterday. With the gala, the expansion, and the possible promotion, it had slipped her mind. That was no excuse. She couldn't be careless. People wanted their art back on time, and she'd promised them that. She'd fix it tomorrow.

Later, after he had left, she wondered why she didn't share the good news with Andre. She didn't want to jinx it, or perhaps, she wanted to savor this moment alone.

OCTOBER 11TH

CHAPTER 5

VERA

"Anything else?" the waitress asked, clinking plates down on the table before Vera and her mom.

"We're set," Eliza said.

Vera wasn't supposed to eat for twenty-four hours before surgery, so Eliza let her choose her final meal. More than anything, Vera wanted chicken and biscuits. Comfort food. Plus, she could eat it without silverware, so no chance of accidently stabbing her plate or the table with her fork.

Eliza had found a place in the neighborhood, Maple Street Biscuit Cafe, guided Vera there, and ordered for both of them. They both had high standards for biscuits, and for Vera, these did not disappoint. Knowing she wouldn't be able to eat for a while, she ordered a second one with honey butter.

When her phone buzzed, she ignored it at first, until it started blowing up. She didn't like having her texts read aloud in public places, and considered her mom reading them the lesser of two evils. She handed her mom her phone and waited, powerless. "There are too many. They're coming in too fast. Can you read them and let me know what's happening?" Vera asked.

"Oh, honey," Eliza said.

"Oh, honey what?"

"It's Zoe. She got a soccer scholarship. To Chapel Hill."

Where Vera wanted to go. That was supposed to be her scholarship. It could have been, at least. The recruiter had come to see her. But by that game with her vision in flux, Vera was warming the bench. Knowing she wouldn't play, she almost didn't go at all. When people cheered, she couldn't tell which team it was for. She had to wait for a cue from her coach to know if she should cheer or not. It wasn't fair. None of this was.

"Good for her." Vera tried to muster some joy for her friend. At Vera's best, she knew she was better than Zoe. "Can you text her congrats from me?"

"I will. I'm so sorry, Vera. I know you wanted that."

"It's over, Mom." Vera buried her forehead in her hands.

"Your coach sent them some of your tapes. I'm sure you'll have a chance."

Tapes weren't the same. She knew her mom was trying to help, but somehow, her false hope made things worse. "Not there, I won't."

"Maybe in a DII school? Maybe they'll have walk-on tryouts?"

"Maybe," Vera said, but she doubted it. Even if her vision came back, her faith in her soccer future dimmed daily.

"I found your college essay, Vee," Eliza said.

"You weren't supposed to read that." They'd asked her to write about something central to her identity, and she didn't know what to write. So much of her life had revolved around soccer that when she couldn't do that, she didn't know who she was anymore. So that's what she wrote. How this terrible tumor took from her what she loved most.

"It was on the printer. I didn't mean to."

"You could have stopped reading when you realized what it was."

"I just... couldn't stop reading. I wanted to know what was going on with you. I know how hard this must be."

Sure, you do, Vera thought. So much for enjoying her last meal. Itching to leave but unable to go anywhere on her own, she distracted herself by listening in on a nearby conversation.

"The usual, Andre?" a female voice asked.

"Just mine," he said. "You have enough plywood for the windows?"

"We're ready. Thanks for checking."

"Of course. That's my job."

Her mother's voice jarred her from eavesdropping. "Ready to go, Vera?"

Vera nodded, standing.

"Still up for checking out the museum?"

"Isn't that why we got here early? It beats waiting around the hotel." Or thinking about Zoe, Chapel Hill, and her mom violating her privacy. What else had she found or seen? Vera didn't want to know.

"Let me get the door for you," the man's voice she'd just heard said.

Chimes jingled and Vera welcomed the fresh air.

"Thank you!" Eliza said, clutching Vera's left elbow, guiding her out of the restaurant. They'd gotten better at this, Eliza guiding and Vera letting herself be led.

CHAPTER 6

LUCIA

Standing at her desk, Lucia reviewed the $38.6 million dollar expansion of the Dalítorium and the proposal to the city. Yes, they were asking for taxpayer money for almost half of the cost, but just think about how much energy this would bring to the downtown. Of the 400,000 museum visitors each year, more than half came from outside central Florida, and they brought $161 million with them. The least the city could do was give people a place to park.

Thanks to her insight from Andre, that was how they were pitching it: as central to the St. Pete Rising campaign. The rebirth of St. Pete as a cultural and arts center was largely thanks to the Dalítorium. She'd done most of the legwork on the proposed expansion, working with the architect, figuring out how to dovetail their goals with that of St. Pete, but Harold had been the face of it. That is until now. Soon, that would change.

After weeks of not getting her hopes up, Lucia let herself indulge in the dream of being the next director. In that role, she would oversee the expansion that included a large education wing and a new digital gallery space other museums would be envious of. She would make the Dalítorium a trendsetter in the art world, using the newest technology to usher the artist into the future.

Even though her door was ajar, a knock jolted her back to reality. She told herself that she didn't like having her creative flow interrupted, but Lucia liked being needed, and she preferred too many interruptions to none at all. "Yes?"

"Busy?" Nick asked.

Seeing him, she smiled and beckoned him to join her. Sometimes Lucia was secretly glad things hadn't quite worked out for Nick at the University of South Florida. She'd missed having him at the Dalítorium. There was no one she would rather work an event or install a new exhibit with. He'd been her sounding board through the development of *Dreams of Dalí in 360°* and *The Lazarus Project.* Being almost two decades her junior, he was better versed in the newest technology and had been studying computer programming before he left school. Lucia often consulted with him on these matters. She wanted to promote him to oversee the digital gallery, but it was too early to think of such things. The role hadn't been posted or even created yet.

"I finished securing the miniatures. They're ready to ship out," Nick let her know.

The miniatures. Of course. What would she do without Nick? "Thank you. With everything going on, I'd almost forgotten about them."

"I've got you, Lu. Any word on the interview?"

She lit up. "Noon tomorrow. Don't tell anyone, but I made the cut. Harold called me last night."

"They'd be fools not to choose you."

"I know, right? But thanks for the vote of confidence." Noting his stubble and tousled corkscrew mane, she asked, "Late night?"

"New video game," he blushed, smoothing his hair down with his hands. "How can I help? Want me to ask you interview questions like you did for me?"

Lucia was typically not one to be sentimental, but Nick was different. "Thanks, but I'm ready."

"So... I should send them out tomorrow? The miniatures?"

"Not yet. There's a storm brewing, and the last thing I want is for transportation snafus. Not with 2.3 million on the line. Oh, and do you mind doing first rounds? I want to finish looking these over."

"Got it, director," he said, turning to leave.

Lucia rolled her eyes, secretly pleased. "Oh, and Nick?"

"Yes?"

"Don't mention this to your father yet." Andre wouldn't like Nick knowing first.

She turned back to her work, opening her desk drawer in search of the purple pen she used for edits. That's when she saw it: that pesky, pixelated photo. She shoved it in the back of her desk drawer and slammed it closed.

CHAPTER 7

ELIZA

"I saw this in Figueres! They must have it on loan. You can't miss the F-Holes, the cello's shadow." Eliza held Vera's arm, basking in memories from Eliza's past and possibilities for Vera's future.

"I'm sure it looks great, Mom."

"Vera..." her mother murmured. Vera must know how much Eliza wanted to come here. Ever since they found out they could save a few hundred dollars flying in a day early, Eliza decided they would come to the Dalítorium first.

"What am I supposed to say, Mom? Why are we even here? For you to describe the art work? You could have come after I was admitted."

"I'm not going to an art museum while you are in the hospital, Vera." But why had she insisted they come today? Why not come together, after? If everything went as expected. If Vera regained her sight. If... She'd answered her own question. She tightened her grip on her bag and her daughter. "You'll see it soon enough. I... I thought it would be nice to get out a bit before... before the hospital."

"I don't want to think about that yet."

"Exactly. Do you remember the first time I took you to see Dalí? When *Persistence of Memory* was on loan at The Parthenon in Nashville?" Eliza could have floated away that day, unencumbered by bills or responsibilities, or even Vera. When she saw that painting, something in her shifted.

"The melting clocks? Time dripping away?" Vera asked, shifting her weight back and forth.

Eliza took a breath. She never fully understood what Vera was feeling. That was parenthood: Your heart living outside your body. "They said recovery can take up to five days, but your sight comes back right away."

"What if… it doesn't work? What if I lose my sight forever? Or worse?" Vera finally asked.

And there it was. The question that had been plaguing them both since her diagnosis. Eliza wasn't sure if the weight of it was heavier now that Vera had said it or before, when it was unspoken. Eliza repeated the mantra that had been playing in her head for weeks, especially when she had doubts about dragging Vera to St. Pete.

"We came here because they are the best. Dr. Madhav does this surgery three times a week," Eliza reassured herself as much as Vera. "You know you can't live like this. It'll keep growing. It will get worse."

"I know."

"Can you pretend with me right now? Can I tell you about the painting?"

"*My last work, The Swallow's Tail,*" Dalí interrupted, appearing from behind today's *Tampa Bay Times*. "*After my Gala died, I lost the will to create. But then I met René. His theories inspire me. I start anew. Dalí dream in glorious technicolor again.*"

Vera turned quickly toward the voice and stumbled.

A young man, dressed in black with a Dalítorium docent nametag, rushed to Vera and helped her right herself. "Are you okay?" he asked.

"I think so," Vera said, "but sometimes I get these dizzy spells."

"Doesn't everyone?"

"Not like me. But thanks," Vera said.

Eliza, grateful for the reprieve, smiled at the broad-shouldered handsome young man. He looked a little older than Vera.

"The sunglasses inside might not be helping," he suggested. Vera did not move to take them off, so he tried again. "I'm Nick, a guide here. Or at least I used to be before we had tours by Dalí himself."

"So, what do you do now?" Vera asked.

"Catch damsels in distress," he joked. "Visitors are pouring in. I can't complain."

"As amazing as Deepfake Dalí is," Eliza said, "Vera needs help getting around, and these Dalís aren't up to that task."

Without probing further, Nick seized the opportunity, "Why don't I take you both around and tell you about my favorites?"

"Sure. I'm Vera."

Eliza, enraptured but unable to wander unencumbered, welcomed Nick's help.

"This… is Dalí's last painted work," Nick explained, gesturing to *The Swallow's Tail*, "inspired by Rene Thom's catastrophe theory…"

"Thanks. We just heard," Vera said.

"Where a seemingly small shift triggers something much bigger, disproportionate, like a bridge suddenly collapsing or someone appearing to be fine and then seemingly out of nowhere reaching their personal breaking point," Eliza said, remembering when she reached her own personal breaking point.

"Or even catastrophic. A butterfly's flapping wings in New Mexico causing a typhoon in Japan," Vera added.

Eliza knew Vera's example was chaos theory and not catastrophe theory, but Eliza was so grateful for the mood-shift in Vera that she didn't bother to correct her.

"You know your Thom?" Nick asked Vera.

"Mom taught me. She even met him once," Vera bragged.

"Impressive."

"Eliza, Vera's mother," she introduced herself. "I studied some Dalí. I studied more math." She had not only studied Thom but also took an overnight train to hear him speak once. Ever since her brother Frank had died when he was in college, she searched for meaning in the catastrophic. Church and therapy had not helped, but in some small way, Thom's theories had. "Thom tried to create models to predict random catastrophic events."

"Between you two and the *Lazarus Project*, I'm going to be out of a job soon."

"I'm sure you could teach us a thing or two," Vera said.

This was what Eliza had come for. For Vera to be interested in something other than her own fate. Eliza remembered Vera's first trip to DC; they had planned on staying two days, but given free admission to museums and Vera's unquenchable thirst to explore, they stayed a week. The flu, she told work.

"Show us more," Eliza asked, happy to see a glimmer of light back in her daughter and excited herself about seeing more art.

"There's one in the next room that will blow your mind. It looks totally different when you are far away. You'll never think of Lincoln the same way again," Nick said, leading the way.

As they entered the next gallery, they practically bumped into Lucia, exactly what Eliza had hoped and dreaded. Lucia still insisted on wearing heels and looked like she hadn't gained an ounce. Her hair, pulled up in a sleek twist, showed no sign of graying or roots. Unlike her own reflection, time had not yet marched across Lucia's face.

As they stared each other down, introductions were inevitable. Nick took the lead. "Lucia, this is Vera and Lisa."

"Vera and Eliza," Lucia corrected him.

"Sorry, Eliza," Nick said. "We were just talking about René Thom. I wanted to show them the *Homage to Rothko* next."

"Go right ahead," Lucia answered.

Lucia should have known they were coming. Eliza had written to her so many times, first with milestones like first words and lost teeth, with birthday photos. And then, with the news. With why they were coming to St. Pete.

"Why don't you tell Vera about it?" Eliza suggested to Nick and Vera. "I'll be right there." She had not only come here for Dalí, but for Lucia. For Lucia to see them. Everything came flooding back. Love, jealousy, anger. The last time they had been together, Eliza was moving out of their flat in Barcelona with seven-month-old Vera in tow.

Without waiting for Eliza to change her mind, Nick took Vera's arm, guiding and steadying her towards the next gallery. Eliza and Lucia watched them leave. They said nothing for a while, dwarfed by Dalí's final work, *The Swallow's Tail.*

"Why is he holding her arm?" Lucia finally asked, breaking the silence.

"She's blind, mostly anyway. And sick. My daughter... is sick, Lucia. I thought you knew,"

"How sick? With what?" Lucia asked.

Eliza was put off by Lucia's directness since she hadn't heard from her in so long. She wondered if Lucia hadn't gotten the letters. Did she even care? How foolish this trip had been. "A tumor in her pituitary gland. A craniopharyngioma." Even if Johns Hopkins was the best, there were other hospitals. Why put her daughter through multiple flights? Why St. Pete?

"What caused it? Do they know?" Lucia asked.

Her first question. Not about Vera, if she would be okay. Not even about Eliza, how she was dealing with this. "They aren't sure," Eliza replied. She'd asked the doctor the same question.

"Will she be okay?" Lucia asked.

Should have been your first question, Eliza thought. Two months ago when Eliza first wrote Lucia, when Eliza needed Lucia. "It needs to come out. Soon. That's why we're here. Johns Hopkins is the best."

"They are," Lucia agreed. "So many of the doctors are also patrons and donors here. She'll be in good hands."

A couple interrupted them. "Can you tell me where the other Dalís are?"

Eliza stepped back, giving Lucia space to do her job.

"Have you been upstairs?"

They shook their heads no.

"I'd check those out."

As they left, Lucia turned her attention back to Eliza. "When?" Lucia asked.

"Tuesday afternoon, if labs are good. They are admitting her tomorrow." Talking about logistics was the easy part. Like the weather, it filled the emptiness and was easier than talking about real things. With quiet confidence, be it a nostalgia for something past or a need to fight for her daughter's future, Eliza broke the silence. "I wrote you."

"You did," Lucia said. "I didn't read them."

Eliza, unsure how to respond, welcomed Nick and Vera's return before worrying what brought them back. She brushed Lucia's arm, turning her attention towards the pair.

"He's a good guy. I've worked with him for two years now and he's never let me down," Lucia explained. "He even has keys to my place."

Eliza looked at her skeptically.

"He checks on my cat when I'm traveling for work," Lucia clarified.

"How old?"

"Twenty-one. He tried going to the University of South Florida, just down the street, but that didn't work out."

Nick guided Vera protectively. "She has a headache."

Eliza took Vera's hand. Vera let her, but she didn't let Nick go either. "I'm dizzy, Mom. I can't…. I need fresh air."

"Let's get you outside," Eliza said to Vera.

Eliza and Nick each took a side and guided her towards the entrance. Only then Eliza realized how incomplete her meeting with Lucia had been and wondered if they would get another opportunity to talk.

CHAPTER 8

LUCIA

After Eliza and Vera walked away, Lucia wanted to cancel her afternoon meetings. She considered rescheduling the film crew that was supposed to do a special on *The Lazarus Project.* She had half a mind to get it over with, but she wanted to prep more for the interview tomorrow. That's what she told herself. It had nothing whatsoever to do with seeing Eliza and Vera.

And yet, she could hardly stand. This was her fortress, and they'd managed to breach it. Lucia forced herself to retreat up the dizzying helix stairs, mentally trying to stabilize herself by going over the script for the film crew, all the details of the structure itself and the new exhibit.

Facts centered her. She told herself the story of the birth of the museum to keep herself from falling apart. When the board was looking to renovate the existing museum more than a decade ago, Yann Weymouth, a local and I. M. Pei mentee, set himself apart by instead proposing to demolish the old structure entirely and build from the ground up. This would enable him to create a stronghold built to withstand a Category 5 hurricane and fully protect Dalí's art inside. They argued the cost of the possibility of a lost collection more than offset the cost of a new building. They were in Florida after all, and it was a question not if, but when, the big one was coming.

Lucia fought hard for this plan, and because of her recommendations, the board agreed. She convinced them. They were particularly impressed with Weymouth's creation for being state-of-the-art in both art protection and climate-change resistant architecture; his innovation set a new bar for architects. This whimsical design, born as a sketch on paper and brought to life through digital technology, took the limits of the human imagination to another dimension. She'd birthed this museum.

The museum was so much more than a concrete vault. Weymouth went to great lengths to create a showstopper. Without wanting to be cliche, he and his team veered away from anything related to melting clocks and instead embraced the juxtaposition of the Euclidean with more organic shapes. Dalí, master of the surreal, explorer of the subconscious, was enraptured by forms of both math and nature. Inspired by the longtime friendship of Dalí and Buckminster Fuller, the architects highlighted Bucky's geodesic dome in the atrium. Fuller's work not only ignited a generation of eco-friendly architects and artists, but also the Spaceship Earth, the jewel-piece of Epcot. She wondered if Eliza had ever taken Vera to Disney World.

Channeling the individuality of snowflakes, or the possible genetic combinations when sperm and egg united, not one of the 1,062 panels of the atrium's liquid glass enigma were exactly alike. More importantly, this "treasure box" on steroids housed the largest collection of original Dalí works worldwide and protected them in eighteen-inch thick concrete walls, illuminating them with natural light filtering in through the geodesic dome. Lucia had done that. Because of her, this art fortress existed. Too bad it wasn't tough enough to keep out her past.

She had gotten Eliza's letters, but letters she could compartmentalize, ignore. She'd lied to Eliza. Lucia had read them all in the bathroom after Andre had gone to sleep. She kept everything Eliza sent her in a false-bottom desk drawer. To date, no prior lover, Andre included, had found them. Sometimes she could even forget those letters existed. It was easier that way, cleaner. But when Eliza and Vera were both standing in front of her, she couldn't pretend anymore.

Gravity and time had both gotten the better of Eliza. She'd put on thirty pounds, easily, mostly around her lower half. Lucia had put on five pounds since their college days, at most. Crow's feet and frown lines, the wrinkles reserved for the joys and sorrows of motherhood, held equal prominence on Eliza's face. Thanks to her skin routine and life choices, Lucia had avoided both.

She couldn't remember the last time she'd seen Vera. Vera was definitely a baby and had one tooth, or possibly two. They argued over her hair color, if it was red or a dirty blonde. Lucia thought that it was red, at least in the right light. She'd worked so hard to forget the way Vera's little fingers couldn't curl fully around Lucia's pinky, how Vera would hum when she took a bottle. The last time she'd seen her, Lucia didn't know it would be the last time, until today.

CHAPTER 9

ELIZA

"There's a bench just outside, near the garden. Let's go there," Nick suggested.

Together, they walked down the DNA spiral of concrete, metal, and glass stairs, through the lobby, and past the final Dalí, who, in sensing movement, came to life and asked, *"Before you leave, you will take a picture with me*?" Eliza smiled, bemused. For a second, she wasn't thinking about Vera.

"Next time, Dalí," Eliza said. As if the past two months hadn't been surreal enough. Eliza would have loved to indulge in this small, otherworldly luxury, but not until after the surgery.

"*Next time,*" Dalí responded, but they were already out the door.

"Wait. Was that another one?" Vera asked.

"Kind of. More like a hologram of him," Nick said.

"How did he know what you said? He responded like he heard you!" Vera delighted.

"Amazing, isn't it?" Nick agreed. "There are sensors and triggers encoded to help him respond. They programmed over 190,000 possible combinations of footage, so every interaction appears unique. It's been Lucia's pet project for the past year."

"Lucia?" Vera asked.

"My boss."

After hearing Vera utter Lucia's name, Eliza held Vera's arm tighter.

"Let's sit here," Nick said, guiding Vera to what looked like half a bench, supported by a large metal crutch. With the massive concrete building behind them, a fortress except for the organic glass window-sculpture hugging and oozing around the building, they faced the water. A huge handle-bar mustache and, in comparison, a few seemingly miniature palm trees, evenly spaced, were the only things separating them from the sea. They sat quietly as Vera began to regain her strength, color returning to her face.

Out of habit, Eliza reached for Vera's favorite granola bar and a bottle of water. Eliza had been bringing them as a go-to snack to Vera on the soccer field for years. Eliza bought them in bulk and shared them generously with other players. With the rise in concerns over nuts, she passed them out under the radar.

When she handed one to Vera, Vera reminded her, "No food for 24 hours, Mom."

"You're right. Sorry."

"Mom, I didn't think I would be able to see any of Dalí's work, but there was this painting Nick took me to, and from far away, it looks like Lincoln's face. He said it's made up of these big squares, but with the lights and darks. Even I could see it, sort of."

Eliza said a quick prayer of thanks that Vera had one of those rare moments of partial blurry vision while she was here. It must be a sign.

"Apparently," Nick said, "Dalí was inspired by this article in *Scientific American* saying that only 121 pixels were required to describe a human face."

"Up close, it's supposed to look like the back of Gala, totally naked. I want to come back to see her, to see the painting again. After, I mean." Vera paused before continuing, almost to herself. "To have that ability, to morph into something else… What if people transform like that?"

Passersby leaving the museum were abuzz discussing the new exhibit with each other, looking back at their selfies with Dalí. One group stopped, interrupting Vera, to ask Nick, "Can you show us where the Wish Tree is? We missed it last time we were in town."

"Of course."

"Hurricane Irma didn't get it?"

"She had a field day with it, but the root ball somehow survived. We righted and replanted it. Third time, actually. That tree will outlast us all. This way," Nick said, leaving Vera and Eliza.

"Is he gone, Mom?"

"Yes."

"I… I don't think I want to have the surgery any more. I know we came all the way here and..."

Eliza sighed. "Vera, we've been over this."

"It's my brain. What if something goes wrong and afterward, I'm not me? Like I've changed into something else? From Gala to Lincoln, or the other way around?

"That's art. You'll always be you. They're operating on your pituitary gland. That doesn't control personality. You may have to take some hormone supplements, but you will still be you."

They were so close to the other side of this. Of course, she would have questions. When Vera voiced them, they echoed Eliza's own doubts, the ones Eliza had worked so hard to suppress. This was the best option, she kept telling herself.

"What if I never wake up, Mom?"

That was Eliza's single biggest fear. Survival rates were 98% or better across the board, and so far, they'd been lucky, catching it as early as they did. Otherwise, Vera's health was excellent. Everything was in their favor.

"Wake up from what?" Nick asked. Unbeknownst to them, he'd returned from his guide duties.

Vera, flushing crimson, fiddled with the edge of her favorite tennis skirt.

"Nick," Eliza asked, "Can you give us some privacy?"

"I should probably head back in," Nick said.

"Don't go. Stay?" Vera asked. "Please?"

"The Avant Garden is full of surprises, from the Wish Tree to the labyrinth. I could take you there," Nick suggested.

Eliza watched her daughter chuckle. Her shoulders settled, and her eyes and smile lit up. "Normally, I'd say yes, but right now, a labyrinth sounds like some level of hell."

"Touché," he smiled.

Glancing back and forth between the pair, Eliza said, "You know what? Why don't I check them out on my own? Give you some space. I'll be quick."

Nick rested his hand gently on Vera's shoulder. "Mind if I keep you company?"

Vera nodded. "Sounds great."

"Which way's the labyrinth?" Eliza asked Nick.

"You can't miss it. Just keep following this path."

Eliza turned to leave, surprised at herself. The old Eliza would have never trusted a stranger. She corrected herself: when she was not that much older than Vera, she had.

CHAPTER 10

ELIZA

Almost 20 years earlier
Barcelona

Her whole life, she'd gone by Libby. But when she met Lucia, her study-abroad roommate in Barcelona, the first thing Lucia convinced her to do was to change her name to Eliza, just to try it. Eliza sounded cooler, Lucia said. Perhaps Lucia didn't want them both having names starting with L. Libby, now Eliza, embraced it. The second thing Lucia convinced her to do was to skip class one Friday in early October to visit the Dalí Museum in Figueres. They took a train, planning to go up and come back on the same day. They stayed for the whole weekend, skipping Monday classes as well, but by Monday, their priorities had shifted.

Even though the rest of the world stopped after 9/11, Eliza had waited her entire life for this kind of freedom and was not going to give it up and head back home, not because of her uncle's rant about otherness, or because of some fledgling fear this experience could alter her life. It was too early to know that.

"It's the boat!" Lucia exclaimed, pointing toward the ceiling. "Dalí and Gala spent days in that boat."

"Wouldn't you get bored, lying around? Just… rowing?" Eliza hated being still.

"But wasn't he more prolific than most artists? If we were still more—like Dalí, would we produce more? Or better quality stuff? My stuff recently has felt like crap," Lucia lamented.

"It's been good, Lucia. Especially the stone-women ones."

"They were okay. The rest was crap."

"He must have loved her," Eliza said. "He put her in a castle."

"The one we're going to…" Lucia said.

Eliza nodded. "He would only visit if she wrote to him. After she died, he buckled her dead body into his car for one last ride and drove her to be buried."

"That's a little weird, right?"

"What do we know about love?"

"This car?" Lucia asked.

"I think so."

They looked from the car up toward the gigantic blue raindrops, dangling in mid-air.

"I read about this!" Eliza referenced her many hours studying Dalí in preparation for this trip while Lucia was otherwise occupied. A boat hung upside-down in the center of the atrium. It was in this boat Dalí and his lover, Gala, frequently rowed into an otherworldly dimension. After Gala died, Dalí upturned their safe haven to mimic his own dishevel, and turned it into a work of art, an outward and visible sign of the grief he felt. He turned blue condoms, filled with various amounts of water, stretched beyond their intended limits, into tears, hanging down from the upended boat. Beneath the boat, he placed a car and created mechanisms for it to rain and play music inside. I want to be grieved in this way, Eliza thought. I want someone to love me so much they create a mechanically-engineered memorial to my passing. She could take or leave the unexpected condom use.

"I didn't know condoms could stretch that much," Lucia said, marveling at the latex teardrops, suspended in time and space.

"I heard you the other night. You used a condom, right? Please tell me you did," Eliza criticized.

"Of course, I did! Is it my fault I wanted to keep learning after he finished the lecture? The accent… The bravado… I can't resist an intellectual, you know."

"Quite an education you got," Eliza said. "Next time you are learning after hours, how about letting me sleep?"

"Okay, so maybe a single wasn't an option, but look at it this way: If I were in a single, we might not have met," Lucia countered. "Think of everything you would have missed out on… Tibidabo… the rager on the roof of Casa Mila…"

"Your delicious biscuits from scratch and mac and cheese… your inability to change the toilet paper… Your searing the image of my professor's butt, or the rest of him, once he realized I was there and tried to cover up and run away, in my permanent memory."

"You know you liked it… At least that last view."

"Lucia. Gross," Eliza said. Realizing a man with glittering eyes was staring at them, she stopped thinking about the professor. This stranger seemed similarly enamored with the boat, tears, and car. She asked, "What's with the mannequin in the car?"

"You haven't seen it," he said, "Until you turn it on."

"Turn what on?" Lucia asked coyly.

"A peseta," he said, gesturing to a metal box with a slot to insert change. "You must see the car rain."

Eliza checked her clutch. "I don't have any."

Bolder, Lucia asked, "Got one to spare?"

"I don't, but you do," he riddled.

Puzzled, Lucia stuck her hands in her pockets to check.

"Not there," the mysterious, Dalí-like man said, reaching behind her ear and producing a shiny new coin. "Here." He handed the coin to Lucia, who handed it to Eliza in turn. Eliza dropped the coin in the contraption. Mesmerized, Eliza stared at the cabin, waiting for something to happen.

Lucia thanked him, offering him a hand.

"Miquel," he offered back.

"Miquel," she said. "I'm Lucia. That's Eliza. It's our first time."

"I figured," he said.

The car sprang to life, rain falling, music jingling.

CHAPTER 11

NICK

Present time
St. Petersburg

As soon as Eliza walked away, Vera relaxed. "Thanks for your help earlier."

"No problem," Nick said, squeezing in on the bench beside her.

"I'm not always this helpless."

"I figured." The truth was he liked helping. It grounded him.

"Tell me about those Dalís."

"It's pretty incredible. They are programmed to interact with people, so it's like talking to Dalí himself."

"How is that possible?"

"It's the same technology used to make it look like politicians are saying horrible things or famous celebrities are porn stars." He looked from the water back toward Vera's face. The mention of porn stars didn't seem to faze Vera. "They take hundreds of clips of someone's face and use Artificial Intelligence to superimpose that face onto someone else's body."

"So, you couldn't really do it for an old artist, someone you don't have video footage of."

"Not yet, at least."

"But you could do it with someone like Einstein? Or JFK?"

"Exactly. It was Lucia's idea, to use this deepfake technology for good. She's brilliant. But I want to go even further with it. *The Lazarus Project* could be so much bigger than just this place. Museums across the country could use this to bring people back to life."

"Or Mia Hamm could give me shooting tips, or I could see my grandparents again," Vera suggested.

Nick laughed. Vera thought even bigger than he did.

"You have to come back and see it. Seriously. It's incredible."

Vera's eyes widened, bright and strong, at his suggestion. "I want to, but…"

"But…"

"It's just this stupid tumor. It messed up everything."

Nick had seen what cancer could do to a family. Not that he remembered much about his mother, but he'd seen how it changed his father. "I'm sorry. That sucks."

"I just want to feel like myself again."

"I'm sure you will…"

"But what if I don't? What if it messes something else up? Would you let someone cut into your brain?"

Nick wasn't sure what to say. This all felt too serious all of a sudden. What if he told her to have the surgery and something went wrong? Or if she didn't because of something he said? "Have you ever heard of a banyan tree?"

"That sounds familiar. In AP Bio, I think?"

"Have you ever seen one?" Reading about them or studying them was nothing compared to seeing them in person. It was his favorite spot in the city, even more than the Dalítorium. A St. Pete native, Nick had grown up with banyans and couldn't imagine not knowing them.

"Only in chalk. Mr. Putnam is the only teacher on the planet that still uses a chalkboard."

"How good of an artist is he?"

"Definitely no Dalí, but memorable." She laughed. "You should see his stick figures. I've missed seeing them this semester."

"I'll take that as a no. These trees are incredible. In other parts of the world, they've taken over ruins, spreading out for miles."

"Just one tree?"

"Sort of. More like generations of trees. The seeds nestle in the branches and drop tentacle roots from the sky."

"Is there one here?"

"A few actually. I thought everywhere had them, and when I realized how wrong I was, how special they were, I wanted to learn everything I could about them."

"Special?"

"So... Thomas Edison brought some to Henry Ford in hopes of finding a cheaper source of rubber. Ours are babies compared to the ones in Thailand and Sri Lanka." Had he overdone it on the nerdiness? Most people agreed they were beautiful but started glossing over when he got excited about them.

"Did it work? The rubber?"

"I don't think so. I don't remember why, but now St. Pete has these amazing trees, right around the corner."

"Could I feel them? The sky roots?"

Nobody had put it like that before. Meredith hadn't been interested at all, but Vera wanted to know more.

"We should probably stay here."

"Please? I need to feel something bigger than me. Bigger than this stupid tumor."

He got that, the need to get out of your own head and problems.

"It's my 'Make a Wish' wish."

How could he say no? "Okay. We'll be quick."

He helped her stand and steadied her as they walked north by the water toward the majestic trees. He didn't tell her that this was an absolutely unforgettable make out spot. She wasn't the first girl he'd brought here, but she didn't need to know that. Besides, this wasn't like that. Not really.

He pushed an arm of roots out of the way, like a curtain, taking her into a private nook near the base of the biggest tree.

"Here," he said, guiding her hand and placing it on one of the thicker shafts.

"This is a root?"

"There are hundreds of them. The lucky ones make it to the ground and begin sprouting their own branches. Some are thicker, like that one. And some," he took a thinner root and caressed it up and down Vera's arm, almost like a feather, "are still young."

"That tickles!" she protested.

"Here. You do me," he said, putting the root in her hand and letting her use it to brush his skin. It sent chills up his spine. This felt more intimate than anything he'd done at the banyan before.

"We should head back," he said.

"You're probably right."

Neither of them moved.

"I'd like to see this tree again, when I can actually see it. And the Dalís," Vera said.

"You know what that means?" he asked, suddenly eager for a second date, if only to know how the surgery went.

"What?"

"That you'd have to see me again too."

"I guess that would be okay," Vera teased. "I'd probably need your number, so we could set that up."

"Give me your phone. I'll put it in," Nick said. Nick had promised himself he was taking a break from dating, after what happened with Meredith, but something about Vera was different than anyone he'd met. It wasn't just her fiery hair. She seemed cooler, more grown up. Most of the girls he knew were caught up in superficial drama, but that didn't seem like Vera at all.

CHAPTER 12

ELIZA

Eliza found the labyrinth easily. The gate, situated between two alabaster pillars, had a diagram of the path. She traced it lightly with her finger first before setting foot on the crushed limestone path flanked by a tall green hedge.

Labyrinths calmed her, or at least they used to. She didn't have to make any decisions. The path did that for her. This wasn't her first labyrinth. St. Michael's, the church she grew up in, had one. It was a bit of a drive from Soddy-Daisy, but her parents liked the Reverend better, so every Sunday, they dragged her and Frank the extra twelve minutes to church on the outskirts of Chattanooga. After the service, while her parents had coffee or lemonade and chatted with other adults, she and Frank used to race through the labyrinth, trying to tag each other. After years of stupid fights, of the inevitable competition that happens between siblings born less than a year apart, they reconnected through an Episcopal youth retreat put on by the Diocese. There, they walked the labyrinth together, this time not racing, scrambling, or clawing at each other to be the first to the center and the first back out again.

A single car accident, that's what they said. He'd barely left for Wake Forest. He was back for a long weekend, out drinking with high school friends. Eliza had begged to go with him, but he'd refused. She'd pleaded, then sulked. They'd fought. He'd left. And then he'd died. More days than not, she'd wished she'd been in the car with him. Or been there to drive him safely home, made him call their parents for a ride, or convinced him to sleep over. But she hadn't been there. He'd died alone.

Funny that the Frank incident hadn't been enough to make her stop drinking. For a while she'd drank more—a lot more. It was only after Vera's diagnosis that she quit for good.

Later, during the funeral service, she left during the homily. She couldn't stand hearing Frank talked about in the past tense. Not one to get caught crying in a bathroom stall, which was likely to be packed following the lengthy service, she went to walk the labyrinth, the first time she'd walked it without Frank. She wanted to find her center again, in this new world without him to balance her. But she couldn't finish it, not that time. Her mother had found her sobbing in the center, or so she was told. Her mother said they walked out together, not following the path. It was the only time she hadn't completed the path.

The limestone crunched beneath her feet, bringing her back to the here and now. Before Vera's diagnosis, Eliza wouldn't have thought twice about letting Vera spend time with friends. Vera always let her know where she was going and only once had broken her curfew. But since Vera's vision became blurry, even before the official diagnosis, Eliza had barely let Vera out of her sight. It was exhausting, constantly worrying. Even more so than in Vera's first months when Eliza didn't know any different, when Eliza didn't have any help. But Vera was okay, now. She was sitting with a museum employee, a good-looking one at that. She had her phone. She was on the bench nearby, happy for the first time in as long as Eliza could remember. Eliza appreciated the break. They were so close to being through this. They'd come to the best surgeon. In a few more days, this would be behind them.

The center. She'd made it there, as she always knew she would. And she would come out again. How strange to have this tall cypress in the center of a labyrinth. Of all the labyrinths she'd walked, mostly in search of Frank, she'd never seen a tree in the middle before, not like this. She hadn't been able to save Frank, but she could save Vera. She had to. She couldn't bear to lose her too.

Empowered by this realization, Eliza began the uncoiling process, the journey back out from the center.

Before heading back to the bench, Eliza stopped, enchanted by the glossy green canopy above a rainbow of dangling ribbons and streamers. The Wish Tree, the placard said. She slowly approached it. The colorful strips of paper, filled with the hopes and dreams of strangers, danced at the mercy of the gusts of wind coming off the gulf. Each dream, inspired perhaps by visits to the Dalítorium, was captured on the visitor's bracelet and tied to this organic maypole. She wondered how many desires had been fulfilled, how many were detached and lost, carried off by a breeze. As she got closer, standing nearer, then under, surrounded by the yearnings of others, she wondered how many were similar to hers, for loved ones to be well or children to be safe. In this whirling frenzy of color, she was not alone.

The unassuming placard dated this practice back to Hindu and Scottish rites. The hopes of her Scottish ancestors, her parents, Nana and Pops, and countless others were here with her, too. She took off her yellow visitor's bracelet, dug in her bag for a pen, and added her own wish to this ancestral cultural tradition. At first, she wanted to write, "Let Vera survive the surgery," but then, she thought the better of it. Thinking of Lucia, she wrote, "Keep my daughter safe." She tied her own wish to a nearby branch, entwining her wishes to the countless wishes of others. Her fears diminished, her hope stronger and her faith restored.

ELIZA

As Eliza approached the bench, she panicked. Vera was gone, and so was Nick.

Eliza turned in a circle, looking in every direction for Vera's long red hair, her signature tennis skirt. Nothing. She rummaged through her bag for her phone. No missed call or message. Leaning on the cast iron crutch that held up half the bench for balance, she called Vera's phone. She waited for a beat. No answer. It went straight to voicemail.

Even though Vera was almost completely blind, she had no excuse for not answering her phone. When Vera started to lose her vision, her first concern was how she'd ever be able to use it, but thanks to recommended apps, Vera was using her phone as nimbly and often as ever.

Why had she trusted her daughter to an almost-complete stranger? How foolish she had been. Eliza tried to turn off her worst-case scenario brain. Maybe Vera had to go to the bathroom or maybe they went for a little walk.

Eliza waited sixty seconds, a small eternity, before trying again. This time, Vera picked up on the third ring.

"Where are you?" Eliza demanded. A cooler mom might have not been so direct, but since Vera had gotten sick, safety trumped appearance.

"I'm fine Mom, really. We just went for a walk. We're not far."

"Where?" Eliza asked.

"By the tree…"

"Which tree?"

"Hold on. I'm giving you to Nick, Mom."

When Nick got on the phone, she asked, "Where are you two?"

"The banyans. Just follow the water. You can't miss it."

"Stay there. I'm coming to you." She hung up and started walking away from the museum, following the water. The banyans were a type of tree. She knew that, but she'd also never seen one. How would she recognize it?

How could she not? When she first spied the tree, it appeared to be a grove of trees, not just one or two. Upon closer examination, the museum itself would pale in comparison to the majestic banyan. The tangled labyrinth of roots and branches—flying buttresses bolstering the mother tree—created an enchanted forest, twisting, spreading, interwoven by necessity, etched with initials and some forgotten promises of forever, dependent upon the ancestors that came before. While initially glad to have found the banyans so quickly, seeing the maze before her, she realized it might take her a while to find Vera.

Eliza, momentarily mesmerized by the maze of tangled sky-roots, could not help but touch them, walk through them, around them, within them. Returning to her mission at hand, she called, "Vera!" undeterred by the gawking of strangers.

CHAPTER 13

VERA

"Vera!" a voice called more urgently. Hearing her mother's voice, Vera's body tensed again. Since the diagnosis and the daily-decreasing sight, Eliza had been treating her more like a toddler than an almost eighteen-year-old. When they should have been visiting colleges, they were researching hospitals and treatments instead. Now she couldn't go on a little walk, much less prom or a proper date, without her mother joining her.

"We're over here," Nick said.

After a brief moment, Vera felt her mother clutching her tightly.

"Vera... I thought you were staying at the bench."

"You knew I was with Nick, Mom. We didn't go far. He started talking about the banyans, and I wanted to touch them." Before the sickness, she'd been learning about banyans and fig wasps in her AP Bio class. How the wasps and the fig trees depend upon each other for pollination, perpetuation, and survival. Just like a mother and child, or, more accurately, the way the mother sees the relationship.

"I didn't know where you were."

"We just went on a walk. What's the big deal?"

"We're not in Soddy-Daisy anymore, Vee. And with your... condition—"

"I told Nick. He knows—"

"We're supposed to meet the doctors soon."

"I know. I just... I just needed some space."

"From me?"

"Ever since the diagnosis, you haven't let me out of your sight..." She couldn't say what she wanted to say, that her mother's hovering suffocated her, that she needed to breathe, to feel something impossible to imagine, like this banyan. Something whose life would continue to grow, seeds nestled into limbs, bearing the fruit of the next generation, even if the host tree succumbed to the strangulation by its offspring.

"I just want to make sure you are okay..."

"I'm not, Mom. I finally got my license, and I can't drive. I made varsity—starting lineup—and I can't play soccer. I can't even see this stupid tree."

"We're so close. This is all going to be over soon. It'll be gone by Wednesday."

"You say that, but what if it isn't? What if it doesn't work? What if I'm not me? What if—"

"It will. It has to."

Vera started to protest then thought the better of it. She changed the subject. "Nick, tell Mom what you were saying about these trees."

"They're pretty special. The biggest one in India covers almost five acres! In other parts of the world, they serve as shelters for cyclones. And if they fall, that means big political change is coming," Nick said.

"So how did these get here?" Eliza asked.

"Ford and Edison brought them. They kept trying new things, new ways to do things better."

Vera laughed. "Sounds like my coach. She's into this growth mindset thing and wants us to get a little better every day. Not just in soccer. In everything."

"You still can, Vee. After they take it out, you're going to be as good as new. Better, even. Right away," Eliza said.

"Right away?" Vera asked.

"That's what they said. You heard them."

"So, what's stopping you?" Nick asked.

"Nothing, I guess." Besides my stupid fear I won't wake up, Vera thought.

"Let me know how it goes then? You have my number..."

Eliza mouthed 'Thank you' to Nick as she hugged Vera once more.

"Maybe..." Vera suggested, "We can meet back here after it's over, so I can see the tree in its full glory."

"My description didn't do it justice?"

"You made it sound like I couldn't leave St. Pete without seeing it."

"Well then, Vera. It's a date. Until we meet again..." Nick squeezed Vera's hand before leaving, and Vera cheeks flushed. She had something to look forward to, after the surgery.

CHAPTER 14

NICK

Nick added paprika, cumin, and chili powder to the InstaPot as he waited for Vera to text him back. He hadn't planned on cooking a full meal tonight, thinking his dad had another campaign event, but cooking was the perfect thing to distract him. Since his mom died when he was five, his dad had done most of the cooking. Nick had helped him in the kitchen, first peeling carrots and measuring dry ingredients and then moving onto more complex tasks like using the pasta maker. They didn't see eye to eye on many things, but they'd always loved to cook together.

Nick read up on newer tech gadgets for the kitchen, and those became birthday presents for his dad. The InstaPot. The immersion blender. His dad seemed to like them, and Nick got to use them when he was home.

When Nick got kicked out of his dorm, he was surprised to find takeout containers piling up, no sign of cooking in sight. Perhaps it had all been for him? Cooking for one, especially during an election session, probably wasn't worth the effort. Nick figured that cooking for them both would be a way to earn his keep. He usually made something big enough that they would have leftovers if needed but also that would keep if his dad worked late, or if he stayed over at Lucia's.

Sometimes he wasn't sure what Lucia saw in his dad. Brilliant Lucia kept eclipsing herself with visions for the museum, first *Dalí in 360°*, and now *The Lazarus Project*. He'd been coding since middle school and had been studying computer science at the University of South Florida in

St. Pete before he got kicked out, but he hadn't thought to apply it to art until he'd met Lucia. She inspired him.

He used to think Meredith inspired him. It was her idea to break into the college's computer system and change her grades. She didn't want to disappoint her parents. A straight-A student himself, he didn't need to change any of his grades. He just liked the challenge. That challenge came with more trouble than it was worth, including student loan debt, a paper trail that would follow him to future schools, and no college degree. At least USF chose to handle it quietly versus contacting the police. Anything to avoid a scandal. It's like he had a politician for a dad or something.

That should have been enough for him to end things with Meredith, but she kept popping up when she needed rescuing—when she couldn't figure out how to install her air conditioner, when someone used the credit card she'd accidently dropped, when her car needed jumping. He couldn't bring himself to turn her down. His dad helped people. That's what Parker men did.

As he set the InstaPot, his phone buzzed. Vera.

He read it, smiled, and responded quickly. She would be going home at the end of the week. He didn't have time to wait. What was he doing, getting caught up with a girl again? But he couldn't get her out of his head. How many girls her age knew Thom's theories? It was more than that, though. She had first felt the banyans without seeing them. She had first heard Dalí's voice without seeing his work. She had the energy and promise of someone who had flirted with death.

After a few text volleys back and forth, Andre came home, surprising Nick. Because of the gala, they'd both been gone last night, but Nick thought his dad had another event tonight. Nick slid his phone back in his pocket for now.

"How can I help?" Andre asked.

"Make the crema?" Nick suggested.

His dad put the avocado, lime, garlic, and sour cream into a bowl and used the immersion blender to whip them into something airy and delicious. It was a recipe Nick came up with, and now they couldn't imagine Mexican cuisine without it.

"Taste it," Andre asked Nick.

Nick stuck his finger into the bowl, happy with the consistency.

"You could use a spoon, Nick."

"No need to make extra dishes to wash." Nick put his tongue to his finger, savoring the extra garlic. "A little more acid," Nick suggested. "And salt."

As Andre made the adjustments, he brought up Lucia and her job. "So, when do you think she'll hear?"

So, Lucia hadn't told him yet. "I'm not sure."

"You don't have inside information? I thought you knew everything that went on in that place."

He did, but he couldn't share. "Not this time."

"I don't know what she's going to do if she doesn't get that job. She wants it so badly."

Nick hadn't fully considered that. What would happen if someone else got it? Lucia would be devastated. As long as Nick had known her, he knew it was her dream. What if the new director replaced her?

"Do you think she can handle it?" Andre asked.

"The job or not getting the job?" Nick countered.

Andre shrugged.

How could he have such little faith in Lucia? Or perhaps he was just being practical. His dad had had his share of disappointments. "I can't imagine anyone else," Nick said.

"That's not what I asked."

"You think I know the Dalítorium? Not like she does. She's got vision: She's ahead of the curve on integrating technology and bringing museums into this century. And she practically lives there."

Andre got a call. Glancing at his smartwatch, he said, "Her ears must have been burning." He headed back to his bedroom.

Glad to have a chance to check his phone, he realized he'd missed three more texts from Vera.

"I'll be back later," Andre told Nick. "She got the interview. Tomorrow morning. I want to help her practice."

"Good luck," Nick said, a little miffed that Lucia had asked his dad but not taken Nick up on the offer to help. Nick almost mentioned he already knew about the interview but decided against it. That wouldn't help Lucia. No longer hungry, he almost turned off the InstaPot, but he knew he'd want that mouth-watering barbacoa tomorrow.

He texted Vera: "Call me later. After your mom goes to sleep."

He played video games while waiting for the call, and they ended up talking for hours, both refusing to be the first one to hang up, falling asleep with the lines still open.

OCTOBER 12TH

CHAPTER 15

LUCIA

As Lucia reached the tip of North Shore Park, the halfway point in her daily four-mile running loop, she found her mind drifting. To the future: rehearsing her pitch for the board in her head, visualizing getting the job, worrying about what would happen if she didn't. To the past: seeing Eliza opened up the floodgates of shame and the dark seeds of regret that she'd worked so hard to repress. Even worse, this could throw her off her game. Why did they show up now? Lucia knew, of course, but the timing couldn't have been worse. She needed to focus on the interview. How could she do that with Eliza here? And Vera?

She was glad she'd called Andre last night and finally told him about making it to the next round. She hated asking for help, but he was an expert in self-promotion. Practicing out loud with a partner was much better than just running through it in your head. Having Andre there took her mind off of Eliza and Lucia, and helped her focus on her dream. Lucia compartmentalized: Because Andre knew nothing of them, if he was there, they couldn't possibly be.

She'd read that most stress came from the past or the future, not the present. From past regrets, from reliving decisions, mistakes, and consequences; From future worries about things out of her control. From worrying about unlikely disasters or tragedies. All of this sabotaged any good happening in the present.

Be present, she told herself. Be here. Feel the sweat bead dripping down your forehead. Hear the waves crashing on the shore. They usually weren't this loud, or were they? Maybe she took them for granted. What else do you hear? Concentrate on your breath. Three in. One out. In in in, out. In in in, out. Lamaze technique. She knew she was terrible at this. Quieting her head was impossible. She lived better in her head than her body. She forced herself to check in with each part of her body. Toes, calves—shaking out the tightness in her left one, thighs sweatily sticking and rubbing together. She shouldn't have had that third glass of wine last night. But it helped me practice my pitch with more confidence, she justified. So much for the body check in. She couldn't make it past her thighs.

She cranked up her go-to running music and leaned into the last half-mile. She loved this moment, when she could see the Dalítorium for the first time in her loop. She loved the way the sunrise ricocheted off the triangular glass panels, a continually-shifting stained glass of ambers, saffrons, and tangerines, of salmons, dandelions, and violets, with every moment and every morning slightly different from the last. On particularly majestic days like this one, she let herself be transported back to the nave of the Sagrada, bathed in a rainbow of light. Not today, Lucia, she told herself. Keep your head in the game. Be present. Be light. Be strong. Be present. Be light. Be strong. She repeated that until she made it home.

Routines calmed Lucia. Predictability calmed Lucia. She turned on the coffee pot before she left on her run, so she could pour a cup—black—when she got home. Cup of coffee. Light breakfast. Greek yogurt, plain, with cut up fruit—peaches when they were in season, a sprinkle of cinnamon and pecans. When the weather cooperated, she ate on her balcony while she scrolled through *The New York Times* headlines. Then she showered and got dressed. She'd set out her outfit the night before. She didn't always do this, but with the interview, she didn't want to take any chances. A black pencil shirt and silk top from Everlane, practically the only place she shopped. Low nude heels. She liked higher ones, but already standing 5'8", she wanted to look the board members in the eye and not tower over them. She thanked herself for deciding to sign up for the subscription box of accessories. Otherwise, she wouldn't have the turtle-shell comb for her French twist that brought out the sun-kissed highlights in her otherwise auburn hair or the drop necklace Dalí would have approved of. She knew she looked good.

When she opened the door to her apartment however, things were not quite as she expected. The sink was overflowing with dishes and food scraps. The juicer, a double boiler, and her favorite mug. Lemon rinds and eggshells—eggshells were terrible for the garbage disposal. On the counter sat a plate with eggs Benedict, her brunch go-to, a note, and a single iris, her favorite flower. Andre must have left them. He did make good hollandaise, but by now, it had congealed, hardened, and had lost its original shine. Dagny probably wouldn't even eat it. She never left anything in her sink, but she didn't have time to handle the kitchen. She scraped the plate off into the trash, skipped breakfast, poured her coffee into her third favorite mug, and headed for the shower.

CHAPTER 16

ELIZA

When they got to the hospital, Eliza was unnerved by the colorful flowers, butterflies, and palm trees painted on the walls. Her daughter was having brain surgery, and it looked like she was taking her to kindergarten!

But they'd come here for a reason. Vera would be eighteen the day after tomorrow. Eliza hadn't thought much about her birthday recently, with so many other things going on, but they wanted this pediatric oncologist, Dr. Madhav, to perform the surgery. Dr. Madhav had gone to med school with Dr. Warren, the doctor who diagnosed Vera, and, at least according to him, Dr. Madhav was the best. If they waited until she was eighteen, insurance wouldn't cover a pediatric oncologist to perform the surgery. They were cutting it close with the labs, and they all knew it.

"Can I help you?" a young man in scrubs, sitting behind the front desk, asked Vera and Eliza.

"We're here to check-in. Vera Garcia. I'm her mother, Eliza Davis-Garcia," she said, handing over her ID. "Vera is scheduled to have surgery early tomorrow morning, provided her labs today go well."

After typing a few things, he printed some forms, put them on a clipboard, and handed them to Eliza. "Please check these over to confirm everything looks right, including the insurance information. Let me know if there are any changes needed."

They settled in as best they could on lime green chairs, and Eliza reviewed the information. With finances as tight as they had been and with her job and therefore insurance on the line given how much time she already had taken off, she'd already triple-checked everything to make sure there were no mistakes. "Date of birth, October 14?"

"You know my birthdate, Mom."

"Yes, but with everything focused on our coming here, we didn't think about how we would celebrate. You know, after..."

"Let's get through tomorrow first," Vera said.

After hearing that, Eliza turned her attention to the remaining pile of paperwork. Eliza carefully, but quickly, finished reviewing them, signing off that everything was accurate, and handed them back to the nurse. She then rejoined Vera to sit. And wait.

She had gotten accustomed to waiting. All they'd done for the past two months was wait. When Vera's vision went out during a soccer game, they called the doctor immediately but were transferred to the weekend on-call service; they waited for his response. When Dr. Abel, Eliza's own childhood pediatrician who caught Vera up on vaccines after they moved back stateside and had been with Vera ever since, referred them to the first specialist, they waited. When that specialist wanted a second opinion before confirming anything, they finally saw Dr. Warren, a pediatric neurologist. He'd seen the first CT, but opted to do a second as things can change quickly, and an MRI scan as well. They waited to do the scans. They waited for him to analyze the results.

When they had been sitting in Dr. Warren's office back in Tennessee, he finally called them both into his office to share the results. Most of the conversation was a blur, so Eliza was grateful that she'd jotted notes on her phone. As she waited again in Florida, she reviewed what she'd written back in Tennessee.

Tumor → Craniopharyngioma
On pituitary gland
Causes dizziness, headaches, blurriness
Caught early
Small
Clean lines
Remove endoscopically versus radiation

After he said "tumor," she heard little else until he started talking about a plan of action. Threats to her daughter's well-being overwhelmed Eliza, but instructions were something she could follow. She jotted these notes so she wouldn't completely fall apart.

"I know this is a lot to process, but we have someone for you and your family to speak with," Dr. Warren continued.

Eliza didn't want sympathy or counseling. She wanted a blueprint to fix this problem and make it go away. She wanted to go back to planning Vera's eighteenth birthday trip—a week in Savannah, just the two of them, and finalize Vera's college search.

"I also have a good friend, a medical school classmate, who has removed hundreds of these before. She's in St. Pete." Eliza's ears perked up. "With a referral from me and with your insurance's approval and your permission, Dr. Madhav would be my best recommendation for Vera. We want to move quickly, before it grows much more and before Vera turns eighteen. Better handle this with pediatric experts." A plan. They would go to St. Pete.

"Vera Garcia?" A new voice jolted Eliza back to the present in the lobby at Johns Hopkins All Children's. They both stood, Eliza placing a light hand on the small of Vera's back.

"I'm Arielle, and I'm going to get you settled. Please come with me." Vera and Eliza followed. After going down a long hall with moons, stars, and planets painted on the walls and ceilings, they stopped in a small room with a scale, a blood-pressure cuff, a computer, and a few other devices. "Let's check your height and weight. Can you please step forward onto the scale?" Vera did, and Arielle took note. "Have a seat for me."

Eliza helped guide her to the chair.

"I'm going to draw some blood, and we will use it to run a few tests, to make sure your levels are ready for the surgery."

"She prefers the left," Eliza told Arielle. "It has better veins." Eliza knew Vera had always hated having her blood drawn, and out of habit, Eliza placed her hand in Vera's for Vera to squeeze.

"This will only pinch a bit," Arielle said, "One… two…" Arielle stuck before she got to three.

After the initial pinch, Vera relaxed her vice grip on Eliza's hand.

Arielle switched in a few vials, and after she had filled them all, she moved onto screening questions. "Any allergies?"

"Not that I know of… Right, Mom?"

"She had an adverse reaction to penicillin as a child, but we think she grew out of that," Eliza said.

"Any meds?" Arielle asked.

Eliza rummaged through her bag, pulling out an index card she prepared for this very moment. "Here's a list… Recent stuff prescribed by Dr. Warren after the diagnosis, in advance of this surgery."

"Family medical history?"

"Nana died of ovarian cancer, and Pops had a heart attack," Vera offered, glad to have something to share.

"They are?" Arielle asked.

"My parents," Eliza said.

"So, maternal grandparents," Arielle noted. Eliza almost corrected her, and then thought better of it. The medical history was important, but the family history was more complicated. She would find Arielle later. With every new doctor, with every new hospital, she wrestled with these questions.

"And on your father's side?" Arielle asked.

Neither Eliza nor Vera spoke. This was going to be more difficult than Eliza initially thought.

"We're not sure," Vera finally said, breaking the silence.

CHAPTER 17

LUCIA

Harold ushered Lucia into the board room. Lucia loved this private room because of how the glass enigma bisected the wall and ceiling, giving them a private view of not just the water but also the sky. He gestured for her to sit at the head of the table. She did. There were three other people there, including two board members she had expected, and someone she didn't recognize. Brief introductions were conducted. Ali, the new face, was from an executive search firm the Dalítorium board had brought in.

Lucia wasn't sure if this surprise would work in her favor, but since everyone else at the table knew about the great work she'd been doing, she now had a new person to impress.

As director, Harold started. "Give me a brief overview of your career so far: what were your greatest successes, and what makes you right for this role?"

Lucia was prepared for this one. "I've spent twenty years in arts management and innovation, working my way from the ground up. I fell in love with Dalí while studying abroad in Spain and went on to work at the Barcelona Museum of Modern Art for a year before moving to New York and working there." Her eyes flashed, electrified, remembering those early years.

"But the Dalítorium is my home. I've been here for a decade, and you can see my influence and vision throughout the museum. When I joined the Dalítorium as Director of Special Events, the architecture competition was just starting. Popular opinion was to remodel the former space," she said, nodding toward Harold, "I embraced Yann Weymouth's hurricane-proof design and advocated for this spectacular building we're sitting in now. After being promoted to Senior Director of Exhibits and Innovation, I channeled Dalí's love of innovation and transformation, birthing numerous cutting-edge exhibits including *Dreams of Dalí, Dalí in 3D*, and the current *The Lazarus Project*. We're seeing more than 400,000 visitors annually, and these exhibits are what continue to delight and drive Dalí lovers back here again and again. We not only support the St. Pete Rising revitalization campaign but also want to make the Dalítorium a beacon of inspiration for art museums around the world."

Lucia caught Ali glancing at her phone. She'd have to try harder. "I'm also overseeing the plans for the $38.6 million addition to the current structure, working closely with both our board and the city to make sure it aligns to our goals and those of St. Pete Rising. I'm uniquely suited to continue to drive the Dalítorium as a leader in community partnership and technological innovation."

A board member, the one she liked, went next. "How would you go about designing the Dalítorium's strategy for the next five years?"

"Obviously our first priority is to preserve the Dalí collection and legacy at all costs, but thanks to Weymouth's design, that's practically taken care of for us. This place is an art fortress. That's what it was built for."

She paused and noticed the two board members looking at each other. But that's what our mission states, she thought: to preserve his collection first and foremost.

"I also want to continue to ensure that the Dalítorium is the center for the cultural life of the community through our partnership with St. Pete Rising and a standard bearer for the larger art world. The mayor wants people to know that if they come downtown, there will always be things going on, and thanks to the Dalítorium, there will. That's how we will get the money from the city for the proposed expansion, a priority over the next few years." Thanks to Andre, Lucia knew how to dovetail her own goals to those of the city.

"We will continue to develop and foster creativity through our Innovation Labs. I want to expand that from working with businesses and women's groups to include more affordable workshops for teens and young adults from underserved communities. I will keep embracing new technology and share our ideas freely with other museums. I have a few new ideas for future exhibits that are in development. I'm also considering a restructuring that divides my current role into two, with someone overseeing just the technology-enhanced exhibits."

"Can you elaborate on those new exhibits?" Ali asked.

Not sure if she should share these fledgling ideas with someone outside the organization yet, Lucia deflected. "They are still in development, but trust me. They will be bigger than Lazarus."

Ali jotted something down. She went on, "Tell me about a time when you had to deliver a message or decision to your team that came from the director, about which you didn't agree. How did you deliver that message?"

Lucia paused, not sure how to respond. "I work closely with Harold, and we almost always see eye-to-eye on strategy."

"What about a time when you didn't?"

"If we disagree behind closed doors, we find a compromise before sharing the plan publicly."

Ali motioned for Lucia to elaborate.

"Most of our disagreements have been about funding, about my expansion ideas being too big, but I'm almost always able to justify the cost and rally the director's support to move my ideas forward. Right?" Lucia asked Harold.

He nodded, and then looked out the glass tessellations toward the water.

After Ali scribbled something down and thanked her, the other board member, the one most resistant to the changes she'd brought to the Dalítorium, asked, "Give me an example of someone who you coached and developed and were about to promote. What did you work on with them to make it happen?"

She smiled broadly, knowing exactly who she wanted to talk about. "When we hired Nick as a docent, I knew he had more potential than what he was being asked to do. With his computer science background, he was an untapped resource. That's why when we started working on *The Lazarus Project*, I wanted him to work directly with the tech company as we brought Dalí back to life. We promoted him to Assistant Director of Special Projects."

"How did you help develop him?"

"I found how his skill set matched our goals. He manages our social media and promotes our new exhibits. I find ideas and possibilities and make them happen. And Nick has done an excellent job in this role so far, given how smoothly this exhibit rolled out."

"Nick's the Deputy Mayor's son," the board member whispered to Ali, thinking Lucia didn't hear.

Ali said, "Thank you so much for your time, Lucia. It's clear you've done a lot for the Dalítorium. Before you go, please tell me about a time you've been really wrong about something. What did you learn from it?"

Lucia thought briefly. She'd made a few mistakes, probably, but being really wrong about something? She trusted her instincts, and those were usually right. So that's what she said. "I know what I want. I have a strong vision for this place, and before I move forward with logistics, I consult the director and public opinion. When we started marketing the Dalítorium as a place for special events to drive revenue for other projects, it was so successful that we began to get pushback from the community as being less accessible and able to be bought for a price, instead of the hub of a vibrant downtown St. Pete.

"So, we shifted strategy to limit the number of special events and increased our less expensive public events like yoga classes and sleepovers for Girl Scout troops. We made sure those, and not political galas and high-profile weddings, got press coverage, helping turn public opinion in our favor. But I wasn't really wrong. Our marketing for special events was a raving success; it just created a distaste from the public that we needed to fix. Which I did."

Glancing down at her phone, Ali said, "I think that's all from me. Do you have any questions?"

"What's your timeline on making a decision?" Lucia asked.

"We should know later this week, but the storm may push it back a bit," the director said.

"Thank you, Lucia," Ali said, standing to walk Lucia out of the room.

CHAPTER 18

VERA

Had it just been two months ago? Vera remembered it like it was yesterday. How Vera tucked a wayward tendril behind her ear, adrenaline pumping through her veins as she crouched with her hands on her knees, waiting for the ref to start the game. For the first game of the season, this Saturday in August, it was surprisingly cool, with the crispness of fall setting in. After he blew the whistle, she pounced after the ball, beating her opponent, dribbled through the fray, and passed it to her best friend Zoe. With six returning starters as seniors, including Zoe and herself as strikers, they had a great chance of going undefeated again this season.

Her mom had taken on the Team Parent-for-life role. She got to the field first, bringing her two chairs. She set up one at midfield and another in front of the opposite goal. The angle was better for pictures. She moved the second chair when the teams switched sides at half-time, and so far, no one had complained. She was Vera's cheering squad of one. As long as Eliza brought snacks, if Eliza wanted to set up two separate chairs, both in prime viewing real-estate, the other parents let it slide.

Deep into the second half of the game with minutes left to play, the score was tied 2 to 2. Vera and Zoe each had scored one goal for their team. They had been the Trojans, but they were in the middle of a rebranding campaign, and for the moment, they had no mascot.

Wanting to avoid overtime, Vera went into beast mode. She stole the ball from an oncoming forward and dodged a midfielder before passing it in a perfect arc towards Zoe. She scrambled downfield to get open and hopefully take the winning shot. They obviously both wanted to shoot, but they took turns when they could, having long ago settled the silly competition between players on the same team. They decided they both could get scholarships and both could be stars.

Zoe passed her the ball. Vera dribbled towards the goal, gauging her best shot. The goalie had a weakness in the top left, as the first half had proven, so that's where she would aim. As she went to kick the ball and win the game for her team, something shifted. The goal disappeared, and everything went fuzzy. She stood there, paralyzed, as the sidelines erupted, "Shoot it!" She wanted to, but she could no longer see the goalie, much less the ball.

A defender stole the ball and cleared it, booting it down the field. Confused, the sidelines began to murmur. Vera still did not move. She knew she didn't look injured, but she didn't know how to get help. She wasn't even sure which side of the field was her team's.

"Time out!" her coach called, and the game stopped, the players likely taking knees.

Zoe reached her first. "Are you okay, Vee?"

"I should have let you take that shot," Vera said. "Something's wrong with me."

"Vera!?!" her mother shouted, taking her into her arms. "Are you okay?"

"I don't know what's happening, Mom. I can't see."

"What do you mean?"

"I can't see you, or Zoe, or the goal, or anything! It just went dark."

Zoe and her mother each took a side and helped her off the field. She wanted to stay until the end of the game, but Eliza overruled her.

As Eliza guided Vera to the car, they heard the cheers of the other side, the painful ending to their first game of the season.

Vera's vision would return and go again in starts and fits, but there was no discernable pattern. She never knew when the next blackout would come. Because of that, the soccer season for Vera—and their chance at an undefeated season—was over. No college recruiters would be able to see her if she wasn't playing.

Even though it was a Saturday, Eliza called Dr. Abel's emergency number from the car after the game, and he saw them that afternoon.

Vera could see her freedom slipping away with her vision. When they got home, the first thing her mother did was take away the keys to the Buick LeSabre that had been Nana and Pops. Zoe came to visit when she could, but she was busy with her travel team and weekend college tours. Until they figured out what was wrong with Vera, she couldn't even go to school.

Vera wanted to keep her social media apps for the moments when she had some glimmers of sight. They kept her sane and gave her a lifeline to her friends, but ultimately, Vera deleted most of her accounts, not only because she didn't want her mother to see them, but also because she couldn't bear listening to videos she couldn't see, wondering what she was missing.

The irony was because her mother worked in the school office, her mother still got to go to high school while Vera stayed home and waited. Her mother tried to keep her up on her studies at night, bringing home work and photocopied notes, but Vera lost motivation quickly.

It wasn't seeing or not seeing that bothered her: what bothered her most was the unpredictability of it. Just when it came back, a light flickering on—a glimpse of freedom, it could disappear again in an instant. She was tired of getting her hopes up and being disappointed.

CHAPTER 19

NICK

Nick lingered outside of the board room, glancing towards the door and away again, hoping to catch Lucia as she left. He was supposed to be downstairs, circulating and talking to patrons, but he figured the Dalís could handle it for now. It's not that he wanted to be eclipsed by a hologram. "I'm a guide here, or at least I used to be," was his go-to joke but in truth, he loved the new exhibit. Instead of having the same conversations over and over, he could tinker with the Deepfake Dalís and make sure they were in running order. Nowadays, he spent more time talking about the creation of *The Lazarus Project* than Dalí's art, but he was okay with that. He'd seen the uptick in visitors, and given how much he'd worked on this project, it boded well for both him and Lucia.

Without *The Lazarus Project*, he might never have met Vera, who was likely having surgery right now. He'd called Vera a few times since he last saw her, and they talked like they'd known each other for years, but hadn't heard from her in a few hours. To pass the time while he waited for Vera to be out, he tried to focus on his work.

Lucia's interview should be finishing now, and he couldn't wait to hear how it went. With her in charge, he may even get to run the new technology wing and virtual reality exhibits. He didn't mind waiting a little longer. The longer the interview went, the better her chances were.

"Nick?" Lucia's voice jarred him out of fantasies of future exhibits.

He turned toward her. Those tortoise-shell glasses picked up the golden flecks in her eyes and her French twist created a sexy librarian vibe that was hard to ignore. He focused on the end of the pen she was chewing on, gross enough to push that thought out of his head. "I thought you were still in there."

"We finished early. With the storm coming, they needed to meet privately, so they cut it short." She twisted a tendril of hair around her finger. "But they loved my ideas and my vision for the future. They thanked me for the notoriety and traffic *The Lazarus Project* has brought to the museum."

Despite her confidence, her frenetic energy coupled with the short interview puzzled him. Not a great sign for her, he thought. "Nice. You've got this. When will you know?"

"They're supposed to make a decision by the end of this week. Oh, and Nick, can you get the miniatures shipped today? Like now?"

"Of course. I'm on it."

"Thank you. I told the board they were shipping this morning," she confided. "The Meadows Museum in Dallas was asking."

It wasn't like her to fudge anything, be it numbers or truths. Most people he knew would say they were 5 minutes away when the GPS said 7. Or even round up to 10 to be on the safe side. Or pretend they knew the person featured on that podcast everyone was talking about, even when they didn't. But Lucia told it like it was. Usually.

"I told you I've got it," he said again, trying to take some of the pressure off of her.

"Good. I'm meeting the film crew in the James Wing if you need anything."

"The film crew? For *The Lazarus Project*? Weren't they supposed to come yesterday?"

"It's a long story. Something came up. I was going to push them till tomorrow, but with the storm coming, I didn't want to chance it."

"Got it." Lucia might have mentioned it already, but if so, he didn't remember. Since he'd met Vera, he'd had trouble thinking of anything else.

Lucia disappeared through the double doors behind them as Nick turned toward the vault.

When he passed the board room, the door opened. Harold held it for a man Nick had never seen. Who needed a black dress coat in Florida in October? Even though the building was air conditioned, the humidity outside was unbearable. "I think you're going to love it here, Stu," the director said, shaking the stranger's hand and patting his back. Seeing Nick, the director addressed him: "Nick. Lazarus is brilliant. A real triumph. Cancel your plans this afternoon," Harold continued. "You're showing my friend Stu around St. Pete. You have to try the oysters, Stu!"

Nick had been hoping to finish up early, so he could check on Vera after her surgery, maybe even show her around, now that she could see better. Whoever this guy was, it meant trouble for Lucia. Although if this Stu became the next director, Nick wanted to be on his good side.

"Next time," Stu responded. "I've got a plane to catch. Should be in LaGuardia by dusk."

"Next time, then. Nick can drive you. Let us know when you decide."

"I will," Stu said. "You have a car, right?"

"Nick," Nick said, extending a hand and reintroducing himself to his possible future boss. "And yes, I do. Pleasure to meet you, Stu." Nick crossed off everything he was planning for the rest of the afternoon, not like he had a choice. If Lucia weren't with the film crew, he'd just call her and have her ship the miniatures. But he didn't want to have to explain Stu to her, and she didn't need anything else to worry about. He'd have to try and catch her later. The miniatures would have to wait; he couldn't let the director know they were still here.

CHAPTER 20

VERA

Exhausted after multiple tests and blood draws, the last thing Vera wanted to do was to talk about it more. Even though she decided to have the surgery, she couldn't bear the thought of having to think about it, much less talk. Before her mom could bring up a new question or memory or idea of something they could do after the surgery, Vera asked her mom to turn on the TV. Even if she couldn't see it, at least she could listen to it. She hated not being able to see the remote more than not being able to see the show.

Her mom obliged. Hearing the tapping of texting, Vera figured her mom must be scrolling social media or responding to well-meaning friends and neighbors, updating them on Vera's status. Like many, her mom loved the escapism and dopamine hits.

She heard the door open, and both her mother's tapping and her show came to an abrupt stop.

A voice she recognized took the lead. "I'm Dr. Madhav, and this is Arielle." Even though this was the first time they'd met Dr. Madhav in person, after numerous video consults, Dr. Madhav seemed to know what she was doing. They were here, Dr. Madhav explained, to review the procedure Vera would undergo.

"As we discussed, we're going to do a transsphenoidal surgery," Dr. Madhav explained, pulling out and pointing to a 3-D model. She was talking to Vera, but the diagram was mostly for Eliza's benefit. "Vera, do you want me to show you?"

Vera nodded, and Dr. Madhav took her hand guiding it over the model.

"We're going to make a small cut at the bottom of your nose, here, between your nostrils, and insert our instruments, including a little camera. That way, we will be able to see the tumor and make sure we remove all of it. Given the size of your tumor, this is the least invasive plan and should fully remove the growth. You will have some follow-up tests to make sure we removed everything, that nothing comes back, but after this surgery, you should be as good as new. Any questions?"

Vera wanted to ask the question she couldn't shake, that kept her up nights, that almost made her walk away from surgery altogether: if she would die. Instead, she opted for a safer, more hopeful, question: "When will I wake up? How long will it take for me to be me again?"

"Good question," Dr. Madhav said. "The surgery could take up to nine hours, and you will be out for longer, due to the anesthesia. But if everything goes as planned when you wake up, your vision will be fully restored. After you gain your strength, you should be back to your old self."

Vera couldn't imagine it, and she couldn't wait to be there. Just in time for her eighteenth birthday, not that she had plans to celebrate yet. She could call Nick. She could finally see Nick. "Let's do this," she said, with resolve and enthusiasm she had not previously had.

"Your mother is still legally your guardian. Eliza, if you consent, you need to sign here first."

"Vera, you're sure?" Eliza asked.

Vera nodded.

"You're sure this is safe?" Eliza asked.

"Nothing is completely safe, but I have done many of these procedures, and if you don't do this, the tumor will continue to grow. The symptoms will continue to get worse," Dr. Madhav confirmed. "Any other questions?"

"I don't think so," Eliza said. "Hand me the papers."

"Arielle will help you take care of that, and you, Vera, will see me when you wake up," Dr. Madhav said, heading out of the room to complete her rounds.

"Here," Arielle handed Eliza a stack of papers. "Read through these and sign anything that is highlighted. Let me know if you have any questions."

As Eliza flipped through the numerous forms, Vera took a moment to ask Arielle a few questions of her own. She liked how sure and warm Arielle's voice sounded. "So kids my age, how do they do with this… this kind of surgery?"

"Dr. Madhav does this procedure at least three times a week, and she's the best. With how early this was caught, you should feel like yourself in no time."

"And my vision?"

"It may be a little blurry when you first wake up, but it should come right back. Only a small fraction of people having this surgery need any corrective vision work afterwards."

"Will you be there?"

"The whole time."

"Good."

Arielle led Vera towards the bed, putting her hand on a cloth object. "Here's the gown you'll wear while you are here. Leave it open in the back. You should take everything off, including your underwear and jewelry. You can put them in this belongings bag," she said, moving Vera's hand to a second cloth object. "I'll knock before I come back in to make sure you are ready."

"Can you go, too, Mom?" Vera asked Eliza. Vera had been dying to check her phone and see if she'd heard back from Nick, and she didn't want to check it with her mom there. Having text messages read aloud and having to say what she wanted to type was awkward with her mom in earshot, and she couldn't find her headphones. Realizing her mom hadn't responded or started to leave, she offered, "I'll text you when I'm done changing."

"I've got a few questions about these forms, Arielle." Eliza said, not waiting for a response. Her mother got the hint, but needed to make it seem like it was her idea.

As soon as Vera heard the door close, she pulled out her phone. Three new messages, all from Nick, plus a few from friends and teammates back home. She checked his first. She wished it read messages in his voice. It wasn't fair that he could hear her voice texts. It wasn't fair that he knew what she looked like while she could only imagine what he looked like. What if he was shorter than her? What if he was out of her league? She'd thought about asking her mom but decided against it.

Still, he'd texted, checking on her, making a joke about bringing her a treat that was better than hospital food. He wanted to see her. Vera's heart soared, and she practiced her response a few times, trying to get the words and the tone just right, before hitting record.

ELIZA

Eliza knew that Vera wanted a moment alone, but Eliza was torn about leaving her. She didn't want to let Vera out of her sight again, and what if Vera needed help? This might be her only chance to clear up family history. Once the door was firmly closed behind them both, she said, "Arielle, can I have a word?"

Arielle nodded. "I just need to scan the consent form."

"It will only take a minute. It's important. The ovarian cancer and heart disease Vera mentioned?"

"Yes."

"That's not Vera's medical history. My parents loved her as their own, but they aren't her biological grandparents."

"Okay. What family history should I know about?"

"I wish I knew."

"You wouldn't be the first," Arielle said.

CHAPTER 21
LUCIA

The local news crew was waiting in the James Wing when Lucia got there. She'd helped many previous shoots, but this time, Harold let her take the lead. He reasoned that she knew more about the exhibit than anyone. Lucia relished the opportunity to play director for the day, to be the face of the museum. She glanced down at her watch. Just before three. She wasn't late. She wondered if Vera's surgery had started, and then forced herself to push that thought out of her head.

She welcomed the local news crew and took the lead on introductions. They were primarily here to showcase *The Lazarus Project*, but because the Dalítorium needed the public on their side to approve the expansion, she never shied away from a chance to show off the building itself.

Instead of letting the Dalís speak for themselves, Lucia found herself over-explaining, talking for longer than she expected, as if she were interviewing for the director role all over again, but saying everything she didn't get to say.

"Let's get a few more with the Dalís," the reporter said, as they approached a Dalí reading today's *Tampa Bay Times*. The headline, "This Could Be the BIG One," sprawled across the cover. Sensing movement, the digital Dalí dropped the paper, warning, "*So little of what could happen does happen. One day, it will have to be officially admitted that what we have christened reality is an even greater illusion than the world of dreams.*"

"Perhaps, Dalí, perhaps," the reporter said before turning to the camera. "If you haven't seen this exhibit, you should." To the cameraman, she said, "We've got enough...

The cameraman stopped shooting. "We may need to cut the newspaper bit."

"The *Tampa Bay Times* was one of our biggest donors on this project," Lucia countered, channeling the director. She knew the museum needed their full support to push the expansion through. Where was Harold? Even though he'd left her in charge, she was almost certain he would stop by.

"Well, we may need to replace that headline then. No point in bringing hurricane doomsday into this." The conversation turned to hurricane prep.

"Sounds like a plan. I can send you a few other clips of the *Tampa Bay Times* Dalí from other days," Lucia offered, not totally sure about the quality of the footage.

"That would be great, Lucia. And thanks for moving the shoot up. We're leaving town now, trying to outrun the storm and get back to the studio in Orlando. We'll send you a copy before we air it."

Lucia nodded. This was going exactly the way it was supposed to. She could do this.

"Give me ten minutes to get B-roll?" the cameraman asked.

"Just ten. We've got one last stop before we leave St. Pete," the reporter said. Turning her attention to Lucia, she asked, "What are you going to do? When are you leaving town?"

"I'm not leaving town," Lucia smiled. "I'm staying here."

"In St. Pete? At what shelter?"

"At the Dalítorium. This place is a fortress."

"Couldn't the glass break?"

"Not a chance. Those panes may look fragile, but they are an inch and a half thick. When Yann Weymouth designed it, he built it to survive a hurricane."

"So, if the water rises?"

She gestured towards the enigma of glass panes. "This place will become an aquarium. Who knows what marine life or debris may come swirling by, or what the Dalís will have to say about it." Dalí would have loved to see that, something straight out of one of his lucid dreams.

"What if we stayed to shoot?" the cameraman suggested.

That was an idea. Dalí Underwater. She could use the footage for a new exhibit, maybe even have special events where she recreated the exhibit. But that would mean having other people here, possibly putting their lives at risk.

"The building hasn't actually been tested before," Lucia said.

"But you trust it."

Out of the corner of her eye, she saw Harold, Nick, and a man she'd never seen before leaving the museum together. As director, shouldn't Harold be here with her? Or in the meeting that cut her interview short? She made a mental note to ask Nick about who that man was as soon as she got the chance.

"But you trust it?" he asked, prompting her again.

"I do, I mean I think I do." She'd been waiting for a hurricane to hit, wanting to test out the limits of the building and witness the impossible. When she got hired, she knew it was part of her responsibilities. They even made her sign a waiver. If the glass broke and the place flooded, the walls were still quite thick, and she could take shelter in one of the windowless rooms on the third floor. She'd still need to be here to salvage as much of the collection as she possibly could.

"But what if you get stuck here for a while? What about power?"

"Weymouth put all mission-critical systems including generators and dehumidifiers on the third floor, above the storm surge level. Nothing is going to get in here."

"So why not open it up as a shelter?" She realized they'd started recording her again. And she had no good answer to that question. She stood there, mute and stumped for a painfully long time until she heard the interviewer say, "You heard it here at the hurricane fortress, the Dalítorium."

CHAPTER 22

ELIZA

When Eliza got the call from Vera, she had been waiting outside the room, coffee in hand, for more than a few minutes, but she wanted to give Vera her privacy. This was a lot for both of them. Eliza had picked up a Peppermint Pattie, an impulse, for sure. Vera's childhood favorite. It was a surprise. For after surgery.

As she entered the room, the reality of what was to happen hit her. Her daughter was lying in a hospital bed, wearing a dinosaur print gown—could they not have found something more age-appropriate? Nana's necklace, the locket Nana had given her on her tenth birthday, the one she never took off, was now cast aside in a heap on the nearest table. Vera was listening to something on her phone, her autumn hair loose, cascading around her shoulders. This was happening.

"Will you braid my hair, Mom?"

"One or two?"

"Two. French."

Eliza sat on the bed beside her, repeating a ritual she'd done more times than she could count. How many more times would Vera let her do this? What was it they said about motherhood? Long days and short years? She'd gone from an inconsolable infant to a senior perfecting her personal statement for colleges seemingly overnight. But that was all still before. Before the diagnosis.

After the papers were signed and Vera changed, things moved quickly, more so than Eliza had expected. Arielle and another nurse came in, put Vera on a gurney and rolled her away.

"You need some rest," a nurse told Eliza.

After the marathon from that initial diagnosis to Vera agreeing to do the surgery, Eliza couldn't remember the last time she'd rested. "I'm fine. I'll just wait here."

"Don't be foolish. She's the last surgery of the day. It could go later into the night. There's nothing you can do to help her right now."

"I know but…"

"Go back to Ronald McDonald. Get some sleep. We'll call you when there's news, so you can be there when she wakes up. She's going to need you tomorrow, and you're going to need your energy."

Reluctantly, Eliza realized the nurse was right. Selfishly, she knew she needed some sleep, but she didn't want to leave Vera. Her daughter was safe here, she told herself. What Vera would need more than anything tomorrow was a mom who wasn't totally exhausted.

CHAPTER 23
LUCIA

Andre and Lucia were lying in bed at her house with the nightly news on, muted in the background. She hadn't had a TV in her room until after they started dating seriously, and when he wasn't there, it was rarely—if ever—on. He'd gotten it for her as a surprise that first November, justifying it as a way to watch the campaign results come in with her. Instead, he stayed at some hall near his campaign office rented out for the occasion. She'd thought about watching the results from home but instead stayed late at work, and when things were looking more promising, joined him at the hall, officially as a guest and not his significant other. It was still early in their relationship, Andre had told her, and he wasn't sure how it would look to voters.

They had met at one of his campaign fundraisers held at the Dalítorium. She'd been in charge of the event. They didn't get photographed together until after he was elected, and to this day, they denied being together if anyone asked. The widowed, unattainable bachelor angle worked better for his campaign, and she preferred keeping their relationship private. She knew that the director knew, and a few close friends, but that was it. Since then, the TV—like him—became a semi-permanent figure in her bedroom.

"How'd the interview with the board go?" he asked.

It had taken him long enough to ask. She could have brought it up. She'd been mulling over every question, every facial expression, everything she could remember saying, over and over in her mind ever since she'd left. "It's over at least. I think it went well. They said they would make an announcement by the end of the week."

"I'm sure you did just fine, babe. You do everything for them. They love you."

"Maybe. I hope so." She didn't share what bothered her most, that it felt like her interview was rushed, cut short, perfunctory even. She couldn't shake the thought that they were leading her on. Again.

Instead of probing further, Andre took the remote and turned the volume up. "Have you heard about this?" he asked Lucia, pointing towards the screen. "This could be the big one… This could be terrible for St. Pete Rising and for my campaign." Across the screen, the words, "Hurricane Phoenix, Two Days until Landfall" scrolled ominously.

A man in an oversized button-down, sleeves rolled up for the long haul, appeared on-screen with a map of the gulf area projected behind him. "Well, it just keeps getting worse now. We've got another update: We have a 105 mile-per-hour category 2 hurricane, and it's rapidly intensifying here right near the Yucatan Channel. It's going to come into the Gulf of Mexico within about 6 to 12 hours. Hurricane landfall is certain in the Florida area. We think Central West Florida is most likely, as a category 4, possibly a 5. We have an extreme event unfolding here with Hurricane Phoenix."

"Do you think this could be the big one?" Lucia asked Andre.

"You heard him…" Andre said. "The possible projected range includes almost all of Florida. You know how unpredictable these things can be."

She knew it would come here eventually. If not this one, there would be another one. It was only a matter of time, and they had eked out of close calls before. She was a planner. Her job depended on it.

As they watched, Andre got a call. Andre sprang up from the bed, looking for his pants, socks, shoes, and other things he had carelessly thrown around the room. "I've got to go in, Lucia. They're triggering evacuation protocols and setting up shelters."

"The stadium?"

Andre shook his head. "I wish. If only the Tropicana were built stronger..."

"Why do you need to be there now?"

"People in St. Pete don't look to FEMA or the president or governor. They look to me. I want to be in Home Depot when they're getting plywood."

"This might be a long haul," Lucia warned. "And you might not want to be in Home Depot when it hits."

"Obviously not. But I need to do something. We can barely handle a Category 4, much less a 5." Andre said. "We need to get as many people out as quickly as possible. These structures aren't built for a big one, Lu."

Except for the museum, she thought, as he rushed out the door. It was too early to think about that now. It wasn't her fault the city continued to feign ignorance through all these hurricane seasons and not expand preparations. After Dennis and Wilma, after Matthew and Irma, and even after Katrina, why wait until a storm's on your doorstep to prepare? He hated showing the public any vulnerability that wasn't preplanned and orchestrated to boost ratings. Only she saw this, and, like the storm, she saw what would come. She tried to put that, and Eliza and Vera, and her continual replaying of her interview out of her head, or at least use one to distract her from another. What she wanted more than anything was sleep, but it wouldn't come.

OCTOBER 13TH

CHAPTER 24

ELIZA

"Mrs. Garcia! Mrs. Garcia!" Arielle said, nudging her back into the present. Eliza had fallen asleep in the waiting room. "Vera's out of surgery. They were able to remove the tumor with clear margins. Her vitals are steady, and she should be waking up soon."

Eliza was embarrassed she had fallen asleep. She'd tried to go back to the Ronald McDonald House, but found sleeping there impossible. Every time she drifted off, she jerked back awake, thinking she'd heard Vera, checking her phone for a missed call from the hospital. She'd slept better in Vera's first few weeks of life when Vera, not nursing, cried through most of the night. She'd slept better the first time Vera missed curfew by more than a few minutes. Eliza stared at her phone and the alarm clock from 2:37 until she couldn't stand it any longer and the clock read the seemingly reasonable 4:30. With Vera in surgery Eliza couldn't sleep, so Eliza ended up wandering the streets of St. Pete. She told herself she was looking for coffee, but instead she walked directly to the water, marveling how the museum's tessellated windows reflected the fleeting pink of early morning light.

When she got to the hospital an hour later, she still couldn't go to Vera's room. She collapsed into the same plastic chair she'd sat in yesterday, nodding off shortly after sitting down. But none of that mattered anymore. Vera, her Vera, was awake. They were on the other side of this catastrophe.

"Where's the doctor?" Eliza asked the nurse. "Shouldn't she be here telling me this?"

"Dr. Madhav would be here with me if there were any concerns, but after operating into the night, she's sleeping. She'll check on Vera later this morning, and if anything at all changes, we will get her immediately."

They must know better, Eliza thought, but it seemed strange to her. Also, Arielle likely had been awake for at least as long. Grateful her daughter survived the surgery, Eliza hungered to be reunited with her. "Where is she? Where is she now?"

"In 321," Arielle said.

"Not 118?"

Arielle explained that given her strong vitals, they took her to a recovery room. Standard operating procedure. She was practically an adult and since she was stable and recovering nicely, she didn't need to be monitored in the pediatric intensive unit any longer. She could be moved to a regular floor.

Eliza grabbed her purse and the overnight bag she'd packed for Vera, and then she went with Arielle, saying a brief prayer, thankful her daughter pulled through. Despite all the misgivings she had had about the surgery, about the risk she would be putting Vera through, she finally absolved herself of the guilt, knowing it was all worth it.

CHAPTER 25

VERA

A rhythmic beeping pulled Vera from the depths of her subconscious. Vera's eyes fluttered a few times, overwhelmed by slats of light. Vertical blinds. A poster-picture with haphazard splotches of color. This wasn't her bedroom. Where was she? Something teal, a chair, most likely. She could see it. She could see! Her eyes jumped from object to object, lingering on some, waiting for her eyes to focus, zooming in and out on others, adjusting to the brightness.

How long had she been out? Was it tomorrow yet?

And her mom... Where was her mom? She should be here. She scanned the room once more, seeing more clearly. The bathroom door was open, but the light was off. Where could her mom have gone? She'd promised she would be here.

When Vera tried to sit up, her head spun. That wasn't working. Something else, she decided. Noticing the controls on the side of the bed, she pressed the button to raise her body into a sitting position. Her tongue stuck to the roof of her mouth, and it was impossible to swallow. She found a ginormous plastic mug with a handle, lid, and straw beside her table. She didn't care what it was. She needed something to drink. The ice-cold, sugary liquid, likely ginger ale, gave her strength. She munched on the bits of crushed ice small enough to make it through the straw. She saw her phone on the same wheeled table. She grabbed it, hoping her mom had called.

Nothing.

She heard a click and turned. The door to her room opened, just a crack at first and then wider. Her mom was there. Backlit with the fluorescent lights from the hall, her mom glowed for a flickering moment before rushing towards her.

"Let me check her first, please," a nurse who looked familiar to Vera said. She'd been with her when they put her under, Vera remembered. Arielle. Her short-term memory still seemed to work.

Arielle checked the monitors to make sure they were firmly attached, and looked at the miniscule incision spot.

"That looks good. I'll leave you for now, but Vera, if you need help, click this button. My shift ends soon, and Giulia will be taking over for me. And, Eliza, she'll need her rest." With that, Arielle turned and left them.

"There you are!"

"Oh honey. I've been trying to get up here for hours," her mom said. "How are you? What do you need?"

"It's the left side. I knew it!"

"The left side, what?"

"This is stupid, but I forgot which side your dimple was on. When they were putting me under, I was thinking about you, trying to remember what you looked like, your purple glasses, the laugh lines around your eyes. But I couldn't remember which side your dimple was on."

"That's not silly at all, and you remembered perfectly," her mom commended.

"It's coming back, my vision. I was worried it wouldn't, or that something would… change."

"You're a champion."

"Thanks, Mom."

"A cop stopped me."

"You? For what?" Vera couldn't help but laugh.

"I couldn't sleep. I was wandering the streets of St. Pete before dawn, and I guess she was worried about me."

"Oh, Mom. I'm turning eighteen, and you're the one having run-ins with the cops!"

"I hadn't done anything wrong."

"But you still got my stuff, right? I can't wait to put on my own clothes, to put on eyeliner." She knew it probably sounded silly, but she'd finally been allowed eyeliner, and then the tumor came. She foolishly tried to put it on in the beginning, but after a few eyeball pokes, she realized it wasn't worth the trouble.

"I left your makeup bag back at the hotel."

"But I wanted to have it!"

"You don't need it here."

"I haven't been able to use it in months! You just don't like it when I wear it. You think it looks trashy."

"We'll leave here soon enough, and then you can put on all the eyeliner you want, and we can explore St. Pete."

When Vera didn't respond, Eliza tried again. "I'm sorry, Vera. I can go pick it up."

"No, it's fine," Vera said, rolling her eyes. Normally, her mother would have been all over her for that, but between the tumor and brain surgery, Eliza let it slide. As much as she'd wanted her mother a few minutes ago, right now, she wanted to be alone, to scroll through her phone and catch up on months of social media, to see which friends had texted, to see if Nick had called.

She'd pretend to be sleepy. Maybe her mom would actually go get her makeup bag. Vera yawned, and in turn, her mom did too. Yawns are contagious like that.

"You should get some sleep," Eliza said. "I'll go get some coffee. Is there anything I can get you?"

"Don't I have to eat their food?"

"It'll be our secret."

Sometimes her mom came through. "A Peppermint Pattie would be awesome," Vera said.

Their favorite. The closest thing to a Thin Mint they could get during the other eleven months of the year when the Girl Scouts stopped selling. She never really got into the outdoorsy stuff, and she'd given up after those early Brownie years, but they both couldn't resist the cookies. Vera would buy her own two boxes and write her name on them just so her mom wouldn't eat them.

"Surprise!" her mom said, pulling the shiny silver wrapper out of her bag.

"How'd you do that?" Vera asked, taking the Peppermint Pattie, ripping it open, and devouring it in a few bites. "This is so good. Thanks, Mom. How'd you know?"

"I know my daughter."

"My makeup bag?" Vera asked.

"I don't really want to leave the hospital again, not until you can come with me," Eliza said.

"Please, Mom?"

"We'll see." Vera's all-time least favorite response.

Her mom had been hovering so much over the past two months. Vera probably needed it then, but not now. She raised her eyebrows at her mom, hoping she would get the hint. She didn't.

"You can go, Mom. The nurse said I needed rest, and they'll keep an eye on me."

"Okay, honey."

Vera closed her eyes and turned away from her mom, curling up into the fetal position. She heard her mom's footsteps leaving, the door to her room opening and shutting again. Vera rolled back over, sat up, and reached for her phone.

CHAPTER 26

MIQUEL

Even though Miquel had been to Figueres a hundred times, he had not yet made it to St. Pete to see the Dalí collection there, at least not until now. That wasn't why he'd come, of course. He hadn't endured the red-eye flights connecting through Newark to see the collection. Eliza had written him—she'd written a handful of times before: after their hasty, brief marriage crumbled all those years ago, when the reality of raising a baby felt too suffocating, when Vera wrote her name for the first time to sign a bright blue duck she had painted, when Lucia's mother had died. He hadn't responded to any of them, but this one was different.

He hadn't told her—them, he was coming. He even bought a full-price ticket, something he never did. Instead, he preferred to draw on some connection, some future promise, or some smooth-talking to gain admission. Miquel's sleight of hand tricks almost always resulted in upgrades.

Miquel had not made plans to see Lucia, but hoped he'd run into her. It had been two years since the last time they'd been together, having run into each other at a gala opening in New York. She was wearing something shimmery, slinky. He noticed her, exuding unwarranted confidence, before he recognized her. She was the constant, the net in the tennis game the rest of them played, the unbeatable force they didn't even realize they were up against.

Over the years, there had been a few planned trysts and a few unplanned run-ins. They were both smarter now, using protection, guarding their deepest selves. It never lasted more than a few days, and they would fall out of contact the minute they parted ways. He stalked her occasionally, mostly through social media when something else in his life fell apart or some other girl had left. He'd known about *The Lazarus Project,* her latest exhibit to bring Dalí back to life. Her name wasn't on it officially, but he saw her fingerprints all over it. Even the last time they were together, she envisioned this future, quoting Dalí as they lay on separate sides of the hotel bed, after.

"When you are a genius," Lucia recited, "You do not have the right to die, because we are necessary for the progress of humanity." She'd taken Dalí's death as a personal affront and made it her quest to bring him back to life. She went after what she wanted; he knew that about her.

The possibility of seeing her vision in person overwhelmed him. Dalí's art enchanted him, but not as much as the goddess who reincarnated him. That trick was beyond his skill set. He still didn't know what he was hoping for: To see her in person? To be close to these holograms, Lucia's professional baby? To avoid going to the hospital?

Miquel, a continental vagabond, preferred drifting from one urban center to the next, dazzling crowds of mostly tourists with magic tricks, making and seeing art when he could, and bedding women when he wasn't performing or creating.

In Newark, he had almost turned back altogether. While Eliza had written to tell him about Vera's tumor, she hadn't asked him to come. She'd stopped doing that a long time ago. Perhaps that's why he went straight to the museum and not the hospital. For Miquel, Dalí provided a solid ground—of melting clocks?—on which to stand.

When he left them—the plump-from-formula, colicky baby who had no interest in him and his study-abroad wife who had not slept or showered in weeks, he thought they would be better off without him. The baby wouldn't go to him without completely falling apart, violently screaming and thrashing, and despite Eliza's inability to produce milk, Vera had not left her arms or chest. He had convinced himself they would be okay to absolve his own history with abandonment and his own guilt about abandoning them.

Since he was here now, he couldn't turn back. Even when he landed in Tampa, he'd thought about catching a return flight without leaving the airport, but most had been postponed or canceled. If he was stuck here, he might as well at least see the Dalí collection. It was Dalí's fault that they'd met and Vera had spiraled into existence in the first place. The least he could do was go back to the source, if only to wait out this storm.

CHAPTER 27

The Dalí Museum
Figueres, Spain

More than eighteen years ago, Lucia and Eliza were climbing the stairs in the Mae West room. Eliza helped balance her friend, who, thanks to her growing belly, was becoming more lopsided by the day.

"You think it's just this sofa," Eliza said. "But when you get to the top…"

When Lucia reached the peephole at the apex and peered through, Mae West's face came into balance. The pictures, eyes; the sideboard, her nose; and the sofa, her iconic lips. From any other angle, the pieces were distorted and disproportionate, but from this spot, Mae sprang to life. Eliza wanted to say the pieces of Lucia's life, similarly distorted, would make sense, but she didn't get a chance. Lucia almost saw it working herself, almost saw her making a life as the mother to this child.

The people behind them nudged them on, reminding them many others were waiting.

As they descended, Lucia confessed what Eliza already knew. "I can't keep it."

"I know," Eliza comforted.

Everything Lucia had been thinking came out at once. "I wanted to. I've thought about it every way I know how and back. I'll lose my scholarship. My mother will disown me. Everything I've worked for to escape her fate. How could I have been so dumb? It's too late to get rid of it. And so now what? Raised in some orphanage by nuns? Raised by strangers?"

Just like Mae West's face had come into focus, Eliza saw her future clearly, pieces falling into place. "I'll take the baby. I'll raise it." And if it was a boy, she could name him Francis. Call him Frank.

"And the baby could be with his father," Lucia agreed. This almost tore them apart last year. Miquel was with Eliza now, and he had been, except for one night that changed everything for them. They'd gone back to Figueres for the weekend, all three of them. They'd intended to go to all three places Dalí loved, including the Gala Dalí Castle Pubol and the Salvador Dalí House in Portlligat, but Eliza had gotten food poisoning before the castle. She told them to go on together, without her. That had been her mistake.

After Lucia confessed everything at the Sagrada de Familia, Eliza eventually forgave them both, not just for her new beau's planting a seed of mistrust in their relationship, but also for planting a child in her best friend's belly. Eliza knew Miquel hated condoms. With her, it didn't matter. She knew long before she came to Spain that she couldn't have children. Something rare, the doctor had told her when she was just fifteen. She was infertile and would never carry a child of her own.

Somehow, they had all gone on living, Eliza and Lucia together, Eliza dating Miquel. Lucia became increasingly hopeful at this newfound possibility. If Eliza and Miquel raised the child, Lucia could get to know her child, keep her scholarship stateside, and not disappoint her mom.

Everything could be okay.

CHAPTER 28

LUCIA

As Lucia headed down the double-helix staircase to the Café Gala for an espresso, her morning pick-me-up, she noticed an eerie, yellow glow across the sky. Such a strange color for midday. A cheer from a crowd below interrupted her reverie, and she noticed people gathering not around one of her many Deepfake Dalís but instead around a salt and peppered performer.

She couldn't see his face, but she didn't have to. She knew it was Miquel. The silvery hair was new, but she'd recognize that spry stature anywhere, his favoring of his left leg due to a childhood futbol accident.

Ironically, the same piece they'd seen together in Figueres almost twenty years ago was hanging behind him, but Miquel seemed more interested in his performance. René Thom's catastrophe theory had inspired Dalí to paint again. After seeing gradual changes triggering unanticipated catastrophes, Thom sought to mathematically represent them. He hoped this theory would help predict sudden shifts in behavior resulting from seemingly small changes, such as a fearful, cowering dog suddenly attacking. Or an absent sperm donor showing up suddenly when his almost-grown daughter's life was in the balance.

He must be here for Vera, or possibly Eliza. Not her. Eliza must have told them. How much did he see them? Even when Lucia had seen him, those half a dozen times after, they never talked about Vera, the daughter they'd both abandoned. Because of Miquel's handiwork, Lucia's name wasn't even on the birth certificate.

But why was he here now? He must know about the hospital. Had he been there? Did he know how the surgery went? For the second time in her life, Lucia found herself paralyzed by indecision. She did not decide quickly enough. Before she approached him, before she had a chance to flee, he turned around, locked his golden-flecked eyes with hers, and time stopped.

They stood there, transported back to Figueres, more than eighteen years ago, the first time she'd lost herself in those eyes. Lucia had no hatred towards him, and despite everything they had been through, had wanted and then had abandoned, there was no one, not even Eliza, who saw her as clearly.

But if he wasn't here for her, why was he at the museum? And not the hospital? He was seeing her most intimate life's work, what she had conceived, nurtured, and brought to life. With deepfake, who needs cryogenics? And this legacy, this technology would outlive her, would outlive them all. She, the first to move, drew her hand to her neck, a visceral reaction to protect her jugular and hide her vulnerability. He, more than anyone, saw the parts of her she did not wish to be seen, the parts she had repressed.

Shaken back to her senses, she descended the staircase and cleared the crowd, ushering them towards exhibits on the third floor. She would be running this museum and couldn't let just anyone come in uninvited to perform. There were appearances to keep up, and the promotion of her dreams on the line.

"*Hola guapa,*" Miquel said, being the first to speak.

"We have a policy against performing without prior approval," she said, noting the hat he was collecting tips in.

"Is your boyfriend jealous?" Miquel asked, nodding toward the closest Deepfake Dalí.

"You think a little card trick could compete with that?"

"Perhaps?" Miquel asked as he shrugged and smiled.

"But why now, Miquel?"

"*Perquè*.... Vera," he said. Miquel uttered the name he hadn't said in her presence, not since he left her as a baby.

"I know. I saw her," Lucia said. He was too much. This was too much. Everything she had been denying converged, more real than she could have ever imagined. She couldn't breathe. She grabbed the nearest railing, because otherwise she—the impenetrable force—would crumble. "Before the surgery," she offered, in response to his hopeful, prying eyes. "I saw them both."

Miquel couldn't help but ask, "Is it over? How'd it go?"

Did he have a right to know the fate of the daughter he had left before her first birthday? Did she?

"I don't know," Lucia said. "I didn't feel like I could ask. They were here, both of them, and then they were gone. The surgery happened yesterday, at least I think it did."

"You didn't ask? Lucia." He looked at her like she was crazy. "Eliza came to St. Pete for a reason," Miquel said.

"Eliza told me. This place is the best," Lucia said.

He shook his head. "She needs you. Especially if things don't go... well... as planned." Miquel said.

"How could you possibly think that?" Lucia asked.

"She wrote me," he said. "So why are you here? And not there?"

"Why aren't you there?" Lucia countered, immediately defensive, feeling a fortress of silent resistance prickle up around her. She had never agreed to any of this. Eliza got Miquel and the child Eliza had always wanted but couldn't have. Lucia had gotten to keep her scholarship and follow her dreams. It was the pact they had made in the Mae West room all those years ago, and even after their falling out, after Eliza left Spain with Vera, nowhere in the pact did it stipulate Vera could re-enter her life and get sick. That she might even die.

"Nervous, I guess. Where would I even begin?" Miquel said.

"So why are you even here?"

"I wanted to see her one more time, just in case..."

"Lucia, there you are," Nick said. "I've been looking everywhere for you. The board wants to see you immediately."

Lucia lit up. Could they have already made a decision about her promotion? That was even faster than she expected to hear from them.

Seeing Lucia's reaction, Nick clarified, "Not about the promotion, about the storm."

"Of course. The storm. I need to go," Lucia said, staying with Miquel's gaze too long before turning to follow Nick.

"*Adeu, amor meu,*" Miquel said after her.

MIQUEL

Miquel stood there, unsure of what to do next. Of course, he must go to the hospital and find Vera. That's why he'd come. He wanted to stay here in the Dalítorium until someone, perhaps that same young man who found Lucia, kicked him out, but for once in his life he made the more responsible choice, heading down the spiral helix stairs towards the door. On his way out, he walked through the gift store, snagging a pack of gum and slipping it into his pocket. After the overnight flight, he hadn't brushed his teeth yet today. He couldn't resist the selfie with Dalí, though. He did it twice because he didn't like the angle of his face in the first one. Not that Dalí would remember or mind much.

He wandered through some of the Avant Garden, stopping to write his hope on his wristband and add it to the tree of wishes.

He checked his phone for directions. Johns Hopkins All Children's was less than a mile away. He decided to walk. He hoped the fresh air would give him the courage needed to see Vera and Eliza again. He had not seen either since he left all those many years ago. He had seen some photos, but those weren't the same. Why did Eliza keep sending them? Did she actually think he would see them and want to get back in touch? To reunite?

Since that marriage had ended, there had been other women, but no more marriages, no more children. After having lived it, he knew children suffocated him, and to suffocate his artistic inner child was a fate worse than physical death. That was what he told himself. His therapist called it commitment issues and a general ego-centric approach to life. At the end of the day, Miquel still paid her, and she wouldn't go as far as to call him selfish.

CHAPTER 29

VERA

There was nothing worth watching on TV, Vera decided. She'd scrolled through the channels multiple times, but it was all kiddie shows, movies she'd loved in elementary school, but nothing she wanted to watch now. She hadn't seen the finale of the newest season of *Stranger Things*, and she couldn't get it here.

Thank goodness for her phone. Even if she couldn't stream her show, at least she had social media. She'd missed so much over the last two months, as most of her content was filtered through her mom's eyes. She'd deleted some of her social media accounts when this started and restoring them was almost as satisfying as having her sight back.

When Vera reached for her phone, she could feel the stickers pulling on the skin of her chest. Then, the annoying beeping started for the third time this morning. She thought little of it and instead, pushed the peas around her plate with one hand, while she scrolled through videos with the other. If the TV wasn't bad enough, the food was terrible. She wanted to go out for Mexican or Indian or maybe even try sushi. They almost went to a sushi place in Chattanooga for Junior Prom but had settled on Italian instead. But bland turkey, mashed potatoes, and peas? No, thank you. If she had to stay here much longer, maybe she could convince her mom to order in. Back home, there weren't a lot of choices besides pizza and hot chicken, but here in St. Pete, she figured she could order anything she could imagine.

The door opened. A nurse, but not Arielle. A new one. "You're off monitor again, Vera. You need to stay still."

"I can't help it. I'm not trying to."

"Just try. Please." The nurse looked down the front of Vera's gown to try and identify the missing lead.

By now, Vera was used to the routine, but she hated having a revolving door of strangers looking at her boobs and touching the stickers that surrounded them, holding the leads in place.

"Next time, ask your mom to help if you need something."

"Do you see her anywhere?"

As if on cue, her mom returned with a coffee and white paper bag in hand. "Everything okay?" she asked the nurse.

"Giulia."

"Everything okay, Giulia?"

"Vera's come off her monitor again. Third time this morning."

"Is that bad?"

"She needs to stay still as much as possible, so we can monitor her progress. If she needs anything, to go to the bathroom, to get something out of her bag, can you help her? We're short staffed today, thanks to Phoenix, and I can't keep coming here to reattach her monitor."

Vera felt her little bit of newfound freedom, simple things like reaching for her phone without her mom seeing it first or going to the bathroom on her own, being taken away from her once again.

"I'll be more careful," Vera said.

"You said that last time."

"We'll do our best. I'll help Vera," her mom promised, and with that, the nurse scurried out of the room. "We're all trying here, Vee. I wish you could too."

"I hate it here. The food is terrible, and they don't get any of my shows. It's all kiddie stuff. And besides, Mom. I feel fine. Can't we leave already?"

"They need to monitor you for 48 hours. You know that. We are so close, Vee. When we leave, you make a list of everything you want to do, and we'll do it."

"Really?" Vera looked at her mom skeptically. "A whole day at the beach? Go back to the museum when I can actually see?"

"Just please, Vera. Please try to stay still. I saw some tourist brochures in the lobby. I can grab them for you to look at."

Vera perked up. "And we can do anything I want? A 'yes' day?"

"Fine, okay."

Excited about her newfound possibility and power, Vera had a sudden urge to put on real clothes. "Can you help me with my bra, Mom?"

"Do you really need..."

"I had brain surgery, not heart surgery. And you heard the nurse...." Vera knew perfectly well that she wouldn't be able to put it on by herself, not with the IV and heart monitor.

"How are we going to get it on you?"

"You can help. Just slide the IV bag through my arm hole and the bra strap." Vera had been thinking about how to do this.

"I don't know if we should, Vee."

"Mom, please? I just want to feel normal again."

Her mom sighed, and then she rummaged through Vera's bag.

"Thank you thank you thank you!!"

Her mom turned toward her with her plain old white bra in hand.

She hadn't worn that bra in months, not since she'd gotten newer ones after she'd noticed all the girls on the team changing out of sports bras into fancier, more colorful bras. Sometimes, her mom forgot how old she was. It was so boring, just little cotton triangles, with no cups or padding. "You brought that one?"

"Which one did you want?"

"The purple one! That one is for middle schoolers, and it doesn't fit anymore. I wanted the purple one."

"Sorry, Vee. I left that one back at the Ronald..."

"Don't you mean the hotel?" How could her mom keep forgetting this?

"The hotel. I'm sorry, Vera. I wasn't sure if you could wear underwire with the heart monitor."

"We could have asked."

"It's this or nothing."

Vera leaned forward, letting her mom untie her hospital gown. She slipped her arms out, with her mom holding the IV bag, gently sliding it through the arm hole and back through the bra strap. Just when her mom was snapping the clasp, they heard it again, the loud beeping.

"Shit," Eliza said.

"At least we tried," Vera said, laughing at the idea of them getting in trouble with the nurse.

As they waited for both the return of the nurse and her impending lecture, Vera asked about the eyeliner.

"Oh Vee, I'm sorry, I forgot."

Vera eyed her skeptically.

"Okay, I didn't forget. I just didn't want to leave the hospital. If it were important…"

"It is important, Mom."

"I found another Peppermint Pattie." A peace offering.

Vera took it begrudgingly from her mom, ripped the wrapping off, and put the entire thing in her mouth.

The monitor continued to drone on, with no nurse in sight yet.

"You're going to be in trouble when she gets back," Vera said, and they both laughed.

CHAPTER 30
LUCIA

Andre found Lucia exiting the labyrinth. She walked it almost every day during her break to calm her mind and center her. She had hated it at first, feeling gluttonous taking time for herself, but a podcast she trusted suggested it, and she tried it, made a habit of it, and it was now so much a part of her routine, she couldn't imagine not walking the labyrinth. Since she'd made her walk predictable, she was occasionally interrupted by something someone else deemed urgent enough to come to find her.

Andre had only come here one other time when she couldn't be reached by phone, when Nick had gotten kicked out of school, and Andre couldn't get in touch with him. For him to come, it must be something important.

"It's bad," Andre said. "The mayor's worried we're under-prepared, but don't quote me on that. I think he was counting on another near-miss. I've been at City Hall for the better part of the morning, and even though they've started the evacuation, they should have started hours ago. We didn't know it would be this bad. No one did."

No one except me, Lucia thought. Despite St. Pete's glaring vulnerability and numerous unwritten checks to Mother Nature, they'd lucked out with a series of near-misses. That's why she had been planning for this moment since before she had taken the interview at the Dalítorium. It was never a question of if but when.

"If it does hit like it could hit, Andre, the devastation would be catastrophic. Buildings around here aren't built for this surge or wind. Even getting everyone out safely will be a challenge, and you know there will be those who refuse to go, who think they can do what they always do: Buy enough toilet paper, milk, and bread, fill their bathtubs with water, and hunker down in a room without windows. And then, there's the bunch that think that if it's my time to go to heaven, then it's my time, but this is my home."

"I never got why they didn't see the evacuation warning as divine intervention," Andre said.

"I know right? But you don't get a merit badge for staying, and if it gets bad, other people may have to risk their lives to save them. Then there are people that don't have the transportation to leave." Lucia knew they agreed on most of this, but the difference was Lucia was prepared. Andre was not. In no way was the city's preparation—or lack thereof—Lucia's fault. If nothing else, it was not Lucia's to fix—not now, not right before her biggest opportunity. Her job, as stated in the Dalítorium's mission, was to protect the art at all costs. She wondered how she could have ever fallen in love with someone who didn't plan.

Obviously, it was his charisma. The first time she'd seen him, Andre had been running for Deputy Mayor for the first time. Lucia had been in charge of the campaign event at the Dalítorium. His campaign had rented a room for current and would-be sponsors. They filled the place. Of course, he thanked her after, but when she first saw him, he was schmoozing with donors, shaking hands, listening deeply, with voracious nodding and look-into-your-soul eye contact. The best politicians could do that: make everyone feel special and heard. The secret was the eye contact, not just that they made it over and over again, but that they lingered a nano-second longer than most people before locking eyes with the next possible voter or donor. People just wanted to be seen.

When he took the podium to address the crowd, she was blown away by his magnetic energy. Perhaps being surrounded by Dalí gave him a similar playfulness, a similar freedom. He shared secrets from his childhood, anecdotes about community members, and a love for the place that she had made her home. More than that, he had shared a progressive vision for St. Pete. His goals for the St. Pete Rising campaign, that he shared to a packed room of wealthy donors, dovetailed perfectly with her own. If she could just catch his eye, get his attention, and stand out from the same crowd he was interested in impressing. How foolish of her. She had not felt this way about someone in such a long time, and yet, she couldn't miss this chance. She had to meet him.

After the event officially ended, while he was still shaking hands and hustling every possible dollar out of the crowd, she approached him and told them they had twenty minutes left. She asked if he wanted to extend the security detail and the length of the contract for another hour. Definitely not a great opening, or a first line anyone writes about, but one that would get his attention.

"Lucia," he said, smiling at her with his eyes, "What a beautiful name. I'm Andre."

"Well, Andre," she said. "It's almost nine o'clock. Do you want to extend the contract? It's $500 an hour."

"Could you consider it a contribution to my campaign?"

"I'm not sure I have that authority. Although it sounds like if you do win, and if you do half of the things you promise, it would be great for the Dalítorium."

"Perhaps we could clear them out more quickly, and you could give me a private tour? Tell me about your vision for the place?" he suggested, putting his hand on her arm and looking deeply into her eyes.

She knew that she should say no and set up a time later, but she did have the keys, and her belly hadn't fluttered like this in so long. She could get in trouble for any after-hours rendez-vous in the museum, but that thought was ridiculous. He just wanted to talk strategy and learn more about the Dalítorium.

"I'll see if I can move them along," Lucia said.

They didn't have sex that night, as she was overly cautious with the security cameras and her career, and he was overly cautious with the upcoming election, but she did give him a private tour of some of her favorite pieces. She almost even shared her dream to bring Dalí back to life, but that seemed too intimate, even more intimate than sex. That night, watching Andre live, she envisioned the project she would dedicate the next two years of her life to make happen. She took him to the labyrinth, and on that dark, clear night beneath a full moon, he kissed her.

"I'd like to see you again," he said. "But, with the campaign and all, we might need to keep it quiet. At least for now."

"Works for me," she agreed. Discreet was better for her anyway. She didn't want a man underfoot or the media attention it could bring her. She wanted someone warm, someone to occasionally stay over, maybe eating Chinese out of boxes on the sofa and watching something on Netflix. She wasn't looking for another reason to get dressed up or be the face of anything. Occasionally being the face of the Dalítorium was more than enough pressure. She wanted to be seen and known in a more vulnerable way than her job or ambition allowed.

"I have a son. A teenager, Nick," Andre shared, before they had been on a proper date. "With the coverage for the campaign, you would have found out online."

"Is his mom in the picture still?"

"She died when he was young."

"I'm sorry," Lucia said. She did not feel compelled to reciprocate any similar information.

"When will I see you again?" Lucia asked, emboldened by his confession.

"I have another event here next week. Could you work it?"

"I don't work them. I run them."

"Well after you run it, would you like to grab a drink with me?"

"I'll think about it." They exchanged numbers. She couldn't remember the last time she had given anyone her number. She didn't know exactly what had gotten into her that night.

CHAPTER 31

VERA

Even though Johns Hopkins' Wi-Fi blocked her favorite shows, she'd figured out how to set up a hot spot and stream them from her phone. Vera tried to stretch her legs long in her bed, to wriggle her toes and twist her back. How long had she been lying here? It seemed darker outside, gray even, but that could just be clouds. She looked around the room. She was alone.

She hoped this meant her mom decided to go get her eyeliner and the other things she asked for. As she mentally checked off everything she had meticulously packed, she remembered her Cucumber Melon lotion her best friend Zoe had given her for her birthday before she left. She forgot to ask her mom for it. She searched for her phone. It must have slid to the side when she dozed off. She texted her mom and asked her to grab the lotion too.

Three messages. Not from her mom. Better. From Nick. Her arms prickled with goosebumps. She shivered and nestled deeper into her bed. He'd texted her, first to ask how the surgery had gone, and then, twice, to see if she wanted to see him—and the banyan tree—before she went back home. She couldn't help but smile. Her cheeks burned. Of course, she wanted to see him. She hoped he was taller than her. She hoped he had dark hair.

But what would her mom think? Where could she even be?

She started to text him back, "Yes! When?" but she edited it before sending, taking out the exclamation mark, rethinking her words. She didn't want to sound too eager.

The thirty-odd seconds it took to wait for a response were brutal.

He was in the neighborhood and could swing by the hospital if that was okay.

Vera didn't want him to see her like this lying down in a hospital bed, hooked up to the IV and monitor. Maybe she could leave the hospital, just for a little bit? Meet up with him and then come right back? She felt fine, and it had been almost a whole day since they started her surgery. The doctor said she did great, and Arielle said she was recovering nicely.

Him coming here would be weird. Mortifying, even, with her in a hospital gown hooked up to monitors. That's not how she wanted him to remember her. Did they even let non-relatives visit patients here? If she saw him in person, then she could be sure that everything she thought she felt for him was real. That there was chemistry. That he wasn't just pitying her. And she would be back before anyone noticed, especially her mom. She'd take her phone.

"I can meet you," Vera texted him back.

"Are you sure?"

"I feel fine," she lied. She hoped when she stood up, her head would stop spinning.

"Where?"

"The corner of 6th and 4th."

Vera hoped she could figure that out, and that it wasn't near the Ronald McDonald house.

"Give me five?" she asked.

Vera channeled her personal heroes, thrilled at the opportunity to sneak out of a hospital, to do anything. With the speed of Mia Hamm and Abby Wambach and the stealthiness of Katness Everdeen, she could do this. Still light-headed, she chugged the ginger ale, guzzling sugar and confidence and strength. She debated leaving her mom a note, so she wouldn't worry, but that would take too long. She'd be back soon, probably before her mom even realized.

She knew she wouldn't have much time once she pulled off her heart monitor. Since it had gotten disconnected a number of times already, the nurse would think it was another accident and not an emergency.

After one last sip of ginger ale, she pinched the part of the IV sticking out of her arm. A quick, clean pull, just like a Band-Aid. She closed her eyes. Three, two, pull. She peeked out of one eye. Just a little trickle of scarlet. No spurting, thank goodness. Her timer wouldn't start until she pulled off the heart monitor, but after the IV, why wait? She went for it, setting off the monotonous drone of the heart monitor.

She threw the covers off and mustered the strength to stand. You can do this, she told herself. She slipped out of her hospital gown and took a moment to brace herself before reaching down towards her bag to grab an emerald-green dress. When she did, the blood rushed to her head, and she thought for a moment she might fall. But she couldn't. He was waiting, and she didn't know how long they would have. She should stash the gown, but where? Under the hospital bed? The nurse might see it. In her bag? Too bulky. In the bathroom trash can? The trashcan, she decided, burying it underneath a pile of tissues.

Looking in the mirror, reacquainting herself with her face that she hadn't seen in months, she wanted to linger but couldn't. She quickly tried to freshen up: brush teeth, run her fingers through her hair, and put on some lip gloss. She wished she had her eyeliner already, but this would have to do. She tried a few different smiles to find the right one for Nick, not too eager or sheepish or childlike.

Vera knew she needed to buy more time. If she left the bathroom light on and the door closed, whoever came back first would hopefully think she was in there, and her bathroom trip triggered the alarm. After a second thought, she rolled the IV stand into the bathroom as well, switched the light on, and closed the door. If she hesitated, she might never leave. Wriggling her wrist out of the hospital bracelet, and she shoved it and her phone deep into her pocket.

Vera cracked the door, overwhelmed by the fluorescent lights in the hallway. She looked back and forth, eyeing an exit sign towards the left. She headed in that direction, trying to avoid eye contact with those she passed.

She heard an alarm going off behind her. Had they realized she had left already?

A nurse she recognized zoomed past her. Room 325, she heard him say.

Not her room. Some other emergency. This could be just the break she needed.

She made it to the third-floor lobby, glancing from the elevator to the door marked "stairs," determining the less nauseating choice.

Alone in the stairwell, she grabbed the railing for strength and balance as she went down as fast as she could handle. She would make it. She would see him! That is, as long as she didn't run into her mom.

She tried to stroll casually through the main lobby, hoping the receptionist wasn't the same one as yesterday, but how would Vera know? Just as she exited the revolving door, she heard over the intercom, "We have an eloper. I repeat, we have an eloper."

CHAPTER 32

MIQUEL

It wasn't hard for Miquel to find the hospital. He'd navigated his fair share of cities, many much bigger than this one. This part of the city was practically a grid, with the hospital being one of the highest structures in the area. It was colder than he expected, the sky heavy and oddly yellow, with streaks of greens and grays. So much for everything he'd heard about Florida. At least he could admire the eye candy on the street.

As he approached the entrance, he practically bumped into one, a leggy collegiate with cascading maple waves, clad in a stunning verde esmeralda hi-low dress, rushing to leave the hospital. He turned to watch her go, admiring the view. On a different day, he might have followed her, but she seemed distracted, and for once, he wasn't here to pick up girls.

Finding it wasn't the hard part. Gaining admittance was. At least there was a woman at the desk: messy bun, dark saucer eyes hidden behind clunky glasses. "*Buna nit,*" he said, reading from her ID card, hanging from a lanyard, "Brandi". His eyes paused there for a split second before drifting northward again.

"Looking for this?" he said, pulling out a pen with Johns Hopkins logo on it out of thin air and handing it to her.

"How did you...?"

"Magic," he smiled, cocking one eyebrow and shrugging smugly as she examined the pen in disbelief.

"Can I help you with something?" she finally asked.

"I'm looking for Vera Garcia's room," he said. Nothing like uttering the name of his deserted daughter to jolt himself out of hitting on this young nurse. Saying Vera's name felt strange on his tongue.

She typed in a few keystrokes and rustled through some papers before saying, "Visiting hours are over."

He hadn't come all this way to not see Vera. And if visiting hours were over, why not just tell him straight away? He wanted to claim parental rights but didn't. He stood there stupidly for a minute. Miquel caved first, channeling some inner strength, voicing the truth he'd been denying, avoiding, and escaping for all those years. "I'm her father," he said.

After a few more clicks, nonplussed, she responded, "You might want to check with her mother?"

Yes, Eliza had reached out to him, but he couldn't just call her, could he? He was kind of hoping to avoid Eliza altogether. To show up, to see Vera, maybe even when she was sleeping, just to know if she had his nose and if she'd pulled through surgery, and then sneak out before either of them knew the better of it. He mumbled something to the affirmative, pulled out his phone, and went to sit on one of the hard plastic chairs in the lobby.

As he scrolled through his feed, pretending to be waiting for a response from Eliza, he heard her name over the intercom. "Eliza Davis-Garcia, Eliza Davis-Garcia, please report to the front desk immediately." She'd be coming here. Why would they be paging her? Because he showed up? Curious, he listened intently to Brandi's conversation.

"Eliza Davis-Garcia, Eliza Davis-Garcia, please report to the front desk." The nurse at the desk had gotten a call from someone, and she then went from waiting and greeting to action. He picked up bits: "an evacuation order… headed this way… bigger than expected… moving patients inland… to Orlando, even." Things around him started to move more urgently, more purposefully, than before. The mood of the place shifted. Brandi caught his eye. He looked away, cheeks flushed: How rarely he got caught. She printed something and went to hang it on the door. Even though Vera was here now, she would be leaving soon. He saw that, from Brandi's hurried conversations with the powers that be.

Miquel saw Eliza first, as she walked quickly to the main desk, looked around, and then started tapping her fingers impatiently. How could he approach her? How could he not? She had the sole power to give him an audience with his daughter. He had told Brandi he would reach out to Eliza about seeing Vera. At the least, he had that cover to persevere. Seeing her there, brown curls now streaked with silver, newfound dimples in her knees, he remembered loving her, why he had loved her. But his confidence still wavered at the thought and threat of talking to her. He forced himself to move past that.

He walked up behind her and considered touching her shoulder then chose not to. "Eliza," he said. She turned, then jumped.

"Miquel? What are you doing here?"

"*L'ocasió s'ha d'agafar pels péls*[1]. I came to see Vera. You wrote me."

"Dozens of times." She stared at him, waiting for a response. "I wasn't sure you'd gotten them. We never heard anything."

"I did."

"So why now? Why is now different?"

"She's—our daughter's—having surgery." Seeing Brandi heading back, he wanted to settle this quickly. If he was going to see Vera, he needed Eliza on his side.

"Had. She's in recovery. And it's a little late to show up for her now."

Brandi returned to the desk, turning her attention to Eliza.

"I can't do this right now," Eliza told Miquel, waving him off. He took a few steps back but stayed in earshot. To Brandi, she said, "Hi, I'm Eliza Davis-Garcia, Vera's mom. You paged me?"

"Yes, Mrs. Davis-Garcia. I'm sorry to tell you this, but Vera's left."

"What do you mean, left? She's sleeping in her room. I was there less than an hour ago."

"Not currently."

"But I just stepped out to get her makeup. She was mad at me for not bringing it earlier. She asked me to go. This must be a mistake."

1 Catalan saying: Opportunity must be grabbed by the hair.

"Apparently, she disconnected her IV and monitors and left the hospital."

Eliza's face turned white, and she braced herself on the front desk.

Watching this, Miquel chuckled to himself, shaking his head, bemused at the surprises that continued to unfold on this trip. Perhaps he and his daughter—a bird in flight—had more in common than he originally thought.

"Not Vera. No. Not my Vera!" Eliza's knees gave out, and just before she crumpled, Miquel caught her. He couldn't just let her fall.

CHAPTER 33
LUCIA

Lucia knew that when Andre shared the city's lack of preparation, it was not her problem. She had one job: to protect the artwork. She would be one of the people who stayed put, hunkered down in the museum. That responsibility was practically written into her job description. Getting people to seek shelter and then worrying about those who stayed put was written into Andre's. But unlike those sustaining on Cheerios, Tootsie Rolls, and boxed wine in bathrooms, partying at first, and then possibly panicking and praying, Lucia could relax. She would be in the only structure in St. Pete built to withstand a Category 5 hurricane: a concrete cube. Alone. Except of course for the Deepfake Dalís and the omnipresent Gala, forever living in his works.

She never envisioned this relationship as complicated. In part, she started dating Andre because of the ease of it all: she could keep her public and private life separate, and they could fill a mutual need in the quiet shadows of semi-regular nights when she wasn't working and he wasn't cutting a ribbon or giving a speech somewhere. For the last two years, that agreement had been more or less satisfactory. He knew she was up for the promotion, but he knew nothing of Eliza, Vera, or Miquel. He also knew she had the keys to the only safe-haven in the greater St. Pete area. As Hurricane Phoenix churned its way towards St. Pete, their relationship became complicated.

As they walked away from the labyrinth and toward the bench, Andre asked, "If there was an emergency and we needed it, would opening up the Dalítorium be an option? If I needed it?" She bristled, and he rushed to fill the silence, not wanting to lose this opportunity. "It came up at city council after they realized the school shelters might not withstand this, that the possible hit zone encompassed most of the peninsula and evacuating every hospital might not be feasible in time. They wanted to reach out to your board."

"Why didn't you let them?" That would have been easier.

"I told them I knew someone."

"Why would you do that?" She knew exactly why. He was trying to be the savior in the crisis he created, she thought.

"I was trying to help. Plus, you know how long it takes the board to approve anything."

"Don't I know it. I bet most of them have left town already." But this wasn't about the board's bureaucracy. Had he let them go to the board, it would be the board's decision to sacrifice the safety of the collection. But by strutting for them instead, he had made her the triage nurse, responsible for determining what to save: the art or the potentially countless, the destitute, the stranded. What did it mean to leave a legacy? Her work at the Dalítorium was her life's legacy. She planned on succeeding the director, running the whole museum, bringing art and inspiration to the masses for a generation to come.

"We can't just open the museum. My first job is to protect the artwork, Andre. You know that." People died every day as a result of wars, famine, natural disasters, random tragedies, or their own choices. When did the city's lack of preparation become her problem? Would there be a way for her to secure the art enough to open their doors? How many would come? Should she pull the lever in the trolley problem, jeopardizing the safety of the collection, Dalí's legacy, and her career; or should she let nature run its course?

As much as she wanted to run the museum, she did not welcome this type of decision. She could pass Andre's request along to the director and the board, but in doing so, would likely reveal their relationship, something they had worked so hard to downplay. Not only would that hurt her chances of promotion, but also Nick's. If the word got out that they were dating, any opportunity for Nick would be seen as favoritism. Nepotism, even. Why had Andre asked her? She couldn't say yes, not now. But if she didn't, the fate of those who didn't make it would be at least in part in her hands. She had never hated him as much as she did now, and yet, she had also never seen him this vulnerable, this much in need of her help. Their relationship—if that's what you would call it—was not built for this level of interdependence.

"You know I can't say yes to this, Andre." Lucia finally said. "It's not my place."

"But you have the keys. You run the facility. You'll be here through the storm," he protested.

"Yes, but it isn't my call. And if we open it now, all of St. Pete could swarm the museum. Who wouldn't want to weather the storm at the Dalítorium? Should we let 100 people camp out here? 500? 1,000? And for how long? We don't have the food or bathrooms, not to mention fire code regulations."

"You know the museum is leasing the land from the city," Andre countered.

A low ball, but one he would play. "Yes, for the next 80 years, at least. But the building is private property." She was obviously right, but he wasn't asking for a rational decision. He wanted a compassionate one, for him and his career as much as for the people of St. Pete.

"We can't make it plan A," Lucia said. "I don't have that jurisdiction, and I'm not sure the board would approve."

"Is art worth more than human lives?" Andre asked.

"A false choice," she said.

It was not her lack of preparation that led to this conundrum, and even though putting a price on one of Dalí's works was hard, it was easier than naming the cost of human life. It would be even harder to predict how many lives would be saved by opening up the museum, how many deaths would happen if they didn't. But Andre wouldn't have asked if it wasn't urgent. He tried again. "Lucia, are Dalí's paintings more valuable than the people of St. Pete?"

"The city must have thought so, given their lack of foresight to protect them." She regretted those words immediately. When choosing to house Dalí's largest state-side collection in a city vulnerable to hurricanes, the board commissioned the best architects to not only build a building worthy of his collection, but also a fortress to protect it through whatever storms it might weather. Why had Andre put the fate of the city in her hands?

"That's unfair," Andre said. "I should have just told them to go to the board."

"It's not too late for that, Andre," Lucia said gently.

"We're out of time. I won't go on the record as opening up the Dalítorium to the public. Not yet, at least. But what if it becomes a real emergency?"

She thought about his question seriously for a bit. Should she sacrifice Dalí's legacy, her career, and the influence the Dalítorium could continue to have as an innovator in the art world to possibly save the lives of strangers who didn't heed the evacuation warning? Depending on how this went, the press would be brutal, regardless of her decision, but there was a chance it could also do wonders for the collection, the museum. Ultimately, it wasn't her call.

"I don't know," she said.

"There are people who won't leave. That can't. Essential workers, those without transportation, people here illegally who may avoid shelters. Phoenix is going to define my legacy," he said.

What would her legacy be? Not her daughter Vera. Lucia had walked away from her. She lived to protect the future of the Dalítorium, to inspire a new generation of patrons and artists, or so she thought. If anything was stolen, defaced, or destroyed, what would be left of Dalí's legacy? Her job was first and foremost to protect it.

Or would that be the legacy? Literature and artwork had been destroyed before, by nature but also by man: the Roman Catholic Church burning books, the Taliban destroying the Buddhas of Bamiyan. Nothing, even sculptures from the 6th century BC, would last forever. Everything eventually would succumb to nature, death, destruction. To losing relevance.

The last one was the hardest for her to grasp, why she fought so hard to preserve Dalí's art.

Practically, if the museum were opened as a sanctuary to the masses, by board generosity or the National Guard, should she still be talking to Andre? Should she be working instead to secure the collection further? Precious minutes were slipping away. She should be taking paintings down, storing them, maybe even shipping some of the more valuable ones elsewhere. No, shipping them was foolish. Air traffic had already limited travel to necessity only. Getting a plane to move part of the collection elsewhere, to the Met, to Spain even, was out of the question. Ironically, each painting, except perhaps a few in the entranceway, was perfectly safe exactly where it was, as long as the door stayed locked. All her work in further securing the art could be for naught.

"You don't know?" he asked again.

"I'm sorry," she said. "It's the best I've got."

Getting a call, he took it. "It's a no-go," he said, looking directly at her. Without actually saying goodbye, he turned on his heel and left, likely in a hurry to come up with Plan C.

She had work to do as well. She must secure the collection further. She needed to call Nick, and ideally talk to him before he talked to his father.

CHAPTER 34

ELIZA

Eliza came to, finding Brandi wafting smelling salts and holding a gigantic plastic mug with a straw.

"You passed out," Brandi said.

After numerous sleepless nights between the red-eye flight and the surgery, Eliza was running on coffee and fumes. Hearing the news of Vera, Eliza's body must have given out.

"She's gone. My Vera is gone," Eliza said, remembering the crux of the problem. She needed to find her fast.

When Eliza tried to get up, Brandi helped her, guiding her to a chair. "You need to take it easy for a bit."

Eliza checked her phone. A few missed calls from friends, seeing how the surgery went. No calls or texts from Vera. She called her. It went straight to voicemail. "Vera, where are you? Why aren't you picking up? You need to call me and come back to the hospital immediately." What else was there to say? She wanted to yell, to cry, but what good would that do? She texted her as well, "CALL ME. COME BACK." She waited to make sure that it had been received. Nothing. Eliza worried if she even had her phone.

"We could check her room," Miquel suggested. "Then we'd know if she had it or not."

Miquel. Miquel was here, witnessing all of this. She couldn't believe her daughter had just up and fled. It was painful enough realizing her daughter was gone without having Miquel here to witness this. Then, she felt even more guilty: she hated that she was admitting failure the first time they'd seen each other in years. She had given up so much to be the perfect Pinterest parent, making sacrifices so that Vera could have a happy childhood. Eliza had given up so much, and she had still failed. Mothers were meant to give their children roots and wings. She just didn't expect her daughter to fly away so far, so fast, right now.

"Why are you here again?" Eliza asked Miquel.

"*Ratolí que no més coneix un forat, està atrapat*[2]."

"You were in trouble in Spain?"

"Something like that. I thought I might be welcome here."

"I lost my daughter," she said.

"Our daughter," Miquel corrected.

Eliza glared at him. "I don't even know where to start."

"She knows you're here. Let me help. Please. I must be here for a reason, right?"

As much as she hated asking for help, especially from him, she needed to find Vera and would take any help she could get.

Giulia approached them both, carrying papers.

"How could she have just left, Giulia? Wouldn't you have seen her? Shouldn't someone have? You'd notice someone walking out of here in a hospital gown."

"They found her gown in the trash," Giulia offered. "She must have changed into regular clothes. Speaking of which, you'll need to clean out her room. We'll need to get it ready for another patient."

"You're giving up her room? She's not done with it yet." Eliza interrupted.

"Here are her discharge papers and…"

"You're discharging her?"

"We didn't discharge her. She eloped. We have her on security cameras leaving the building."

"But she's a child!"

2 Catalan saying: A mouse that knows only one hole is caught.

"That's why I'm giving the paperwork to you. You'll want to have this information when you find her. Trust me."

Eliza took the papers, finally coming to terms with the severity of what her daughter had done.

"Here are her prescriptions, one for pain meds and the other for steroids—"

"Steroids?"

"They decrease brain swelling. The local pharmacies are closed, but you can still fill them in the hospital pharmacy. It's just over there, next to the gift shop," Giulia said, pointing. "And Eliza, when you find her, keep an eye out for vomiting or seizures. Keep the incision clean and dry and have her avoid touching it. Pay attention to any other changes in behavior."

"Like running away from a hospital?"

"I'm just doing my job, Eliza. I'm trying to help here."

Eliza didn't move.

"I've got to get back to the desk, but I'll let you know if we hear anything," Giulia said, walking around them, leaving them alone.

"You've got my number?" Eliza called after her.

"So, you don't know where she is?" Miquel asked.

It's not like he had known where Vera had been for years.

"That came out wrong, El. I meant, where could she have gone?"

Eliza checked her phone again hoping for something from Vera, some momentary escape from this time and place. Still nothing.

"We could report her as missing," Miquel suggested. "You can do that here, right?"

"She'll be eighteen at midnight. I'm not sure they'll consider her missing. She's almost an adult, and she ran away, Miquel."

"And with the storm coming…"

"The storm?"

"They're evacuating the hospital soon, at least I think they are. I overheard the nurse talking."

"My daughter ran away in the middle of a storm, and she's not picking up her phone, if she even has it?" She checked her phone again for the dozenth time in the past few minutes. Still, nothing, except a weather advisory about the impending hurricane. Great.

"Does she even know anyone here? Has she been here before? Where would she go?" Miquel asked.

"Not really. We basically came straight here once we got into town... Except..."

"Except what?"

"She met a boy, Miquel."

He chuckled and shook his head.

"I took her to the Dalítorium first. I know I shouldn't have, but I just wanted to go," Eliza went on. "A guide there, Nick, escorted her around."

"And?"

"And we ran into Lucia, and I let them go off while I talked to her."

"I thought you two weren't talking."

"We weren't. We hadn't been, at least." What a mistake. Every bit of it. Why had she ever taken Vera to the museum? This was all her fault. She should call Nick, or text him at least. Thank goodness she'd found his number and added it to her phone while Vera was still unconscious. Nick might be with her, or know where she is, or at least be able to help Eliza navigate the city.

But what if he didn't know anything? Or didn't pick up because he didn't recognize her number? Would it be crazy for her to reach out? But what other choice did Eliza have? To call Lucia?

"She left you to go chase a boy? Sounds like someone I know."

"That's not helping, Miquel."

"*Quan el gat no hi es, les rates ballen.*[3] She's eighteen," Miquel said.

"Almost eighteen. And she just had brain surgery!"

"So, text him," Miquel suggested.

"And say what?"

"Have you heard from Vera? Have you seen her? I don't know. Something? Anything?"

"Okay." Eliza pulled out her phone, and she did. She tried twice before deciding what to say.

3 Catalan saying: When the cat is not there, the rats dance.

"Let's go get her stuff from the room. At least then we'll know if she has her phone. And by then, we might have heard back from one of them at least."

Eliza didn't want to leave the lobby, and didn't know if she had the strength to walk, but what else was there to do? As they headed toward Vera's room, Eliza kept checking her phone to see if Nick had responded. He hadn't. Trusting him when he was working at the museum was one thing. It was entirely different for her daughter to possibly be gallivanting around town with a practical stranger. How old had Lucia said he was?

When they got to the room, the first thing Eliza noticed was Vera's locket on the side table. Something must be wrong. Vera loved that necklace and always put it on in the morning. She would never have left her locket. Had the doctor nicked something in her brain making her do crazy things like forgetting her necklace and up and leaving the hospital?

Eliza began rummaging through Vera's bag to figure out what was missing. At least she could figure out what Vera was wearing by mentally ruling out everything still in the bag. Finding her charger knotted up, she lamented, "Her charger! She doesn't even have her charger! She's terrible at keeping her phone charged." She must have taken her phone. She never left without her phone. But no charger? Eliza panicked further. How much battery could Vera's phone have left? Vera had been streaming shows and checking social media basically since she'd woken up. She gathered Vera's belongings and shoved that stupid tube of eyeliner, the one that cost Eliza her daughter, into her pocket. When they reported her as a missing person, if it came to that, please don't let it come to that, she wanted to be able to tell the cops what to look for. "She's in her bright green dress, Miquel. She's got to be."

"Green like grass?"

"More like *verde esmeralda*..." Eliza said, savoring the Spanish on her tongue. Seeing Miquel and hearing his accent brought back so many Spanish words she'd thought she had forgotten.

"*Verde esmeralda*... Do you have a recent photo?"

He didn't even know what his own daughter looked like, Eliza thought as she pulled out her phone one more time. Still nothing. After scrolling through pictures, she settled on a recent one. They'd been hiking, surrounded by leaves changing colors, Vera's hair practically camouflaged in the fiery foliage.

Miquel looked at it, raised an eyebrow, and shook his head.

"So, what next?" Eliza asked.

"I think we need to stay put. You've left messages. We can't alert the police yet. It's hardly been an hour. She knows you are here. We'll need our strength and energy. *Fotem un café?*"

"*Un café*?" Eliza was immediately transported to Spain, the first time he had asked her, or something of the sort.

"Unless you'd like something stronger?"

"No thanks. I quit that when Vera got sick."

If Vera knew she was at the hospital, that's where she'd stay. If she went anywhere else, how would Vera ever find her? She'd told Vera when she was younger, if she ever was lost and didn't see an adult that could help, to stay put. That was the best way to be found.

Eliza could use another cup of coffee after this roller coaster of a day. To distract herself from checking her phone every five seconds, she played "Rose, Bud, Thorn", a game they used to do at the dinner table with Nana and Pops. Her rose? Vera pulled through surgery splendidly and the tumor had been removed with clear margins. Her thorn? Vera disappeared, right as they started evacuating the hospital. Her bud (even though she wouldn't ever admit it)? Her ex-husband showed up unannounced. Possibly another thorn? Having Miquel here made her feel doubly guilty about Vera's leaving. What she needed was a confidant, someone on her team. What she needed was Lucia, Lucia before.

CHAPTER 35

VERA

After living in darkness, Vera exited the hospital, overwhelmed by the technicolor world around her. She'd never seen colors this vibrant, except maybe in a candy store. She turned her attention to the more practical problem of finding Nick. He'd said 4th Ave and 6th Street, right? Or was it the other way around? And which way did the grid go? The overly saturated green of the street signs glowed, hurting her eyes. She started looking for him and then realized foolishly that she had no idea what he looked like. Even if he walked up to her, would she recognize him?

Just as she was about to pull out her phone to text him again, she heard his voice calling her name. After their hours on the phone over the past few nights, she'd recognize that voice anywhere. She turned, taking in his square jaw, crooked grin, and corkscrew hair. She wanted to touch it. "Nick?" she asked, wanting to be sure.

He nodded. "Hope you aren't disappointed…"

Vera laughed, shaking her head no. He was definitely cuter than any boy she knew back home. Not that she'd pursued any of them. Soccer always came first.

"So, you're okay? The surgery?"

"Went great. I feel better than ever," she said, grinning at him.

He grinned back. He brushed an auburn strand of hair out of her eyes and behind her ear. Electrified by his touch, she tingled, goosebumps formed up and down her arms.

This is what she'd come for, but she didn't want to get caught and have this end before it even started. "Are we just going to stand here, or are you going to show me around St. Pete?"

"I could do that, but how do you feel?

"Fine... Amazing, actually."

"Really?"

"I'm fine. I told you. I promise. Just maybe a little hungry." Sensing his hesitation, she went on, "You heard my mom. She said I'd be better than new."

"We could grab a quick snack first? Then you could go back?"

The faster they could get off this corner and preferably off the street, the better. "That's more like it. What did you have in mind?"

"There's this ice cream place you have to try..."

"Ice cream?" Did he think she was a kid? "I can get ice cream back home."

"Trust me. St. Pete is famous for it. They scrape it and roll it. Thai-style. Bet they don't do that in Arkansas."

"Tennessee."

"I know," he teased. "It's only a few blocks away. Then I'll bring you right back here. And when else will you get to explore St. Pete with your own personal tour guide?" He held out his hand for her.

She took it.

"That's my girl," he said, squeezing her hand with one of his hands. Even though it was warm, her skin prickled with the thrill of being held. He carried the weight of her hands in his, and she felt lighter.

"Welcome to Sunshine City!"

"Sunshine?" Despite her vivid surroundings, the sky was definitely gray.

"361 sunny days a year, give or take a few. Bummer today happened to be one of the overcast ones."

She let him lead, and as he pulled her away from the hospital, she left any worry behind. Wandering the streets of St. Pete, she took in the sherbet rainbow of signs, murals, and buildings. Compared to the brick and brown from back home, St. Pete looked like a child splattered downtown in neon and tropical Crayola paints. A little silly, but much more fun. A plastic bag, caught in wind, twisted unpredictably down the street, reminding her of herself on the soccer field. She might have gone to grab it, so it didn't end up in the ocean, but Nick stopped abruptly, ending her fantastical daydream.

"Hmmm… That's strange," Nick said.

"What?" Vera asked. She looked towards where Nick was looking. Virgin plywood, not yet touched by spray paint or time, covered everything beneath the Iceberg sign.

"They should be open. They don't close for the season."

"Maybe they're renovating?" Vera suggested. If Vera hadn't been so enamored with Nick, she might have noticed the plywood going up, covering doors and windows all around her. Instead, she took in the tropical trees, the huge colorful murals with faces she probably should recognize but didn't.

"I didn't want rolled ice cream anyway. Too gimmicky. Totally overrated," Nick said, brushing it off. "There's an even better popsicle place down the block."

"You're taking me to get popsicles?"

"Of course not! I'm taking you to get gourmet ice pops," he corrected. "They're Mexican-style, whatever that means, but they are delicious."

"Okay," she laughed. "Gourmet ice pops."

"They use a ton of fresh fruits, and the flavor combinations are out of this world."

"What's fresh in Florida in October? Oranges? Bananas?"

"No idea. But that's part of the fun. There's one way to find out."

She hoped for something exotic, something she couldn't get back home. Holding his hand, she let him lead the way. They wandered down broad streets with mostly two-story buildings. There weren't many cars parked on the road or as many people out as she expected. At that moment, the entire city belonged to just her and Nick.

Something in the distance caught her eye. It wasn't another scrappy tree trunk but instead four spindly metal trunks leaning in awkward angles.

As they got closer, she looked up the stilt-like legs to see an animal, a horse perhaps, complete with chains for a mane and tail. She laughed, as much amused by the fact that the few other people on the street didn't even think twice about this ginormous horse sculpture and for her, it was the strangest sight she'd ever seen. The chains seemed so lifelike, giving the tail texture and movement. She traced her hands on one of the back legs, reaching up to feel the tail. What kind of artist would look at old chains and think horsetail?

"We're here," he announced.

The storefront seemed plain, windows and white with a big orange Hyppo sign. Nick held the door for her, and she entered the wooden and white room, taking in the sea mural of colorful fish and coral on the left wall. "Come here and check out your choices, Vera." he said.

She walked towards the ice chest, reading the names off the wall: "Avocado Coconut, Watermelon Hibiscus, Espresso Horchata, Strawberry Datil!" delighted by selections she couldn't find in Tennessee, combinations and flavors she'd never even heard of, let alone tried. She hated decisions like this. Too many choices! What if she missed out on something great? Nick would have a recommendation. "What do you usually get?"

"They change them a lot, but I like the spicy ones. They have a nice kick."

"I was looking at those! I can't decide between the Mexican Hot Chocolate or the Mango Habanero..."

"Why don't you get one, and I get the other? You can try mine," Nick suggested. There wasn't a line, and they were the only people in the store. Only then did Vera realize that there wasn't even someone at the register.

A man in his thirties came in from the back room. "Sorry, I didn't hear the bell," he said. "Been trying to get all the pops into the back freezer, the one hooked up to the generator. What can I get you?"

They placed their orders, and he rang them up. Only then did Vera realize she didn't have her wallet with her.

"My treat," Nick said, to Vera's relief. He opened his up and headed toward the nearest table.

When Nick started to take the chairs down, the employee interrupted: "You'll have to go somewherc else. We're closing." As they walked out, he said, "Thanks for stopping by! Stay safe."

Once again, Nick held the door. Vera licked her ice pop and shivered at the habanero heat, fanning her mouth to cool off her tongue.

"Try this one," Nick said, holding the Mexican Hot Chocolate pop towards her. He traced her lips with the popsicle, teasing her. She tasted it, tentatively at first, then more greedily. Definitely better than hers. The heat was more subtle and the milkfat sweetness calmed her tongue. "You keep this one," he said, smiling and switching with her. She took it.

"Mind-blowing," she said.

"I know, thanks," he said, and she laughed. She'd meant the popsicle. There were no seats outside the pop shop, so they stood beside the horse sculpture, finishing their sweet treat.

"Did you grab napkins?" she asked Nick, showing him the chocolate trickling down her fingers.

"I've got one better," he said, taking her hand, licking the sticky sweetness. She could feel herself blushing. Be cool, she told herself.

"Are you cold?" he asked, tracing the goosebumps on her arm. "Do you want my jacket?"

"I'm good, thanks." As they savored their popsicles, she couldn't help but stare at him, occasionally blushing or looking away when it felt too intense.

When they finished, he took her trash to throw away. She held onto her popsicle stick.

"I can take that too," he said.

"It's recyclable," she said, putting it in her pocket. Really, she wanted to save it, so she'd know that this afternoon had been real. "So, what next?" she asked eagerly, changing the subject.

"You're sure you don't want to go back?"

"Just one more. I'm fine. I feel great." She smiled extra big on purpose, trying to convince him as much as herself. "I want to do something I've never done before."

"Never, huh?"

"Never ever."

"How do I know what you've never done?" he asked.

"Try me," she challenged, wondering what he was thinking, what experiences he'd had.

He looked her up and down curiously.

"Okay. I think I know the place," he said, clasping her hand and guiding her down the street. "Just out of curiosity, have you ever ridden a horse?"

"Maybe half a dozen times? I did a few pony rides as a kid, and I went to a summer camp that had horses," she said, suddenly embarrassed to be talking about camps and birthday parties. She didn't want to come off as too young. He'd already been to college. "There are farms in downtown St. Pete?"

"Not exactly."

They got to a plain storefront with fluorescent beer brand signs in the window. The sign read, "One Night Stand." She knew what that meant and was suddenly embarrassed to be here with a practical stranger. Neon fliers fluttered in a sudden gust of wind. The salty air prickled her face. They should probably head back to the hospital. What if her mom was looking for her?

"Are you sure I can go in here?" Vera asked. She'd never actually been in a bar before, and almost eighteen wasn't twenty-one. She'd asked for an adventure, but this was even more than she'd imagined.

"It's the middle of the afternoon, and I know the owner," Nick said. "It's practically a restaurant until dinnertime."

Should she tell him that she didn't really drink? That she'd tried a few sips of Boone's Farm in the bathroom during junior prom but didn't really like the taste?

"And besides," he said, "We're not here to drink." Had he read her mind? And if they weren't here to drink, what were they here for?

He said hi to the manager, and they strolled in. Country music she didn't recognize was blaring from the many freestanding speakers. It didn't take her long to figure out why they were there. To their right was a mechanical bull, surrounded by a pit of duct taped gymnastics mats. The smell of cheap beer couldn't mask the sweat-stink. The place, between lunch and dinner shifts, was almost empty. There were giant versions of Jenga and Connect Four, as well as a few ping pong tables set up in the back.

"You expect me to ride that thing?" she asked him, pointing to the black and white patched beast.

"His name is Moustache."

"You expect me to ride Moustache?" She wasn't even sure how to climb on top of the mechanical bull, much less ride it.

"If you want… You said you wanted a thrill."

"Is it hard? I mean… Have you ever done it before?"

"Once or twice," he lied. "Plus, you wanted to try something you'd never done before."

She didn't answer.

"Wait. Don't tell me. You haven't ridden one of these before, have you? Do they have them near you?"

"Probably somewhere?" But not anyplace my mom would take me, she thought. That made her want to try even more. "Will you go first?" she asked, her heart pounding.

Nick did, hopping on with glee and ease. He shifted his balance, seemingly anticipating the random jerks, veers, and shifts. He crouched low and gave into the erratic ebbs and flows of the mechanical beast. Instead of getting bucked off, he slid off the side, almost as if on purpose.

"Could've stayed on longer," he mumbled to her, smiling.

"Sure," she said.

"You're next, Vera."

She wasn't sure if she could do this in a dress, post-surgery, but what other choice did she have? She didn't want him to think she wasn't up for fun. This was exactly what she'd been looking for.

"Go easy on her, it's her first time," he told the man operating the bull.

Vera walked into the pit, unsteady on soft ground. She imagined gracefully swinging a leg over the machine, but it took her two tries to get on.

She felt behind her, making sure her dress was still covering her backside and hadn't ridden up. She wondered if it would vibrate.

Vera held tight to this bucking machine, trying to keep her balance and stop things from spinning, just like she had done throughout her tumor scare. When she couldn't hold on anymore and was bucked off, in losing control of the bull, she let go of everything she'd been bottling up and sobbed. Then, she laughed at the ridiculousness of her situation: legs-over-shoulders on a duct-taped mat in a seedy bar on a random weekday afternoon. At least she wasn't wearing a thong, not that her mom would let her. Her Nana had always quoted *Steel Magnolias*: "Laughter through tears is my favorite emotion."

She broke a record, the operator told her, even though she didn't believe him.

Nick handed her a bar napkin and pulled her close, praising her verve and style. "There's one more place you've got to see," he said, leading her out of the bar and towards the water.

CHAPTER 36

ELIZA

Amidst a whirling frenzy of activity, Eliza and Miquel alone stood still. They had agreed to hunker down and wait for Vera's return. At least the cafeteria hadn't closed yet. With relatively little effort, they were able to procure two medium coffees.

Where to begin? With Vera's first steps? Her first lost tooth? When her fish Cee-ay-tee died and she cried for days? When she missed the penalty kick that would have won it for their team? The first time she drove a car? There was so much he had missed, but she could never fully convey. He didn't deserve that. Neither did Lucia. That was hers and Vera's. On this point, she felt fully entitled being selfish. Instead of catching him up on the almost seventeen years he had missed, she opted for something simpler, something safer, just catching him up on today.

"*Le café*? Terrible," Miquel said, drinking another sip.

"Your standards are impossibly high, but yes. Terrible," Eliza said.

He led her to a small cafe table, gesturing for her to sit. When she did, he launched into his lame justification. "I thought about reaching out a hundred times before today," Miquel said, "But every time I got close to calling, mailing a birthday card, or emailing, I stopped."

"What do you want me to say?" said Eliza, emboldened by the vulnerability and the desperation of her current situation.

"Maybe you could help her understand…"

"Vera got nothing from unsent emails, undialed phone calls, and unsent birthday cards. She told people you had died. When people asked her questions about her father, why he wasn't at father-daughter dances or campouts, why her mother was teaching her to drive when all of her friends relied on their fathers, that's what she said. That her father died when she was a baby." Eliza failed to mention that Vera thought this because that's what Eliza had told her. It was easier than telling her the truth.

Was she trying to hurt him? Was she looking for an apology? An explanation for all those years he had been gone? With Vera now missing, none of it mattered. Still, thinking about the hard questions she had to face alone and the times his absence put a burden on their daughter gave Eliza the slightest bit of verve on what was an otherwise very bad day.

"When she started complaining of headaches," Eliza said, "I was beside myself. After her colicky baby months, she was rarely sick. Even when she was, I knew it before she did: her cheeks turned bright pink. So, when her headaches wouldn't go away, and then the vertigo started and she lost her vision on the field mid-game, I knew something was wrong."

Why was Eliza telling him this? He'd walked away from the right to know. But she didn't have anyone else to tell, she realized. And he was here now. 'Why now? After all those years?' her inner therapist asked, but she didn't wait for the answer.

"The surgery went well, better than expected. I said more Hail Marys than I have in a long time," Eliza said. She checked her phone again. Still nothing. "Would you say them with me again? *Si us plau*?"

A cradle Catholic, happy to hear his own tongue, Miquel obliged.

They settled into long pauses and awkward silences, with Eliza wondering what they were both doing. She thought about asking him to keep watch for Vera while she went to the bathroom. How many cups of coffee had she had already today? She should also get those prescriptions filled before they left the hospital. By now, Vera had missed at least one dose, and she'd need her medicine when Eliza found her. If she found her. She was still blaming herself for getting that eyeliner. If she hadn't left Vera's side, Vera would still be here, getting evacuated with the rest of the hospital.

Eliza still worried about the charger. Did knowing Vera didn't have her charger make things better or worse? But even if Vera had it, where could she use it? Perhaps Vera wasn't ignoring her texts, but instead wasn't getting them? But if she didn't have cell phone service, she could be anywhere with no way of knowing how to get back in touch with her mom. Eliza realized she wasn't even sure if Vera knew Eliza's phone number. The first thing Eliza did when she got the phone for Vera was to put her own number in as speed dial 1, as 'Mom', and 'ICE Mom', in case of an emergency. She'd put her number in as three separate things, but she'd never bothered to teach it to Vera. Of all the things she hadn't taught Vera...

Before she went to fill the prescriptions, she left Miquel with a few pictures of Vera, so he could show them to anyone who asked or may be able to help. Would he even recognize her? It had been so many years. She sent pictures, but it was hard to know if he got them or kept them as he was often moving around. Sometimes they came back undelivered. At least this way, he'd have a point of reference.

"I'll be back soon," she told him, hurrying to the pharmacy before it closed.

MIQUEL

Even though Miquel wasn't sure he should have come in the first place, he was glad he was here now, so Eliza didn't have to go through this alone. People were still scurrying, emptying the building, evacuating patients. A few men in army green fatigues showed up and started giving directions. Men in coveralls were screwing sheets of plywood to the glass entrance to the hospital. Miquel kept watch for an emerald-clad Vera with one eye, the other tuning into the weather report playing on the TV in the lobby.

A female anchor said, "We are now directly in Hurricane Phoenix's path. At this point, we have all the hurricane watches in place. And I do hope you've started to make all of your preparations for your family, pets, and belongings because evacuation orders are in effect. And the storm surge could reach 20 feet, or possibly more if this does make landfall as a Category 5 hurricane." Miquel glanced at his leather loafers. Not exactly hurricane shoes.

This was not going to be a small storm. He'd come across the ocean to see the daughter he'd already abandoned and ended up stuck in the middle of a hurricane. He realized they should be evacuated as well. Even if Eliza had gas in the rental car, the roads were already crammed with people trying to get out of central Florida, and she'd never leave without Vera. And without Eliza, he was pretty much stuck here. He'd Ubered from the airport, realizing only later as the driver tuned into the local news, that his flight was one of the last inbound flights allowed to land, given the impending storm.

They couldn't stay here. The hospital security guards would make them leave soon enough, and just sitting here, waiting and hoping for Vera to return, was not working. They would need to try something else, at least one of them.

The news showed shots of supermarkets in Pinellas County, long lines of buggies filled with water, toilet paper, and non-perishables. Lines of people waiting for gas in Tampa. They then cut to an aerial shot of the bridges. The Skyway was at a standstill, and 92 wasn't faring much better, with over-packed vehicles crawling and creeping along. 295 Northbound was practically a parking lot, and it was already starting to rain. "Thousands heeded the warnings," the reporter voiced over. "This is the largest evacuation in history." Miquel read into the subtext: If you are out there, or if you are leaving, go quickly, because you are going to be on the road a while. He hoped Eliza would get back from the pharmacy soon. They clearly needed another plan.

CHAPTER 37

VERA

"Where are we going, Nick?" Vera laughed as a few droplets of rain fell on her face.

Nick didn't tell Vera, and instead, just led her by the hand, pulling her toward the water. Propelled by the surging winds, their fast stride broke into a full-out run as the trickles turned to downpour. Even though Vera's vision had returned, this onslaught of rain transformed the city into a gray blur. What looked like a forest grove in the distance became stranger to decipher the closer they got. They were going to a place she'd been before, but could not fully appreciate, given her compromised vision and overall dizziness.

The rain pelted the pair as they raced. She may have just had surgery, but she was one of the fastest sprinters in her district, faster than Zoe, faster than all the other girls on her team. And she was certainly faster than a 21-year-old boy who played video games for sport. She broke his hand and sprinted ahead, unleashed from her blindness, wild with newfound freedom.

The banyan tree stood unmoving as the storm whirled around it. Waves surged, spraying salty brine that stung her eyes. Vera ducked into the shelter of the banyan. What seemed like many intertwined trees was just one mother tree, surrounded, supported, snarled with generations of her descendants. Vera couldn't get enough of it, first tracing generations with her eyes, and then with her fingers, following life cycles and entangled destinies.

Nick—breathless—caught up to her at the base of the tree.

She stood waiting, her back against the trunk. By now, they were both drenched, and her wet dress clung to her body, droplets dripping down her legs.

"It's amazing, right?" Nick asked.

Vera laughed, electrified. "Yes. So much. I've never seen anything like it!" Now that Vera could actually see, she savored the banyan in all of its tangled, gnarly glory with branches and aerial prop roots deeply interwoven, growing and changing each other, interdependent for survival. People are like that, she thought. At least some people, whose lives became so deeply entangled that survival apart feels almost impossible.

Was that why she had left? Because she wanted to stand on her own? After the tumor? Without her mom and doctors and nurses hovering? She wasn't completely sure why she'd left. But she did know how good it felt to be free, to see, and—at least for a moment—to not feel entwined. That wasn't entirely true. She wanted to be here with Nick.

"So, are you some track star?" Nick asked, yelling to be heard over the roaring wind and crashing waves.

"Soccer," she said with a grin, glad he'd noticed.

She brushed a number of roots aside, as if she were pulling back a curtain, and held it for Nick as they entered one of the many semi-private alcoves created by the older roots. Even though the wind howled outside of the tree, beneath the banyan's protective branches, time and air stood still.

Vera felt the warmth of Nick's body as he now stood just inches in front of her. She wasn't breathy from the run—that was merely a warm-up jog for her, but having a boy, this boy, stand so close to her took her breath away.

Numerous lovers and would-be graffiti artists carved their marks in these branches, thinking the depths their pocket-knives reached might outlast nature. "Why would anyone dream of defacing this tree?" Vera asked as she turned, tracing a R+D with her finger.

Nick came up behind her, gently resting his hand on her hip. "You don't want to add ours?" Nick countered playfully.

His breath on the back of her neck as he pressed up behind her. She turned toward him, smiling coyly. The banyan branches enveloped her and Nick, creating their own private cave.

Nick entwined his fingers with hers. They were eye to eye, hand to hand, bodies almost touching.

Vera had never really kissed a boy before: she didn't count playing spin the bottle at church camp. This was different. Her entire body wanted him to kiss her. After facing death, knowing she would have to leave in a few days, what did she have to lose?

Under those tangled banyans, Nick leaned towards Vera, but she kissed him first. She pressed her lips against his. She could have lost herself, secluded among the roots, surrounded by Nick's arms. Even though they were steps away from the main drag of downtown, they were alone.

Her hand on his chest moved southward, to rest gently on his hip, as they explored each other's mouths, shyly at first, and then with more curiosity and less restraint. The banyan's canopy shielded them from most of the rain, but Nick wiped a few wayward drops off her face.

Electricity coursed through Vera's body. Nick cupped the back of her neck and head with his hands. Vera found her arms pulling him closer, their bodies now touching just as their lips. As the rest of St. Pete anxiously prepared for the Phoenix, these two tangoed with lips and hands, oblivious to the storm and its consequences.

CHAPTER 38

ELIZA

"Still no word?" Miquel asked as Eliza returned to the lobby, clutching a small white bag.

Eliza shook her head. She was glad she'd gotten Vera's prescriptions filled.

A security guard approached them. "You both need to leave."

Eliza and Miquel didn't move.

"We just got orders: everyone should seek higher ground. All remaining nurses and doctors are leaving on the next military flight with the last round of patients." He gestured toward the two National Guard officers in the front of the lobby and reiterated, "All patients are being evacuated before nightfall."

"What would you do, if you were a mother whose daughter disappeared right after brain surgery? Would you stay here, in case she returned? Would you go to the nearest shelter? Would you evacuate, not knowing if she was safe?"

As she mulled over these undesirable choices, Eliza distracted herself by worrying about another looming catastrophe. How would she explain Miquel to Vera? How could Vera forgive her for lying to her about her father? Would she ever understand what Eliza had been trying to do?

"I'm just following orders," the guard said. "Shelters are filling up, and people are leaving. And I can't leave until you do."

Eliza obviously couldn't leave Vera behind. Instead, she needed to get into Vera's head. Pre-tumor, Eliza had a pretty good idea what Vera was thinking, but post-tumor, Eliza was lost and desperate for answers.

"But my daughter," Eliza protested, "is out there somewhere. We can't just leave. And neither should you! She still needs medical care! And you let her escape!" Eliza had already almost lost Vera to this brain tumor. Never again. At the end of the day, it was the hospital's fault Vera had left. "How else does a child, just hours after brain surgery—walk out of a major hospital unnoticed?"

"But where else could she be?" Miquel asked.

"You could try the police office, to see if she has shown up and file her as a missing person. They will be swamped soon, so I'd go now. There are also a few shelters. There's an elementary school just up the hill that's probably the closest. I'm sorry, ma'am, but you can't stay here."

Around her, everything else was moving. Patients much more vulnerable than her child were rushing by on gurneys with teams of professionals ready to take them anywhere else but here. With Vera gone, Eliza was in limbo. Should she wait and hope for Vera's return? Or, should she go out into this wild night, in search of her wayward child? She disliked both options.

"We'll go," Miquel said, taking Eliza by the arm. He hadn't hugged her when he got there, or when she told him Vera was gone. This was the first time he had touched her in such a long time. She needed strength. He took both his and Vera's bags, and she took her own. They left the lobby. She wished she had spray paint to leave a message for Vera. She wanted her daughter to know she hadn't abandoned her.

"But where? Where should we go?" Eliza asked Miquel. "I can't leave St. Pete. Not without my daughter."

"Let's go report her as missing," Miquel said, taking charge, "and ask about the closest shelter on high enough ground in case of a storm surge."

She still didn't want to go, but she knew they must. Upon leaving, they ran into an officer trying to help with the evacuation. When he asked why they were still there, Eliza told the officer that her daughter had left the hospital, just after surgery, and they couldn't leave town without her. He told them the nearest police station was a mile and a half away, but there was a small office at the University of South Florida, just across the street. Once at the station, they could report her missing, maybe even track her phone, and then get directions to the local shelter as evacuation now was highly unlikely. They went there quickly.

CHAPTER 39

VERA

Vera spun in wild circles until she noticed Nick staring at her. "What?" she asked.

He smiled. "You're just... so happy. More than I've ever seen you."

"There's just something about this tree. I've watched other people I love die. And I didn't know why I deserved a different ending. Ever since I lost my vision, Mom wouldn't let me breathe."

"What about your dad?" Nick asked.

"I don't know him," she said. "He died when I was a baby. That's when we left Spain and moved in with my Nana and Pops. My mom doesn't like to talk about it, but I found a picture of him once. At least I think it's him."

"My mom died too. Cancer. I was young."

"I'm sorry about your mom," Vera said, grateful that hadn't been her fate.

"Thanks. Your dad too. I have some memories of her, but I don't know if that's better or worse. Sometimes I wish it happened when I was a baby, so I didn't know what I lost," Nick said.

After a long pause, Vera asked, "Is he still single?"

"Not really," Nick said. "He's been dating my boss, Lucia. Almost two years now."

"The woman at the museum?" Vera asked.

Nick nodded.

"Who knows my mom?" Vera asked.

"I was wondering..." Nick said.

"You noticed that too? At first, I thought I was imagining things," she said. "It's weird, right?"

Suddenly, the rain picked up, blowing almost sideways. "Here, take my jacket."

"I'm fine! I love the rain." Vera flung her arms wide, face toward the sky, trying to catch a few drops. She began to spin and dance, darting in and out of the protective banyan cover, and he joined her, and held out his hands for her to take. He pulled her in close and started slow dancing back and forth. Cotillion class had been good for something.

He took off his jacket and wrapped it around them both, this time not taking no for an answer and guided her back toward the mother trunk of the tree, safest from the onslaught of rain. With her back to the tree, and their arms entangled like the roots and branches swirling around them, he leaned in for another kiss.

She felt the buzz first, something in his pocket.

"Ignore it," she said. He did, at least at first.

They kept starting to make out, but by the fourth interruption, a full half-minute of vibration, they couldn't ignore it anymore.

"Turn it off?" Vera suggested.

He shook his head. "I'm sorry Vera, but I should probably check it. Then we can get back to what we were doing," He grinned.

"You don't have a… girlfriend?" Vera asked.

He shook his head. "But it might be important," he said, sucking out any romance their tryst had had.

In that void, she remembered that she'd fled the hospital without permission, and she was here with a practical stranger, making out in public. She dropped her arms, clutched his jacket tightly around her, and walked a few feet away, pretending to be interested in the tree. She was trying to decide if she should be annoyed or not. What had happened to her? Had the surgery nicked something in her brain? How long had she been gone? Her mother was probably sick with worry by now.

"It's Lucia. She needs me back at the museum," Nick said.

"You said you were off today. Can't she figure it out on her own?" Vera asked.

"Storm's-a-coming," Nick said. "They are moving the collection into storage."

"Isn't that place a fortress?"

"I just take the orders. I don't ask questions," Nick said. "This was, uh… nice. Thanks for hanging out."

"I want to come with you," Vera said.

"I'm not sure that would be a good idea. I don't know if Lucia would like it," he said, "And besides, don't you need to check in with your mom? Go back to the hospital?"

She knew he was right. If Vera went with him, her mother would have no idea where she was. The hospital should be safe enough. Plus, she'd been gone much longer than she ever planned. What if her mother had come looking for her?

"Let me take you there," he said. "To the hospital. It's practically on the way."

"I've got it."

"What will your mom think? That I left you in a storm? You're soaking wet."

"I'll be fine."

"No, let me, please," he begged.

"I said, I've got it," she said.

He took both of her hands up in his. "Okay, I get it. You're independent. I'll see you soon. Before you leave. I promise. Text me when you get there. And if I don't hear from you in ten minutes, I'm coming to look for you." He stole one last quick kiss, then left the protective embrace of the tree, heading towards the museum. She watched him go, waiting for him to turn back. Right before she gave up hope, he stopped, turned around, and gave her a crooked grin and a little wink.

Raindrops landed on her head and the sky was considerably darker than it had been earlier. Or perhaps the change had been more gradual, but she'd been too distracted to notice. Regardless, with the hurricane quickly approaching, her phone battery almost dead, and her mother probably worrying, she needed to get back to the hospital fast.

But fast wasn't her problem. Directions were. She barely had enough power to load her map app to figure out how to get back to the hospital. She realized she hadn't been paying attention to which way they were walking when she was wandering around the city, fingers interlaced with Nick's. She didn't even have her wallet, much less any food or water with her. How foolish she had been. She wondered if anyone had ever up and left the children's ward before undetected.

When the map finally loaded, Vera tried to memorize it, the street names where she should turn, and then she shut it off, trying to save the little battery she had left. She had multiple missed calls, but she didn't think she had enough battery to check them. Most likely her mom. Just as she tried to text her back, to let her know she was okay, and that she was headed back to the hospital, her screen went blank. She jammed the phone in her pocket, suddenly chilled by the uptick in the wind's speed, the wet hair sticking to the back of her neck, and the absence of Nick's warm arms. Shivering, she headed in the direction she thought the hospital would be.

CHAPTER 40
MIQUEL

Miquel was glad to be out of the hospital. He couldn't stay in one place too long. Once they entered the station, they found the desk empty. Perhaps the officer on duty was helping evacuate students, helping secure the campus as much as possible in advance of the impending storm. After a few minutes, a female cop greeted them.

"*Hola senyora*," Miquel said.

"Officer Jiménez," she corrected.

"We've come to report a missing person, my daughter," Eliza said, taking over from here.

"Is she a minor?"

"Just barely. She's turning 18 tomorrow."

"How long has she been missing?"

"Less than two hours."

"What's her name? I can start a report."

"Vera Garcia. Please hurry. She just had a brain tumor removed. Her cell phone is probably dead, or she's not getting reception, and I'm not sure if something happened during the surgery, I can't imagine why else she would up and leave. And with the storm coming?" Eliza fought back tears and then, finally, just let them come.

Miquel knew they must get to higher ground, and this was not helping things.

"We're short-staffed and busy, but I'll see what I can do. I'll search for her phone number and check traffic cams in the area. Wait here,"

Officer Jiménez said, leaving them in the waiting room, unsure of what to do next.

An evacuation map pinned to the bulletin board caught Miquel's eye and Miquel started looking for the closest shelters, calling to see if they still had availability. Miquel was nothing if he wasn't a survivor. It didn't matter what it cost.

CHAPTER 41

LUCIA

"Thanks for coming, Nick," Lucia said when he arrived. "What took you so long? And where's your coat? It's pouring out there."

Nick shrugged.

"We've got our work cut out for us," Lucia said. If the National Guard decided to open this up as a shelter, they needed to move a lot of art quickly.

"Why are we moving the art into storage? Isn't this place built for this?" Nick asked.

"Everything in the lobby needs to be secured, and anything in rooms exposed to the glass panels. They should be fine in theory, but just in case..." Lucia said.

"Lucia. What are you not telling me? Those hurricane preparation plans you made me read didn't mention any of this."

She hesitated for a brief second, not sure if she should tell him or not. She hated putting him between her and Andre. By now, she depended on Nick, but there were times she wished she hadn't hired her boyfriend's son.

"It's your father. He's worried about not having enough space in shelters, about people ignoring evacuation plans."

"But what does that have to do with the collection?" Nick asked. "Or my dad?"

"If this becomes a shelter, I want all the art, or at least the most valuable pieces, secured."

"Did you tell him yes?"

"No, of course not. But if it needs to happen, we might not have a say in the matter. The least we can do is secure the collection."

Even though they thought they had prepared for everything, they hadn't prepared for this. Not yet, at least. Lucia had a list of assets, ranked by objective value and proximity to the door, and Nick helped her begin to wrap and move those pieces, starting with the top of the list, in a futile effort to triage the collection.

Together, they moved pieces that she could not move alone. As they were carrying a painting, Nick asked Lucia about Eliza. Lucia couldn't evade the question with a massive Dalí in her hands. "That woman the other day… The one you knew."

"What about her?" Lucia asked.

"How do you know her?"

"Why?"

"Just curious."

"Eliza and I were roommates in Barcelona together, when we were studying abroad in college," Lucia said. "I've known her longer than I've known many people, but we hadn't seen each other in a while. I thought she might show up one of these days."

"Roommates! You must have stories."

Lucia did, but she didn't share.

"Do you know her daughter?"

"Why?"

"No reason… I was just wondering."

"No really, why?"

"I spent some time today with her daughter," Nick said. "I was with her when you texted me."

Lucia stopped walking and signaled to Nick to set the artwork down. "Vera's in the hospital, recovering from her brain surgery."

"She needed a break," Nick said.

"She left the hospital with you?"

Nick didn't answer.

"Does Eliza know where she is?"

Nick shook his head.

"Do you?"

Nick's head fell. "No. I left her to come here."

"You left a girl from Tennessee who just had brain surgery outside alone in the middle of a hurricane?"

"She was headed back to her mom at the hospital. She said she'd be fine."

"Does she even know where the hospital is? Do you know if she made it back there safely?"

Nick didn't respond.

"Oh, Vera." Lucia made sure the art wouldn't fall and then raced to her phone. The police probably couldn't do anything, if they even picked up. The hospital would be of no help. She wanted to call Eliza. She should let her know, but what would she even say? Their last meeting ended abruptly, and Lucia hadn't bothered to come to the hospital. Better wait till they found Vera. Then call Eliza. She almost got her jacket to head back to where Nick had last been with her, but thought the better of it. Nick should go.

"Go back there and look for her. You need to find her," Lucia told Nick. "Now."

CHAPTER 42

LUCIA

As much as she wanted to go with Nick, Lucia knew she should stay at the museum. But she would have to tell Eliza, if she could get a hold of her. This would be the second worst thing she'd ever had to tell Eliza. The first, when they were in Barcelona studying abroad so many years ago, had almost broken them.

After months of meaning to make it to Gaudi's famous cathedral, La Sagrada Familia, they finally had. By then, they were no longer roommates. Eliza had moved in with Miquel, leaving Lucia alone. They should have waited for the elevator, but as an unspoken competition between them both, neither wanted to admit she was intimidated by the stairs.

When they finally got to the top, at least the top of what had been built to date, they could look out over the whole city, all the way to the Mediterranean.

"It's been a while since it's just been us," Lucia said, still sore that Eliza had left her.

"I know," Eliza agreed. "I'm glad. I've been meaning to talk to you about something, alone."

Lucia waited.

"I don't know if I can talk about it."

"Tell me, Eliza."

"It's awful. At first, I thought it couldn't be true, that I was seeing things. But then, I knew I couldn't ignore it anymore."

"Ignore what?"

"It's Miquel."

"Oh Eliza! I'm so sorry! I didn't think you knew. I was going to tell you today."

"You knew?"

"How could I not?"

"You knew about Miquel's stealing, and you didn't tell me?"

"Miquel's—?"

"How long have you known?"

"—stealing?"

"During his acts, or slightly after. You think the trick is a coin appearing behind your ear, but after you've left the show, you realize your wallet or watch, or both, are missing. How could I have been so foolish?"

"You didn't know, Eliza."

"But I did, at least I suspected. After seeing his routine many times, I started watching other things. And then, I pretended not to see. But it's gotten worse. He's dropped items in my bag more than once. I could get caught. I could lose everything."

"You could leave him."

"But I love him. It's stupid, I know."

"What does he even need the money for? Don't your parents pay for your flat?"

"He keeps buying art supplies, but it must be more than that. I think he has debt. He won't talk about it. I've tried."

"Move along," the guard motioned. "Other people are waiting to get to the top."

"Wait, you didn't know?" Eliza asked, heading toward the exit. "Then what were you talking about? What were you going to tell me about Miquel?"

"It's nothing."

"It's not nothing. I see it on your face. Tell me."

"Eliza, I'm pregnant," Lucia confessed.

"But how? You're not seeing anyone, not since that professor months ago."

She had to tell her. She couldn't keep it a secret forever. "It's his, Eliza. It's Miquel's."

The guard approached them again, motioning for them to move along. Welcoming the break in the tension, Lucia headed to the staircase first, not giving Eliza a chance to take the lead, or push her off the top.

Together, they descended the dizzying conch shell of a staircase, not talking or looking at each other. Lucia went first. She could feel Eliza's cold fury piercing her back. Lucia did not look back or up. Instead, she continued to plunge into the depths of her own private hell.

Since she didn't have the courage to get rid of the baby, she knew she would eventually have to tell Eliza. She was already starting to show, and she knew it couldn't wait much longer. But that was only half of it. She also didn't want to raise this child alone. After growing up with a single parent, after seeing her mom pack up her own paint brushes and canvases and dreams when her dad left, she didn't want that for this child. She'd thought about how the conversation would go a thousand times.

It wasn't just her fault. Lucia wasn't sure if Eliza was madder at her or Miquel. Probably her. Lucia was grateful for the labyrinth-like walk of shame stretching into infinity, giving them both some time to process.

When they finally got to the bottom, out of the narrow canal of a stairway and into the prismatic kaleidoscope of light and color, painting an ever-changing mosaic on a blank canvas, Lucia could see tears streaming down Eliza's face. There they stood, not speaking. What could either of them say? And then, Eliza abruptly left Lucia alone in that marble forest.

Lucia had foolishly hoped for forgiveness, maybe even compassion or support, but got neither. Lucia stayed there for a long time, bathed in the reds and oranges of sin, fire, and shame. Even though she was surrounded by a revolving door of tourists and visitors, she was completely and utterly alone.

CHAPTER 43
VERA

Despite Nick's jacket, rain trickled down Vera's back, making her twist and twitch, sending shivers up her spine. She mostly stuck to sidewalks as the streets were already flooding, storm drains overrun, but she arched around the horse sculpture's chain-link tail as it furiously and unpredictably lashed in every direction, clanging against the horse itself. She squinted, trying to keep the sea spray out of her eyes.

Vera's phone was definitely now dead, but she was able to find the hospital. Since it was a few stories taller than the buildings around it, she could see it sticking up. But by the time she got to the hospital, the front doors had been covered with plywood, screwed shut. Spray-painted on the plywood was the location of the nearest shelter.

She asked a pair of men who were continuing to prep for the hurricane if they knew what was going on.

"They evacuated the entire building already. The last of the patients just left. They are flying them out on a military plane."

"And their families?" Vera asked, now realizing she didn't know where her mother was, nor did she have a way to get in touch with her.

"Probably taking shelter. You should too. There's a place open just a few blocks," he said pointing away from the water and the museum.

The museum: Where Nick was headed. If she could get there and find him, she wouldn't be alone. She could borrow his phone or maybe a charger.

She thanked the men and then turned on her heel, going exactly in the opposite direction of where he had said, towards the impending storm, towards the water.

"Not that way! The other way," the man shouted into the wind, but Vera ignored him and just kept walking.

CHAPTER 44
ELIZA

Eliza and Miquel continued to fret in the cramped waiting room of the police station. There were no chairs, sending the message this was not a place to get comfortable.

"We might need a new plan," Miquel suggested, "If this doesn't go anywhere."

While Eliza wanted to wander the streets in circles, looking for any sign of Vera, that would be foolish. They would need a safe place to wait out the storm. The shelters were likely filling quickly, so every moment they waited could contribute to future problems for them.

Because Eliza still couldn't get in touch with Vera, she finally broke down and called Lucia. Lucia picked up. Eliza spoke in a hushed whisper, as if saying the words out loud would make her less of a mother. Eliza had promised her friend she would protect and raise her daughter, and Eliza had failed. She had gotten her through these eighteen years and even gotten her through brain surgery, and then, when she thought she could take her eyes off for a second, she lost Vera. She had failed Vera and Lucia. She'd failed herself.

"Vera's gone," Eliza said. "Her surgery went well, and while she was recovering and napping in her room, I went to get a cup of coffee and pick up some things Vera wanted. When I came back, she was gone. We haven't been able to find her anywhere, and this storm's getting worse."

Why had she waited until now to reach out to Lucia? But Lucia hadn't come to the hospital. If she cared, she would have come. How would telling Lucia ever help? She thought herself foolish, wasting time on this call when her daughter was still missing.

"I know. I'm sorry," Lucia said.

"Wait. You… know?" Eliza asked.

"Nick told me. Vera left the hospital to meet him. They've been exploring St. Pete this afternoon."

"Why didn't you call me? We've been beside ourselves."

"I just found out. We?"

"Miquel's here."

Eliza did not get a response. Was Lucia still there? Had they been disconnected?

Eliza tried again, "So she's with you and Nick? Vera, I mean?"

Lucia paused. "No."

"Didn't you say she was with Nick?"

"He left her near the banyans about half an hour ago to come help me. I didn't know she was with him. I swear. I just needed help with the art."

"Does he know where she is? Where she could be? Why aren't you looking??" Eliza accused.

The cop came back into the room, with something written on a Post-it. "I've got to go," Eliza said to Lucia, not waiting for a response. "Call me immediately if you hear anything. I need to find my daughter."

"I was able to track her cell phone, and it looks like the last place she had a signal was a block from the hospital. I pulled up the traffic cam footage, and it looks like she returned to the hospital, talked to two men hanging plywood, and then turned and walked towards the water… This is the last angle I have. From 4:37 p.m., just seven minutes ago."

"The Dalítorium!" Eliza exclaimed. "She must be going to the museum."

"*S'ha acabat el broquil*[4], Vera," Miquel agreed.

As they headed out the door, the officer said, "The Dalítorium's closed, with the storm coming and all. You need to find higher ground fast. It's not safe to wander around these streets, especially near the water. The expected storm surge will be deadly."

4 Catalan saying: There's no more broccoli.

"Thanks, but that museum was built for this," Eliza replied confidently. She knew the Dalítorium was the safest place in town to be. Plus, what choice did they have? They had a lead on where Vera was. They had to follow it, lest they lose her all over again.

CHAPTER 45
NICK

Nick had to find Vera. Nick realized what an idiot he had been. He should have stayed with her. He never should have lured her away from the hospital. He thought he was being responsible, returning to help Lucia store the collection. He had tried to call Vera, but couldn't get an answer. He texted. They went undelivered. He would make it right now. He was going to go back to where he left her, to try and retrace her steps, to do whatever it took to find her.

When he went to open the door, he had to brace himself against the crushing wind, using more force than he could muster. Needles of raindrops riddled his face. How could he possibly find her? How could he possibly not try?

Luckily, Nick didn't have to look very far. There was a figure in a bright green dress, wrapped in his jacket, walking right towards him. He sprinted towards her, enveloping her in a bear hug. He wiped streaks of wet hair off her face and kissed her cheeks.

"Oh, Vera. I'm so sorry. I should never have left you!"

Her electrified eyes danced from him to the museum to the water and back again. "Do you feel that wind? Hold me tighter, or it might blow me away!"

"Let's get you inside. Once you dry off, I can show you around properly." He huddled her back towards the museum.

LUCIA

Lucia had just gotten off the phone with Eliza, or more accurately, Eliza had hung up on her. Why wouldn't she? Eliza must blame Nick—and her by association—for losing Vera. And if anything were to happen to Vera… she couldn't fathom it. She would make calls: to local officials, to local shelters, to businesses between the banyans and the hospital. Nick would do a sweep of the area, although Lucia had given him strict instructions to come back within the hour, or earlier if things got bad. She couldn't lose him either. Andre would never forgive her.

Lucia heard a clamor and turned to see Nick opening the heavy door and guiding Vera inside. When Lucia saw Vera, she dropped her phone. She ran to her and hugged this stranger. She ran and hugged her daughter. She would send Nick in search of a towel, something to dry her off and make her more comfortable. She should have texted or called Eliza immediately, but she didn't. Instead, she was so overcome by relief and happiness that the daughter she had given up all those years ago had not been washed away in the hurricane or died on the operating table. Instead, she was in her arms again, like she had been almost eighteen years ago.

She and her daughter would reunite at the Dalítorium. It was thanks to Dalí, and his shower of blue raindrop condoms in Figueres, that the three vertices of the love triangle that would collectively birth and raise Vera were joined. Under an upturned boat, a symbol of Dalí's love and grief in his wife's passing, Vera's existence began. And in his jewelry-box fortress would their relationship begin anew.

Before fetching a towel, it was Nick who texted Eliza, finally responding to Eliza's previously unanswered texts. "She's here," he wrote. "Vera's at the Dalí."

ELIZA

When Eliza got that message, they were already en route to the Dalítorium. Now, this family of strangers with intertwined stories and lives would hunker down together, at least until the storm passed. Thankfully, Dalí could offer some sort of refuge, some talking point that wasn't the storm or their lives, some surreal escapism, but had she stopped and really thought about it, she would have fully realized the storm into which she was walking.

What would Miquel think? What would Lucia think? That she'd raised their daughter to sneak out of hospitals and chase boys?

And what of Vera? She wanted to scold her. She wanted to yell. She wanted to ground her for three Sundays. But those things were increasingly less effective. By law, Vera was almost officially an adult and could make her own choices. And when Eliza tried to create boundaries or enforce consequences, she drove Vera further away. After spending Vera's entire life together, Vera would be leaving. They had been tangoing this fine line, this dance for power and autonomy, since Vera was little. Vera had always tested boundaries, seeing how far she could go before someone, almost always Eliza, drew that line and reeled her back in. It was exhausting for Eliza, always being the limits in a world where each day presented new tests, new lines needing to be drawn. She wanted her daughter to have spirit and wings, but this was not what she intended.

Eliza and Miquel approached quickly, having Vera's location confirmed and seeking shelter from the torrential rain. Once they were under the overhang, a concrete umbrella providing the first reprieve they had had since Vera had left, Eliza hesitated. To enter would mean to come face to face with Nick, the boy who had drawn Vera away; Lucia, Vera's biological mother and a person she'd barely spoken to in years; and Vera, who had recklessly left her, jeopardizing both of their safety.

And what if Vera found out the truth? About her birth parents? That Eliza had been lying to her all these years? Eliza might just lose her, this time possibly forever.

She didn't have to make the first move. Nick opened the door, and then, with urgency, said, "Come in! Now! Storm's getting close, and we have to close down the entrance." They heeded his warning, seeking refuge and reunion in this concrete monstrosity.

PART II: THE EYE

"The eye of a hurricane is an excellent place to reflect upon the puniness of man and his work. If an adequate definition of humility is ever written, it's … done in the eye of a hurricane."
Journalist Edward R. Murrow,
after flying into the eye of a hurricane

CHAPTER 46
NICK

Nick pulled down the metal gate intended to protect the entrance from water seeping in or wind breaking the glass door. Ironic that it said "Welcome" in two dozen languages, many he didn't recognize. He then headed through the museum to the back door, furthest away from the surge, to repeat this ritual at the loading dock. The preparation for hurricanes, particularly of this magnitude, had been extensive. Pulling down the second metal barricade, he wondered how Vera could forgive him so easily. He'd left her in the middle of a freaking storm. What an idiot. He lingered at the door, not ready to face Lucia or Eliza's wrath for taking Vera away from the hospital. In theory, they were all safe now, but all these people would be stuck together in this hall of dreams and nightmares for the foreseeable future, or at least until the storm passed.

Nick knew he would have to join them eventually, or they would worry about him. For now, he enjoyed the peace and quiet of this storage area, more fully packed than usual due to their recent defensive purging. The miniatures were still safely in the vault; that was the first thing he would do after the storm. He checked his phone. Glad to have some service, he scrolled to find the most up-to-date forecast. He watched a local update:

Hurricane Phoenix, now a category 5 hurricane, is expected to make landfall around 8 p.m. in central Pinellas County, where it's bringing heavy rain, damaging winds, and life-threatening storm surges. With the expected damage to bridges and causeways, if you haven't left yet, you should stay put, or seek shelter and higher ground locally.

It cut from the weatherman to the news desk where Lucia's face appeared on the screen, her name in the headline. "I'm staying here. At the Dalítorium. This place is a fortress."

"Couldn't the glass break?"

"Not a chance. Those panes may look fragile, but they are an inch and a half thick." It panned across the vast expanse of the glass enigma and then cut to an aerial view. The ticker bar across the bottom read, "St. Pete protects Dalí—not citizens—from storm."

"But what if you get stuck here for a while? What about power?"

"Weymouth put all mission-critical systems, the generators, the humidifiers, on the third floor, above the storm surge level. Nothing is going to get in here."

"So why not open it up as a shelter?" Lucia stood there, paralyzed. Painful seconds passed. He thought it was frozen until the reporter said, "You heard it here, at the hurricane fortress, the Dalítorium."

He shut off his phone. What was Lucia thinking? So much for the money for the expansion. He wondered if Lucia'd seen the clip yet. He should probably find her and let her know, but the damage was already done. Thank goodness he'd already started to get on Stu's good side. If Lucia didn't get the job, it looked like Stu would. With the external lockup complete, as per hurricane protocol, he headed back into the museum. He needed to find Vera.

CHAPTER 47

ELIZA

Nick had opened the door for them, but then he disappeared, likely to finish some last-minute preparations. It was better this way, Eliza thought. She wanted to see Vera first: to yell at her and hold her. Having him there would definitely complicate things. With just the power-saving emergency lights on, the museum took on another quality, where the bluish-purple shadows seemed more real than the walls and sculptures themselves. There was still some natural light, at least in the lobby, but without the sun, it did little to illuminate the collection, much less indicate where Eliza should go next.

Once Eliza grasped her bearings, she looked up at the triangular glass prisms that almost split the building in half. She knew they were thick, built to withstand the storm, but they were currently being tested, thanks to an assault of raindrops ricocheting in every direction. She thought of standing under showers, waterfalls; she thought of that boat in Figueres.

And under it all, stood Lucia comforting Vera, drying her off with a blanket. What nerve.

"Vera!"

Vera spun around, and Eliza rushed to her, enveloping Vera in her arms. "I thought I lost you," she said. Ready to chastise her, Vera surprised Eliza by hugging her back.

"I'm so sorry, Mom."

"I'm going to go check on..." Lucia excused herself, taking Miquel with her.

"Vera..." Eliza started.

"I saw the tree! The banyan."

"You left the hospital, Vera," Eliza said, holding back tears and rage.

"I shouldn't have. I know. But I'm fine, Mom! That crazy gnarled tree, dancing in the wind? Have you ever seen anything like it? It's incredible."

"You left me, Vera. I was terrified. I texted. I called. Nothing."

"You know I don't keep my phone charged."

"And you know how much I hate that." She had threatened on more than one occasion—before the tumor—to take Vera's phone away if she didn't keep it charged, but Eliza never followed through. Maybe she should have.

"I'll work on it. I said I was sorry."

"I went to the police, Vee."

"The police? Really? I'm practically grown!"

Why was her daughter looking at her like she was the crazy one? It wasn't like she missed curfew by a few minutes. She'd eloped the hospital after surgery in the middle of a hurricane. Eliza was not the crazy one.

"You could have been lost in this storm!" Eliza said. "What if you had some post-op complication from the surgery? You already missed at least one dose of medication, and you missed your post-op evaluation."

"They said I was fine. You heard them."

"I could have lost you," Eliza confessed, giving voice to her greatest fear.

"But I'm okay."

Vera was right, thank goodness. All of the tension and stress of worrying left her body and Eliza said a quick prayer of gratitude that her daughter was standing in front of her, whole and safe.

"At least take your meds." Eliza said, pulling a few prescription bags out of her purse. As she did, her beloved Red Rose teal seagull fell out, shattering to the floor.

"I'm sorry, Mom," Vera said, bending to try and clean up the shards of glass.

"I'll do it, Vee. We'll find a broom after you take your meds."

Eliza feared losing Vera to anything, be it a boy, a state college less than two hours away, or even death. The threats changed over the years, from a blind cord to a falling dresser to a car backing up to an accessible, unlocked gun at a friend's house. The worry morphed based on Vera's age and new tragedies featured on the nightly news or Eliza's social media feed, but there was always something. It was natural, wasn't it? For mothers to think about the ways their children could die, and then replay those worst-case scenarios when they couldn't sleep at night? When they got the tumor diagnosis, it was as much as an actualization of all those other imaginary fears and possible deaths that they had avoided.

"I didn't mean to worry you. I didn't even mean to be gone for that long." Vera dropped her head and then looked back up at Eliza.

"Why did you leave? Where could you possibly have gone?"

"I went to see Nick," Vera admitted. "He came to check on me, and I wasn't sure they'd let him come up to my room, or if you'd approve."

"More than your leaving, Vee!" How could she not see the difference? This was not the child she raised.

"I just wanted to say hi, to actually see him now that I finally could."

"But leaving the hospital?"

"We got caught up in an adventure. We crammed three or four dates into one afternoon. He's a really nice guy, Mom. I like him," she paused. "A lot."

Getting Vera to see why this was wrong wasn't working. Eliza tried differently. "You scared me, Vera."

"That's not fair! You weren't even there. I woke up and you were gone."

Rummaging through her bag, she pulled out something. "I went to get your eyeliner. And the bra you wanted. That's where I was."

Vera looked at the eyeliner and then back at her mother. "Okay, I believe you. You don't need to pull out my bra, Mom."

"I know better than that." Eliza laughed at the thought of pulling it out in the middle of the museum, even if it was basically empty.

Eliza handed her the locket and the eyeliner, and Vera snatched the eyeliner, stuffing it into her pocket.

"Your locket?" Eliza asked, holding it out for her to take.

"You can hold onto it for now."

"But you always wear it."

"Because you want me to. If you like it so much, why don't you wear it?"

Nick and Miquel wandered into the gallery, making their flashlights dance on the walls.

"Since we're stuck here anyway, can I go exploring?" Vera asked her mom, testing the limits of their tentative truce.

"I'd be happy to show her around," Nick offered.

Eliza looked from Nick to Vera and back again. If Vera went with Nick, she could find Lucia and finish their conversation from the other day. This might even be a chance for Vera to get to know Miquel. "Do not leave this building."

"Really, Mom?" Vera rolled her eyes. "Don't you know me better than that?"

"I thought I did."

As Vera left, Eliza looked from the locket to the shattered seagull and back again. She put the locket safely into her purse and went to find a broom, only then realizing Vera still hadn't taken her medicine.

CHAPTER 48

LUCIA

After Lucia pawned Miquel off on Nick, she finished her walk-through of all vital systems. She wanted to marvel at the architect's attention to detail, how everything was working exactly as they had designed: all critical systems, from the solar-powered dehumidification system to the HVAC, were up and running. But all she could think about was Vera. The relief and release of finding her, of wrapping her in a blanket, of feeling the same electric spark for Vera that she once had for Dalí. Looking around the museum, she wondered if this had all been for nothing, if she'd missed out on something she could never have back.

She stopped in her office, hoping to check in with the director before she gathered necessary supplies and hunkered down to weather the storm. She knew better than anyone that in this museum, it didn't matter how strong the storm got, at least in theory. Although this building had been built to survive the big one, up until now, it had only been tested in labs.

Even though the landlines were down, she still had cell service. She had the director on speed dial, and Harold picked up after the second ring. She had hoped he wouldn't, that she could just leave a message.

"Everything's working as planned so far, but this storm will definitely put Weymouth's design to the test." She was secretly thrilled to witness what this building could withstand. "The collection should be fine."

She considered asking if he was safe but knew he'd flown out on a private helicopter the night before. It was not a time for small talk. She had work to do. "Yes, the miniatures have shipped," she answered. "They went out yesterday. We also secured the collection in the lobby further, at least the most valuable works."

He asked about the 'we' and her voice fell.

"Nick's here too." She couldn't let Harold know about the others. They'd be gone before he returned from Atlanta. She knew the plan was for her and her only to be there during the storm. She had to sign a waiver with HR in case the systems failed.

"I called him in to help move heavy pieces and troubleshoot in case any of the systems shorted. I know, not exactly the plan, but I needed another set of hands in case of emergency."

While she listened to his lecture, she opened her desk drawer, pulling out the grainy, gray picture of Vera's ultrasound. She'd tried to be gentle with it, but the edges had worn ragged from handling. She looked from it to the expansion plans and back again.

"Okay. I'll get him to sign the waiver. I've got it under control. I promise." She hoped she was right.

When he told her the pressure the board was getting to open up the museum as a shelter, she countered, "If the systems fail, and we had opened up the museum, we'd be a walking liability target. It's counterintuitive to send people into the storm surge, where the water could rise more than twenty feet." She hoped the area's death toll would be minimal.

"That's a change in tone."

"I'm just following the plan we built."

"You've seen the footage?"

"The storm footage?"

"We're going to have a PR nightmare on our hands after this, Lucia."

"What are you talking about?"

"Just Google yourself, Lucia."

He hung up first without saying goodbye or good luck. Confused, she opened her laptop. Her screen saver, a picture of Dagny, popped up. Only then did Lucia realize her cat would be weathering the storm alone in her apartment. She hoped she—or more likely Andre—had at least set out food for Dagny. But Lucia was here with what mattered. Dalí's art and legacy would outlive them all, thanks to her. She couldn't even keep a cat safe, much less another person. She had done the right thing in giving Vera to Eliza to raise, hadn't she? With Vera here now, she wasn't so sure.

She opened a search bar and typed in her name. She was the top story.

CHAPTER 49

VERA

Even though the Deepfake Dalís were shut off now to conserve energy, Nick wanted Vera to see them, so he turned them on. Nick then handed Vera a flashlight of her own. Her warm beam of light contrasted with the underworldly blue of emergency lights shifting under shadows of a fast-moving, howling sky. She darted it this way and that, flitting from the helix staircase that seemed to disappear into midair to the glint in Nick's eye. It was too much to take in all at once, and she was grateful for the laser-like focus her flashlight provided.

An accented voice from behind her caught her off guard. "*Knowing how to look is a way of inventing*." She spun around just in time to see the trademark handlebar mustache of the now-flickering Dalí.

Looking at Nick, she marveled, "You created this?"

Sheepishly, he nodded. "I mean... kind of. I helped. I'm hoping we can sell the technology to other museums."

"Wax museums will be a thing of the past, Vera," interrupted another voice, mimicking Dalí's lilt and cadence.

"Aren't they already?" Vera asked, turning towards this Dalí-like man in the flesh, minus the mustache, the one who'd been with her mom.

Miquel held his flashlight beneath his chin, pointed toward the sky, casting contrasts of light and dark, more surreal than the apparitions themselves. "Touché. Once upon a time, I worked in one, the Museu de Cera in Barcelona."

She looked at him more curiously as he took her hand and kissed it. "Miquel. How did you know my name?" Vera asked.

Miquel shrugged. "Your mother told me. We're old friends." He reached behind her ear, revealing a coin. He nodded toward the car. "You haven't seen it until you turn it on."

Vera did as instructed, delighting in the absurdity of rain falling inside this old-timey black car.

"Let me show you both around," Nick said, interlacing his fingers with Vera's, pulling her towards him.

"I was just here," Miquel said. "I don't know that I need a tour."

"We can make it a game. A scavenger hunt? One point per ant, two for crutches or praying mantises, and five for communion bread," Nick said, pulling her towards a room where all were plentiful.

"What makes the bread so special?" Vera asked. Miquel smirked and glanced at Nick and then back to Vera. Nick blushed.

"You'll see," Miquel said. "If you can find one."

Miquel was quick to point out an army of ants, but Vera found the first praying mantis and the first crutch. With each new one, found independently or with some nudging from Nick, Vera delighted in the dopamine rush of discovery, but relished the vivid feast of strangeness laid out on the walls even more than the victory of finding them first. They bantered back and forth, racking up points and marveling in their conquests.

After fluttering from painting to painting, she stopped, taken by the multitude of Venus-like statues, similarly missing arms, and the arresting reds and yellows: *The Hallucinogenic Troubadour*.

"Isn't that a Dalmation?" Vera asked, pointing to seemingly random black and white dots in the lower left corner of the massive painting.

"No…" Nick said. "I would have known that."

"Look closer. Look here," Vera said, pointing to the dog.

"She's right," Miquel chimed in. "Dalí's sleight of hand. Hiding things in plain sight, creating optical illusions."

"How did you see that? You're amazing, Vera."

"I think that means I won," Vera smiled.

"*De l'arbre dolent no esperis bon fruit*[5]," Miquel said. Miquel pulled out a 100 Euro bill and a purple marker from his brown leather messenger bag. He handed both to Vera. "Sign this," he said.

"Are you sure?" she asked.

He nodded. Vera signed the bill, putting her signature smiley face in the final 'a', and Miquel took it back and ripped it into tiny pieces. "Can I have my bill back, please?" he asked her.

"I don't have it," Vera said, wide-eyed at the scraps on the floor.

"Check your pocket," he said.

She reached into Nick's jacket pocket and pulled out a 100 Euro bill with her signature, smiley face and all. She turned the bill over and held it up to the light in disbelief. "How did you do that?"

"Magic, of course," Miquel said with a wink.

"No, really! That's impossible!" Vera said.

"Keep it. Consider it a birthday gift," he said.

There was no end to the surprises she would experience on her last day of being seventeen. The universe was conspiring to fill her up with as much wonder as possible before she crossed that imaginary threshold from childhood and adulthood.

She looked back and forth from her new love Nick to this familiar stranger Miquel. How did he know her? And how did her mom know him? And if her mom had known Lucia so well, why hadn't she introduced them the first time they were together?

She had found this strange picture recently, a blurry polaroid of her mother, another woman, and a spry, dark man, in front of some old car, nestled in the pages of her mother's copy of *The Fountainhead.* She read it the summer after her sophomore year, never asking her mom about the picture, but wondering, all the same, who these people were and why her mother kept it. When Vera returned the book, she kept the picture, studying it from time to time and then forgetting about it for months until they started invading her dreams again. The stranger standing in front of her looked so much like that man in the picture.

5 Catalan saying: Do not expect good fruit from the bad tree.

As they explored more, they passed one of the Deepfake Dalís. It was glitching, now, with the museum in emergency-only, energy conservation mode. Dalí's body sparked like a flame in the corner, fading out and then dancing back in separate parts like the Cheshire Cat. His hand flickered here; his mustache and face flashed there. Body parts came in and out of focus in a random rhythm.

To Vera, Dalí said, "*Surrealism is destructive, but it destroys only what it considers to be shackles limiting our vision.*" Even though the image was flickering in and out, the voice remained mostly steady.

"Do you think this technology can read us? Was that just for me? Like some sort of futuristic fortune teller?" she asked Nick, looking for reassurance that it had been random.

"What do you think?" he asked her.

For Vera, her peripheral vision had expanded exponentially in the span of just a few days. Before she'd been trapped in her tumor prison, she'd been so focused on soccer that she'd never experienced the thrill of romance. Also, she'd never seriously defied her mom. In the span of a few days, everything changed. She would live: The tumor shackling her brain had been removed with clear margins. The dizziness and blurred vision she had experienced were both gone, and she could see the world anew. For the first time in her life, she was giddy from being properly kissed. She did not feel giddy easily. She knew it was foolish to hope this was anything more than a fling, but she loved having these previously buried emotions now churning through her body, making things that used to matter pale in comparison.

And then, there was her mom. Her mom had been her rock. They were—at least more recently—like sisters. She deferred to her mom on almost everything. They rarely spent a night apart, and when they were apart for more than a few hours, they were calling and texting. For Vera to leave not just the hospital but also her mom was something pre-tumor Vera would never have done. She realized how much her leaving must have hurt her mom. And yet, her mom survived. They both did.

But it was more than that. Vera realized that if she hadn't left the hospital, she would still be stuck in the cave of her former life. In kissing Nick, she'd seen the sun, and the shadows of love and life that used to comfort her would no longer suffice.

As Miquel passed, the Deepfake Dalí said, "*Mistakes are almost always of a sacred nature. Never try to correct them. On the contrary: rationalize them, understand them thoroughly. Only then will it be possible for you to sublimate them.*"

Thunder snapped and cracked. The intimacy of being seen so clearly by an abstract projection rattled her. He was cat-like, Salvador. They knew he would be back, but for now: poof, gone. Relieved that Dalí's flame flickered out for at least a second time, with this barrage of roaring thunder, Vera suddenly remembered the severity of the hurricane. She snuggled closer to Nick.

"Will we be okay here?"

"We should," he said. "This is the safest place we could be. Well, maybe not the lobby. Let's get further away from the glass, just in case, see if we can help Lucia with any last-minute preparations, maybe find some real food. That ice pop was delicious, but it doesn't count as dinner."

Vera fingered the wooden ice pop stick in her pocket. As they walked down the hallway to find food, Vera thought of something. She turned to Miquel. "Yours was about mistakes. What mistakes have you made?"

They were momentarily jarred by a loud banging from the storage area.

"Wait here," Nick said, going to check it out.

"Mistakes? *Jo*?" Miquel laughed. "No mistakes. Not even you, *amor meu*."

"Me? But... that's impossible!"

CHAPTER 50
LUCIA

Lucia slammed her laptop, not bothering to close out the tabs or shut it down properly. She hadn't meant for any of that to be recorded. The director didn't come out and say it, but she knew that he was pissed and this would jeopardize any chance she had of getting the promotion.

That didn't seem fair, though. How many people could have seen that footage? And she didn't say anything that wasn't true. The Dalítorium was hurricane-proof. She believed that now more than ever. She would obviously be here for the storm. It was part of her job description. How could they possibly hold that against her? She was just doing what they hired her to do.

And yet, watching herself on that screen, something seemed off. She never particularly enjoyed watching footage of herself, but this wild-eyed reflection came off like a thrill-seeking storm chaser, not the deliberate planner who'd worked so hard to get to this point. There was no shred of empathy in that mirror image looking back at her.

Vera and Eliza showing up left Lucia unhinged. When Eliza fled their flat in Barcelona without leaving as much as a note, taking Vera with her, Lucia had fallen apart. Until then, Lucia hadn't realized how much she cared, but by then, it was too late. When she saw the freezer, empty of milk bags, she knew they weren't coming back. The milk was for Vera, but it was Lucia who coaxed it out, pumping in where she could, in dirty bathroom stalls with questionable locks. As her breasts hardened and cried, staining shirt after shirt, Lucia quit leaving the apartment for weeks, holding out hope they would return one day. She knew it was foolish, though. Eliza had taken Vera's forged birth certificate and her passport. When Lucia finally got off the floor and decided to leave the apartment, she vowed to never get attached to anyone again. She couldn't let herself be shattered. She focused solely on her art career in order to make losing Vera worth something.

And then she threw it all away in one fickle moment, in one stupid interview. In an instant, everything she had built and been working for disappeared, and the rubble of nothingness left behind terrified her.

For the second time in her life, she didn't know what to do next.

Lucia preferred to continue to hide in her office, avoiding the impending reunion. There was nowhere for any of them to escape to. For Lucia and Eliza, former best friends. For Miquel and Lucia, and for Miquel and Eliza, former lovers, and now co-parents of Vera, the child two of them barely knew. They were all headed to this inevitable impasse where all truths and indiscretions would converge, and there would be no real way out. Given the severity of the impending storm, she knew they'd be here for a while, dealing with whatever was to come, be it environmentally catastrophic or personally devastating.

But Vera was here. What if this was a chance to make things right with her? If not to make up for the last twenty years, to have the chance to begin again? Unfortunately, she knew she'd need to talk to Eliza first. She had to understand why Eliza took her daughter.

LUCIA

Barcelona, Spain

Under that bruised purple sky so long ago, Lucia had navigated the streets of their little neighborhood in García, hoping to make it back before Vera's bedtime. Once its own little town, García—like so many other towns—was swallowed up as Barcelona expanded. Thoughts of Paris flooded her mind. She couldn't wait to tell Eliza about the gala in I. M. Pei's glass pyramid, the never-ending hors d'oeuvres, about touring both the Rodin and the Van Gogh museums with the little time off she found.

Lucia felt guilty that she'd been gone longer than initially planned, but once they asked her to stay, how could she not? Eliza understood. They asked her to move to Paris that summer and take a job full-time. She hoped Eliza would support her. Eliza always did, and where better to be than Paris in summer? With Miquel coming around less frequently, the three of them could move to Paris, she reasoned. He could visit there as easily as he visited them in Barcelona. Plus, their lease would be up soon.

Just as it was starting to feel like home, they would be leaving. She reached their flat and unlocked the exterior door, still charmed by the overly ornate keys. Places with a lift were too expensive, so they joked that climbing the four flights saved them on a gym membership. It was less funny when they were hauling the stroller up and down the stairs. She started taking the stairs two at a time, suddenly ready to get back to Vera.

She opened the door as quietly as possible just in case Eliza had already put Vera down. It was eerily quiet and the lights were off. Odd. Had Eliza forgotten to pay the bill? She walked across the room feeling for the button. She pressed it on and even though everything seemed in place—the table and chairs, the sofa they took turns sleeping on, the lamp—something was off. Miquel's art supplies still cluttered the corner, but he hadn't used them in a while. A suffocating emptiness filled the stale room.

"Eliza?" she whispered. No response. "Eliza!" she called out, opening the door to the bedroom and then the bathroom. The flat was empty. She was alone.

Frantically, Lucia had started opening drawers and cabinets. Besides what was hers, they were empty. The onesies, the diapers, the bottles, all gone. Eliza's clothes, all gone. Senyor Conill, gone. Not even a note.

She threw open the French doors onto the Juliette balcony, craning her neck looking for them. Where could they have gone? Where could they be? Lucia had talked to her last week. Or had it been the week before?

Lucia had racked her brain and the apartment for some clue where they might have gone.

She'd opened the freezer. The milk Lucia had painstakingly pumped was gone. Had they run out? Or had Eliza taken it with her?

Something on the side of the refrigerator had caught her eye: Vera's ultrasound. The only trace that Vera or Eliza had been there. Lucia had un-taped that pixelated picture, collapsed on the sofa, and cried.

CHAPTER 51

VERA

Vera couldn't breathe, move. How could this stranger be her father? How could her mother have lied to her all these years? "But that's impossible," Vera said.

"You don't believe me?"

"I don't know what to believe."

Miquel scratched his chin. "I think I can prove it. You know Senyor Conill?"

She reached into her pocket, reaching for him, fingering his thread-barren ear. How did he know about Senyor Conill?

"I got him for you. When you were born."

"Mom said you died."

Miquel's eyebrows shot up in feign surprise. "*Jo? Mort?* Do I look dead to you? Or perhaps I've been born again? A cat with—how do you say—nine lives?"

A crack of thunder followed by a flash of light startled Vera.

"But why would she tell me that?"

"It was easier than telling the truth? She didn't want you to hate me? Ask her. I have no idea. I came home, and you were both gone."

"Why are you here now? What do you want from me?"

Miquel shrugged. "When Eliza wrote me about your surgery, I wanted to make sure you were okay."

Vera wasn't sure what to do. Should she reach out a hand to shake? Go in for a hug? There was no prior experience of how to handle meeting the father who you thought was dead, no cotillion lessons she could fall back on. This wasn't the expected experience of children who participated in those white-gloved dancing and etiquette classes her Nana made her take all those years ago.

"I'm Vera," Vera said, reaching out her hand to this stranger, her father. Miquel seemed unaccustomed to the American greeting and instead leaned in to kiss her cheek. She turned hard left. Awkward.

As stupid as it seemed, she worried she'd done the wrong thing. That he wouldn't approve of her, that he'd leave her all over again. Why had he even bothered to come now? He'd basically missed everything that mattered, and she'd gone through the entire grief process, finally making peace with the fact her dad wasn't in her life, just in time for him to show back up out of nowhere. What if she blew it? What if she disappointed him?

Vera couldn't bring herself to make eye contact with him and instead looked up to the complex matrix of triangular glass panes above her head. She watched the swirling of yellow and gray, the bombardment of raindrops attacking the fortress she had made her home until the threat of the physical storm had passed. He must have come to St. Pete for her. Her father had no other reason, at least that she knew, to be here right now, besides the opportunity to make sure she survived, to make sure she was okay. "How could you do this to me? How could Mom?"

Miquel had no answer. The thunder rolled, shattering his silence.

Disgusted, Vera turned to leave him. She had to go find her mom.

How dare her mother lie to her? About her own father? Had Eliza been keeping them apart? Why had Eliza not taken her to meet her father before now? Why hadn't she told Vera that he was alive? That he was coming? Even if she wasn't completely sure, even if she didn't want to get Vera's hopes up, the least she could have done was give her a heads up.

This was her first opportunity to get to know her dad, to show him she'd grown up into someone worth sticking around for, and instead of seizing it, she was fuming at her mom. This might be her one real shot at having a real, proper family like her friends had. Even if they wouldn't have 2.3 kids or a dog, she could have a mother and father.

But where had he been all these years? It was Miquel's fault as much as her mom's, maybe even more. When her mother cursed under her breath when yet another bill showed up. When she made up stupid excuses why she was the only girl without a dad to make a Father's Day gift for. She gave Pops the things she made, at least as long as he was alive, but even now she cringed at the memory of the pity she got from other girls and their parents. Even though her Pops cherished the Father's Day back-scratcher and the grilling apron with her handprints, they constantly reminded her of what she was missing.

Her mother probably had a thousand reasons for keeping him from Vera, but none of them that she could think of were any good. She wasn't a child anymore, but her mother insisted on treating her like one. And how could she lie to Vera about her father? How could Vera ever trust her again?

CHAPTER 52
ELIZA

At first, Eliza had hovered from a distance, reluctant to let Vera out of her sight. Once she felt confident that Vera was okay, that she wouldn't be leaving, she decided to seek Lucia out. There was hurricane prep to do. Lucia obviously hadn't planned on having them here for the storm. More than that, so much from their conversation the other day had gone unfinished.

She left the main gallery, walking up that double helix staircase in the direction Lucia had gone, and headed down the hallway. How far Lucia had come since her long hours at whatever small art gallery would have her. Eliza couldn't believe that all this would be Lucia's. She couldn't help but wonder what she herself could have done, what she might have become.

Armed with this new realization and suddenly not particularly eager to see Lucia, she stopped and studied *The Archeological Reminiscence of Millet's Angelus.* Under a menacing, eerie sky, two towering monoliths, reminiscent of a collapsed civilization, loomed over the landscape, backlit by moonlight. In the shadow of the statues, a miniature parent, holding the hand of an even smaller child, pointed up towards the taller statue, the female. How similarly small and insignificant she had felt when she left Spain with Vera. How large Lucia's career had become.

A Deepfake Dalí nearby materialized out of nothing, startling her. "*The thermometer of success,*" he said, "*is merely the jealousy of the malcontents.*" Lucia's stupid holograms called her out on her jealousy. If they could sense it, she was sure Lucia would be able to as well. Maybe she should go check on Vera instead.

She didn't get the chance. Lucia came at her, whirling.

"We had an agreement, Eliza. In the Mae West room." Had Lucia heard Dalí's fortune-telling? Did she see Eliza looking at the painting?

"I know." Eliza couldn't hide any more. She would have to atone for her choices, but what could she say to make it right?

"You were going to raise her as yours, but I was supposed to be part of her life."

"I know, Lu. I tried. I promise I did. But I just couldn't do it."

"You broke your promise."

"I was by myself. Miquel left me. And you were off who knows where."

"I went to Paris for work. You knew I was going. You said it was okay."

"I said a weekend was okay. And then Miquel left me. And then the week dragged on, and then another..." Eliza turned away from Lucia, but Lucia wouldn't let her leave, moving between Eliza and the exit.

"They asked me to stay and help unload a new exhibit at the Rodin. I couldn't say no to that."

"I was alone in Spain with a needy baby I couldn't even feed. I needed help, Lucia." After holding everything together for as long as she could, she'd reached her personal breaking point.

"Why didn't you ask?"

"I thought I did." That was the whole reason for getting Vera's passport. Because Eliza knew she would need help over the holidays when Lucia and Miquel were both working, they'd agreed Vera would go to Tennessee and meet Eliza's family.

"But when I called you from Paris to let you know I was staying longer, I asked if it was okay. I said I could come home, but you said you'd figure it out."

"I guess I did."

"I didn't think you meant leaving Spain! You didn't have to pretend you had everything under control and then up and leave the country with my baby. I didn't get a say in it. I didn't even get to tell her goodbye."

"You wouldn't have been able to. You would have done this: made me feel guilty, and talked about Mae West promises from before either of us knew what we were getting into, and then I would have caved, and I wouldn't have had the courage to leave. Our flat was no place to raise a child. You shackled me there and then went off gallivanting to the City of Lights."

"We could have made it work."

"I tried. But you were running out the door to the newest art exhibit whenever you got the chance. A solo trip to Figueres, another to Madrid. You can't have it both ways."

"You never said anything."

"I shouldn't have had to. Don't you think I wish I were frolicking across Europe with you? Not stuck at home with your kid? Trying to calm her colic, walking her for hours, not knowing where money for our next round of bills was coming from?"

"Miquel and I both were chipping in."

"How much of that did Miquel actually earn? What kind of life is that for a child? But the stupid part is that I didn't even care. It's when he left, that I knew I had to leave too. I needed more help. I needed money, stability, something familiar. Yes, I wanted a child, I wanted Vera, but not like that."

"So, you left me. Without saying goodbye."

Eliza hung her head. She knew Lucia was right. Eliza hated confrontation, especially with Lucia, and she knew she wouldn't have been able to tell her she was leaving. "Look at you, though. You have everything you've always wanted: your dream job, the body of a 25-year-old, and the freedom to go anywhere whenever you want."

"I'm not getting the job, Eliza."

"What do you mean? Why not?"

"I messed up. I made a mistake. And now it's all over the news. I'll be lucky if I have a job at all after this is all over."

"I'm sorry, Lu." So, neither of them had led a full life. Each had pursued half a life, be it motherhood or professional success, and now they would both be left with nothing. What were they missing? How had they let these things define so much of them? When they had just been roommates, they had none of these things, and they had been happy. Hadn't they?

Lucia interrupted her. "She's beautiful, Vera. So strong-willed."

"Can you believe she just up and left the hospital?"

"No… yes, actually. Sounds like something I would have done."

"I know, right?"

"I'm glad she's okay."

"Yeah, me too." For the first time in such a long time, this felt easy, like they were a team again, like they had unwritten possibility. "You know, Lu. Tomorrow's her birthday. What if we threw her a party?"

"In here? In the middle of a hurricane?"

"What else are we doing? She's only turning eighteen once."

"We need to make sure everything is set and secure first, but I like it. People pay good money to have parties here."

Eliza's head started spinning with possibility, a cava toast, a Deepfake Dalí fortune teller. The Gala cafe must have some food. A tapas spread would be fitting. The guest list was a little small, but Nick was here. Vera seemed to really like him, and they wouldn't be able to run off again, at least not until this storm blew over.

"Nick? You like him?"

"Yes. Absolutely. He got into some trouble in college. Hacked into a computer to change his girlfriend's grades. But she's long gone, and his heart is in the right place."

As Eliza dreamed of an epic party, Lucia pulled out her phone, checking her list to see what else needed to be done. Eliza watched the color drain from Lucia's face.

"What, Lu?"

"Nick texted: SOS: Loading Dock."

As Lucia left to investigate, Eliza cursed herself for leaving Vera alone. What could have happened to her? She waited for Lucia to take the lead, only because she didn't know where they were going. She needed to find Vera.

CHAPTER 53
LUCIA

Lucia rushed down the stairs, noting the water already beginning to rise, sloshing against the bottom triangles.

Racing down the long hallway, Lucia heard the pummeling before she saw Nick. "What in God's name is that?"

"I don't know," Nick said. "That's why I called you."

Even with the shriek of wind, they could hear frantic, desperate voices through the metal door Nick had barricaded earlier that evening. "Help! Hello? Can you hear us?"

Lucia knew she was supposed to protect the art at all costs, to not open the museum to anyone, but now lives were on the line. She'd broadcast to the world how safe the museum was. What if they'd heard her and that's why they came? If she ignored them and then something happened to them, it would be her fault. How long had they been out there? The water was already rising.

"Open it, Nick," Lucia ordered. She had no idea how many were on the other side, but they obviously needed help. She began formulating a backup plan, possibly to set up a shelter area separate from the more valuable pieces of art.

"Once the gates close, we're not supposed to open them. We're supposed to protect the art. Director's orders."

"The director's not here. I'm in charge now, and we're not going to let people die. We can do both. We can help them and keep the art safe. Open it!"

He pulled the heavy chain, raising the metal barricade. The manual control was built in just in case the circuit shorted. Water sloshed in, even with the elevated loading dock. Feet were visible, then legs, then torsos. Perhaps a dozen. When there appeared to be enough clearance, without waiting for an invitation, the bodies ducked under the heavy door, seeking shelter from the onslaught of rain.

Most appeared to be young, college students perhaps. All were drenched and shivering. Some were clutching oversized sippy cups with colorful liquids or silly inflatables, including a flamingo and a palm tree. One was even wearing an adult-sized unicorn floaty. At least the loading dock floors were concrete. A woman dressed in a cop outfit with a badge that said USF Police department addressed Nick.

"We need help," she said. "I got an emergency call saying the windows of one of the dorms blew out. These kids thought it would be smart to ride out the hurricane in their dorm, and somehow, when we were evacuating students to nearby shelters, we missed them. And now it's too late." Behind them, palm trees bent almost sideways and small debris swirled like just-blown dandelion seeds. Two cars stranded in the parking lot were tire-deep in tidewater.

"Close the gate, Nick, and then get the Shop-Vac to clean up this water!"

Nick struggled to pull down the gate against the gale-force wind until three other students joined him.

"Why'd you think to come here?" Lucia asked the officer. "It's currently not on any of the evacuation plans."

"A couple came to my office less than half an hour ago. They were looking for a girl, and based on the video footage I found, she was heading here." She waited, looking to Lucia for an answer. "And then I saw you on the news. It was built for this, right? Isn't that what you said?"

"Something like that." That video was out in the world. No way of knowing how many others saw it, how many others might be coming. "You can stay, but there are some ground rules. You're going to stay in the staff offices by the board room. There are bathrooms there. No one touches the artwork. And you..."

"Officer Jiménez… The kids call me OJ."

"I need you, Officer Jiménez, to keep an eye on them."

"Got it."

"And you're setting up a post down here, for the next hour at least, just in case anyone else comes knocking."

"I doubt anyone else is out in this," OJ said, wringing out her jacket as Nick returned with the Shop-Vac.

"Just do it," Lucia said. "Nick, can you get some art blankets for them to dry off? And then show them where they are staying? And clean up this water!"

But Nick wasn't listening. He was staring at a gap-toothed, curvy brunette, likely one of the girls from the university.

"Nick!" She ran and wrapped her soaking wet arms around him, planting a big kiss on his cheek.

"Meredith?"

CHAPTER 54

ELIZA

Eliza and Vera practically collided on the spiral helix stairs, both looking for each other.

"How could you not tell me, Mom?"

"What are you talking about?"

"Like you don't know."

Eliza's face fell.

"You lied to me," Vera said. "You told me my dad was dead, but he's obviously not! How could you?"

"Oh Vera, I'm so sorry. I didn't know what to do—"

"I don't know, tell me the truth?"

"I can explain."

"Explain what? Why he deserted me?"

"He was working, at least at first."

"As a magician? And you—"

"It's not what you think, Vera."

"Then what is it, Mom?"

Eliza's face crumpled. How could she tell Vera the truth about this without telling her the whole truth? How would Vera ever look at her the same way again? And where should she begin? "He left me, Vera. That's the truth. He left us for another girl."

"So, tell me that!"

"Let me finish." Eliza waited until she was sure Vera would. "I waited for him to come back, hoping he would come back, with no way of making money or supporting you, with woefully lacking language skills, and with a visa about to expire. I didn't know what had happened to him, and so I convinced myself that he had died."

"That's terrible, Mom."

"That's what I told myself. That's what I had to tell myself to move on. Otherwise, I would have never left Spain. That's what I told Nana and Pops too. When you got old enough to ask, it was easier to tell you the same thing. Before social media, there was no way to—"

"And you just killed him off?"

"I didn't know what else to do. On your tenth birthday, he found me online. We exchanged a few messages—"

"Why didn't you tell me?"

"He kept ghosting me, not responding for months. I didn't want to hurt you—"

"This hurts!"

"Like he hurt me. What could I have said?"

"That my dad was alive? Maybe if I'd written him…."

"You'd quit asking about him."

"Because I assumed he was dead! Because that's what you told me! I didn't want to keep hurting you by asking over and over again."

"I didn't want to get your hopes up. It just seemed easier—"

"I can handle it, Mom."

"I wanted to introduce you two. You have to believe me, Vera. He kept promising to come visit, but those plans kept falling through."

"You still could have told me..."

"I didn't want to disappoint you. Even this time, I didn't know he was coming until he showed up in the hospital, after you'd left. You have to believe I meant to tell you, once I knew there was a reason to. I'm so sorry."

Vera didn't respond.

"Vera…"

"Yes?"

She wanted to say, "There's something else you should know…" but instead, she offered their secret sign, the ASL sign for "I love you."

Somewhat reluctantly, Vera made the sign back.

She remembered Vera's medicine. They'd missed a dose already. "Let's take your medicine, and then, find a place for you to lie down. It's been a long day for everyone."

Thankfully, Vera agreed.

CHAPTER 55

NICK

Meredith, Nick's first real love, had shattered his heart. Apparently, she didn't want to be with someone who got kicked out of college, even if it was for fixing her grades. She pretended not to know that he was going to do that, and when the Dean of Students asked him, he didn't say otherwise.

And now she was here with a number of her friends, a few he recognized. Meredith didn't think rules applied to her. She was exactly the type to ignore evacuation warnings, probably even hiding from campus officers who were doing rounds and checking for stragglers.

As he tried to brush off her wet embrace, he couldn't help noticing the Malibu on her breath. She had a thing for Malibu and Dr. Pepper. Thank goodness Vera hadn't seen this reunion. If having to apologize for leaving her in the storm wasn't bad enough, now he'd have to also explain why this college girl couldn't keep her hands off of him. But how could he explain Meredith? Without hurting Vera?

"The blankets, Nick?" Lucia interrupted this daydream, bringing him back to the present. He welcomed the reprieve, tipped an invisible hat, and headed to grab them. The museum kept a decent number of blankets to protect the artwork when in storage or transport, and even though they'd gone through a dozen already today, there were plenty to spare. He walked toward the closet where they kept them and grabbed an armful, stacked up to his chin, which helped steady them.

"Nick?" He turned to see Vera standing in front of him, Eliza to her side. He thought about dropping the stack of blankets and wrapping his arms around her, but he didn't. Instead, he looked behind him to make sure Meredith wasn't in sight.

"What was that noise?" Vera asked.

"Looks like we have company," Nick said, jerking his head toward the exit. "Some lady cop from the university brought a bunch of undergrads here. They tried to wait out the storm and then needed rescuing."

"A lady cop?"

"Sounds like you might have met her?"

"Here, give me some of those," Eliza said, taking more than half the stack of blankets. "They aren't doing any good right here."

She had a point. He led the way, and they walked toward the glowing emergency exit sign, Vera trailing behind.

Lucia intercepted them before they got to the group. "I was wondering what took you so long," she said to Nick.

"I ran into Vera and Eliza. They're helping me."

Nick couldn't help but notice how much Vera and Lucia looked alike, seeing them side by side, tall and thin compared with Eliza's fuller curves. They had the same hawk-like noses, the same auburn hair, the same tiger eyes.

Cheers erupted before they got to the students. The clamor was a welcome reprieve from the resemblance questions swirling in Nick's head, but surely their applause wasn't for some thick, gray blankets. The students couldn't see them yet anyway. He then saw Miquel, bowing deeply before the enraptured crowd.

"Magic tricks," Eliza muttered. "He's full of them."

Nick and Eliza began passing out blankets to grateful students, who wrapped themselves up as soon as they got them. Nick tried to avoid Meredith, but she beelined toward him. "My hero! Warm me up?"

He could see Vera's raised eyebrow before she turned and left them, giving him no chance to explain. He couldn't shake Meredith off fast enough.

CHAPTER 56

ELIZA

"Lucia," Eliza started, wondering how she would explain their relationship to Vera. She didn't get a chance.

"Should we tell her?" Lucia asked Eliza.

"Do you want to?" Eliza responded.

"Do you?" Lucia said. "I'm ambivalent."

"Me too," Eliza agreed. Eliza didn't want to tell Vera, but what if she found out anyway? She couldn't decide what would be worse: trying to keep hiding it or telling her the truth. She knew Vera would hate her for lying to her all those years, maybe even for taking her back to Tennessee in the first place.

"She must wonder, right?" Lucia said. "She looks almost exactly as I did when I was her age."

"She'll figure it out eventually, if she hasn't already. Even with the forged birth certificate, DNA tests are easy enough to come by. She's going to hate me, Lucia."

"You don't know that."

"If you were her, wouldn't you?"

"Yes, probably. So, when do we tell her? How?" Lucia asked.

"Um… does this place have Wi-Fi?" a college student asked Lucia.

"This isn't an Airbnb," Lucia told her, sending her sulking back to her friends.

"But the Wi-Fi is working, though, right?" Eliza asked.

"The last thing we need is more people heading into a storm surge."

"But..."

"I need to deal with these people you brought, Eliza, and I need to check on the artwork. Let's not decide about Vera right now," Lucia said, prolonging the inevitable.

Lucia instructed, "Nick, take Miquel and make sure all the doors and exits are secure, all the possible areas water can seep in are plugged. Then meet us in the boardroom on the second floor." As Nick and Miquel left towards the concrete double helix in the center of the building, Lucia explained to Eliza, "The office space has bathrooms, some ability to cook, at least as long as the generators keep working."

They were alone together, and Lucia was talking about generators.

"I'll get the kids settled, Lucia. I'm good at this." Eliza said. She was grateful for a break from Vera's wrath. If Vera was that upset about thinking her father was dead, how would she take the news about Lucia? Eliza couldn't let herself think about it.

"There's probably food in the café. You can check the supply closet for anything else you may need. Take them upstairs."

Eliza, a natural organizer, rose to the occasion. She put OJ in charge of taking half the college students to get toilet paper, flashlights, trash bags, and more blankets from the closet downstairs, and she was planning on taking the other half to the café, when Vera interrupted. "We're not done with our conversation, Mom."

"Now's not the time, Vera. Let's talk about it later."

"Well, at least you could let me help."

"Thank you, but you should rest. You've been through a lot, and your meds should be kicking in soon."

"There's a sofa in my office she can use," Lucia offered.

"But Mom, I feel fine. Please?"

"Later, Vee. I promise. Now, I need you to rest."

When Eliza and Vera got upstairs, they found Lucia's office easily. Eliza set up a palette for Vera on the sofa, then got her some water and tucked her in, turning out the light and closing the door. She hoped the howling wind would be like white noise.

Eliza then found some benches in the common office area that could serve as beds, instructing students to take blankets and claim sleeping areas. Many of them welcomed the opportunity to go to the bathroom, if only to check out their reflections and fix their makeup, post torrential downpour. While few brought changes of clothes, wet layers came off and were draped over bathroom stall doors, anything metal or plastic. Eliza chastised a few who tried to put wet coats on museum benches and was glad none were foolish enough to try and drape them on statues.

Eliza then led her team toward the café, where they found not just flats of bottled water and soda, but also non-perishable Spanish delicacies in bulk, including Manchego and other cheeses, cured meats, olives, figs, almonds, and dried apricots. She grabbed a few bags of coffee beans, hoping there was a grinder on the second floor. They could come back here if they needed anything, but she didn't want to take the chance of weathering this storm under-caffeinated. They got stacks of disposable plates and cups as well.

To those students who had brought up food, Eliza gave other instructions. Inspired by the authentic ingredients, Eliza spearheaded the creation of a generous tapas spread, still saving enough in reserves in case the rations needed to last them many days.

After a solid hour of hustling, directing, and coordinating, Eliza looked around, invigorated to see the students happily mingling, snacking, and taking selfies. "Nice work," OJ complimented.

Proud of her efforts, her outlook soured when she thought back to her conversation with Vera. She cracked the door of the office to find Vera sleeping peacefully, finally. How could she make it up to Vera? How would she ever understand?

The party. Vera's eighteenth birthday party in the Dalí museum. Vera's father would be there for it. It wouldn't make up for all the ones that he had missed, but it was a start. Something to remember. Something to build from. Something to turn Vera's spirits around.

CHAPTER 57
NICK

As they made their rounds, Miquel asked Nick many questions about the art exhibits. Nick was surprised at how much Miquel already knew, not just about the permanent collection but also the special exhibits, including the miniatures.

"I've seen them before," Miquel said, "When they were on tour in Spain."

"Sorry you missed it here," Nick said. "They're already packed up to be shipped out."

"So, we'll be safe here?" Miquel asked, as they closed up the vault and Nick entered the security code.

"If any building will survive this hurricane, it's this one. The walls are a foot and a half thick, and all mission critical systems are above the storm surge line. We'll have water and power, and the art will stay safe."

"What about the glass?" Miquel said, asking the obvious. "Won't it just blow out?"

"Not likely," Nick explained. "Even the glass is almost two inches thick. They tested it against hurricane-strength winds."

"They thought of everything," Miquel said.

"Even when it opened. At 1:11 on 1/11/11. The attention to detail is otherworldly," Nick agreed, glancing at the security camera by the vault. The red light was off. That's odd, he thought. Perhaps the emergency generator didn't back up the security cameras? He would ask Lucia about it when he saw her next.

"Miquel. Can I ask you something?"

Miquel nodded.

"Lucia and Eliza knew each other. They recognized each other."

"That's not a question."

"How do you know Lucia?" Nick hadn't liked the way Lucia looked at Miquel the other day. He'd never seen her look at anyone that way, not even his father.

"*Les persones es troben, les muntanyes no*[6]*.*"

Thanks to his limited Spanish, Nick could make out some of Miquel's riddling, but not enough to understand what it meant. Something about people and mountains? Nick looked at him quizzically, hoping Miquel would give him some explanation. He clearly knew them both, didn't he?

"Perhaps we trade? How about you tell me about that mysterious girl first?" he asked, tracing an hourglass outline with his hands in the air. "Who couldn't take her eyes off of you?"

"She broke my heart," he said.

"How?" Miquel asked.

Nick hated thinking about it, but since she was here now, he couldn't get it out of his head. "We dated when I first got to college, but she was in danger of flunking out. I fixed her grades, and a few others. It became a side hustle, but then I got caught. Her dad paid the college a lot of money, so she didn't get kicked out. I was the one who got kicked out. And dumped. The funny thing is I had a 4.0 without the fixing. I did it for her."

"*Això* és *amor,*" Miquel said.

"What?" Nick asked, tired of riddling.

"That's love," Miquel's smile rivaled the Mona Lisa. "And your parents?"

Suddenly self-conscious about how much he'd shared with this stranger, Nick thought of his own father. Nick realized he hadn't let his father know he was okay.

---

6 Catalan Saying: People meet each other. Mountains never do.

He pulled out his phone, hoping it still had power and that the internet still worked. Two bars. That should be enough. "I need to call my dad," Nick said, turning away from Miquel, not sure he wanted to be near him anymore anyways. Nick walked towards the stairs, leaving Miquel alone at the threshold of the vault.

He called. No answer. He tried again, and his father picked up. "I'm okay, Dad," Nick said. "I'm at the museum, with Lucia and the others."

"The others?" his dad asked.

"It's a long story," Nick said, not knowing how to explain this odd collection of family gathered here in Dalí's jewelry box or the more recent surprises. His dad hated Meredith more than he did. "But you. You're safe?" Nick asked.

"Yes, but trying to deal with overcrowding shelters. We don't have enough beds. Too many people didn't evacuate when ordered," he admitted.

"Love you, Dad," Nick said. He rarely said that, but now, amidst the chaos, he felt like he should. He didn't know when he would see his father again.

"You too. Tell Lucia to call me," Andre said before their connection got cut off.

Nick checked to see if he could get an update on the storm's status. The local weatherman oscillated between a doomsday preacher and a slightly excited former high school actor, knowing this was finally his shining moment. "Here's the latest on Hurricane Phoenix: This is now a category 5 hurricane, and it just made landfall in Central Pinellas County. The storm surge could reach 21 feet, leading to unprecedented flooding in much of the region. Expect 160 miles per hour winds that will damage at least half of the structures around the Tampa Bay area, especially along the beaches..."

Nick had to stop watching. Even though he was fascinated by natural disasters in other parts of the world, seeing his beloved city and thinking about all his neighbors and friends possibly stranded felt voyeuristic. He'd reached his doomsday threshold for the day, and he was powerless to help or change this force of nature. Here he was getting information from satellites a million miles away instead of trusting his senses and looking out the window.

This was the big one, the reason this building had been built, and there was nowhere else he'd rather be right now. For many years, people predicted it was coming. But only Lucia and her team had the foresight, or perhaps access to resources, to adequately prepare for this once-in-a-century travesty. Thanks to Lucia, he was safe.

What if the building became its own island, at least temporarily, completely surrounded by deep water? He loved the thrill of testing the safety features of the building to its limits, of being locked up in a building with lots of dark corners and his newfound paramour with a new lease on life.

He eagerly headed back towards Vera, hoping to avoid Meredith, realizing only then that Miquel was gone.

CHAPTER 58
VERA

Vera awoke to find herself alone in a dark room. She wandered down the hallway, past mounds of sleeping students in the cover of shadows. She ducked behind partial barricades that cast long silhouettes, losing herself in a maze of artwork and suspicions.

Who was she looking for? Not her mother. Eliza wouldn't let her do anything, not even help move supplies or set up sleeping areas. Vera had thought after her vision came back, after the surgery, it would be different, but Eliza was even more protective than before. And she'd betrayed Vera, lying to her about her father. No apology could erase a lifetime of lies.

Not Miquel—her father—she corrected herself. What did her mom ever see in him? How could he have abandoned them? Abandoned her? That's what her mom had said, but if her mom lied about him, what else could she be lying about? Maybe if she could find Miquel, he would tell her the truth.

Not Lucia, her mother's former friend. Vera had the most questions about her, but had no idea where to start. Why Eliza hadn't introduced them the first time they came to the Dalítorium. Why Eliza had brought her to the museum when she couldn't see anything. So, Lucia could see Vera but not the other way round?

Not Nick. Most of all not him. She had trusted him and had left the hospital for him. Had that just been this afternoon? She couldn't think about him without picturing that stupid girl all over him. She'd been played. She knew it happened, but she'd thought Nick was different. How could she trust her own judgement if she'd been so wrong about him?

After wanting her vision back for those endless weeks, now that she had it, she missed blindness. Not seeing was so much easier than this.

A voice flickered to life behind her, startling her. "*For what are you searching? May I be of assistance?*" She laughed in surprise and delight that it was only Dalí, in hologram form.

"I wish I knew," Vera said. "The memory of a lost afternoon?"

"*The difference between false memories and true ones is the same as for jewels: it is always the false ones that look the most real, the most brilliant.*"

At least that explained Nick. Miquel, too. Why did she fall for false jewels? She should know better. As the wind howled outside, she vowed to herself that she wouldn't let herself make that mistake again, that she wouldn't be fooled by their shiny brilliance.

"Vera, there you are!" Nick said in a hushed voice, rushing towards her. "I'm so sorry, Vera." He reached for her, but she stepped back.

Her muscles tightened, and she crossed her arms across her chest.

"I can explain."

She brought her left hand instinctively to her neck, protecting her jugular. "I'm fine."

"But Vera…"

"I don't want to hear it." What could he say that would change the fact that he had a girlfriend. That she had been a fling. That he had lied. That this afternoon didn't mean anything.

"Don't be like that…"

"Like what? Okay with you cuddling up to another girl, a college student, just hours after we were together?" How stupid she had been to think Nick would be interested in a high schooler.

"She's nobody."

"She didn't look like nobody." Vera's face flushed, wondering how far Nick had gone with this girl, and how recently he had been with her.

"You have to trust me."

"I did, and look where it got me."

"Okay, she used to be somebody. But not anymore."

"Does she know that?"

"I thought so."

She looked at his sorry eyes. He seemed sincere. She hoped he was, but how could she tell? "What happened?"

"She's the reason I'm not in school. I did something for her and got burned."

What could Nick have done? Not something terrible, Vera hoped. Was Vera his rebound? She couldn't ask him that. She opted for a safer question: "Why is she even here?"

"Because that's who she is. She gets herself into trouble and waits to be rescued by suckers like me."

She'd hurt him, broken his heart maybe even. "Okay…"

"I don't care about her. I care about you. About us."

This was too much, too sudden. Why was she letting herself fall in love with someone out-of-state, wounded at least and possibly still unavailable? After losing Chapel Hill, she couldn't put herself through another heartbreak. "There is no us, Nick," Vera shot back. "Today was a mistake."

He looked down at his shoes, shuffling them back and forth.

"I need space, Nick. Could you please leave?"

He didn't move. She waited, looking from him to the door. She could leave, but she was here first, and anywhere else she went, she was likely to run into someone else.

"Will you think about it? About giving me another chance?"

"I don't think that's a good idea."

"Please, Vera? I know I messed up."

Just when she started feeling sorry for him, Meredith interrupted them, placing her hand on Nick's arm.

"There you are, Nick! I've been looking all over for you," she purred.

He shook it off, glaring at her.

She didn't seem to notice and instead addressed Vera. "You're Vera, right? Your mom wants you—both of you—on the second floor."

Meredith didn't seem to want to leave without them, so Nick turned, taking Vera's arm, and headed toward the door. So much for any privacy or reconciliation.

CHAPTER 59
ELIZA

Eliza took one last look around the room. The Crema Catalana was perfectly warm, with candles ready for lighting. Using eighteen for a toast seemed wasteful under the circumstances, but Eliza wanted to make this birthday unforgettable. Eliza prided herself in creative DIY birthdays, from tie-dying underwear for Vera's third birthday, to a Mad Hatter's Tea Party for her eighth, to taking some girls to see a play of *The Secret Garden* before letting them take daffodil and tulip bulbs home to plant. Eliza would have planned something epic for Vera's eighteenth if it hadn't been for the tumor. But good mothers threw great parties. It was the least she could do.

And this one would be the best one yet, because Vera's father would be there. Miquel was reluctant to have a starring role in the night's festivities, but when Lucia pointed Miquel and a few others in the direction of the education center to get out art supplies and set up a Dalí-inspired paint night, he agreed to help.

With the surgery behind them, Eliza recruited anyone who was remotely willing to help to make this birthday special. She'd challenged a few college students to come up with the most creative tapas.

At Eliza's prodding for decorations, Lucia had also managed to find a disco light and some glow sticks from a prior gala. Eliza put OJ in charge of being the lookout for when Vera returned and sent Nick after her to keep her company and distract her for a bit. When she sent Meredith to bring them back, all the college students were hiding behind partitions and doorways.

She and Lucia crouched together behind the table with the spread of food, closest to the door Vera would enter from. Maybe Lucia welcomed the distraction, but Eliza thought this was more than that.

"You think she'll like it?" Lucia asked Eliza.

"How could she not? I would have died for a party like this one."

"You and me both. You don't think she knows, do you?"

As they waited, they giggled like two girls in church trying to be quiet during the sermon, giddy with anticipation. Eliza was thrilled to be on Lucia's team again. "Shhhh! I hear something."

Meredith entered, coughing loudly. This was the agreed upon cue for when Vera arrived.

"Surprise! Happy Birthday!" Eliza and Lucia and the rest of the college students shouted, popping out from behind wherever they had been hiding. OJ turned off the lights, cuing the disco ball and the party music.

Vera just stood there awkwardly as the colorful flecks of disco lights danced across her blank face. Vera should have been laughing and hugging Eliza and sampling tapas and taking it all in, but instead, she scowled at Eliza. "What is this?"

"Your birthday party! Come blow out the candle at least."

Vera stayed put and looked at her watch. "It's not even midnight yet, Mom."

By this time, a few of the college students had looked out the sliver of window, pretending to be interested in the swirling, steel-gray storm, but most decided to watch the train wreck.

"It's a Crema Catalana, your favorite," Eliza said.

"My favorite is Hummingbird."

"Well, they didn't have any canned pineapple in the pantry," Eliza said, trying to lighten the mood for the seemingly hundreds of eyes staring at her. Looking around the room and then back at Vera's face, she realized she'd done too much. But if she hadn't done anything, Vera would have been upset about that.

"Okay, but don't say it's my favorite. Crema Catalana's your favorite, Mom. Not mine. Do you even know me, Mom?"

After her behavior today, Eliza wondered if she did. "I was just trying to make your birthday special," Eliza apologized, conscious of the dwindling candles puddling on the cake. "Can you just blow them out and make a wish, Vera? Please?"

"I wish you hadn't thrown me this party! I wish you'd never lied to me! I just want to be alone! How's that for wishes?"

Eliza's face flushed, and she stood there dumbfounded. She hated that Lucia and Miquel were witnessing her epic failure and then hated herself more for caring so much about what they thought.

Lucia took the lead in clearing the room. "Nick's going to show you all how to paint your own Dalí-look alike."

Most reluctantly followed Nick, but a lanky sophomore lingered and asked, "But what about the dessert?"

"Later," Lucia said, ushering him on, leaving Vera and Eliza alone under the disco light, music still playing.

Eliza wished OJ was still here, if only to turn it off, but OJ had stepped into the hallway and was on the phone.

Eliza broke first and asked, "What's wrong, Vee?"

"Nothing… Everything. This is too much. I don't even know these people."

"I know you'd rather be home celebrating with Zoe."

"It's not just that—"

"I thought this was what you wanted. I'm trying here, Vera."

"It's what you wanted, Mom. Not me."

Vera still knew her. Eliza had wanted to throw the perfect party so Lucia and Miquel could see what a good job she was doing, to make up for lying. And it backfired spectacularly. "I'm so sorry. I just wanted your birthday to be special. I wanted to apologize for not telling you. For everything."

"None of this is real, Mom! I thought I knew what I wanted, who I was, but I knew nothing. I don't know what to believe about anything anymore."

"You know I love you? I never meant to hurt you?"

"I know. But you did."

"I know. I'm so sorry, Vee."

"I'll try the food. It looks good, Mom."

"Here, let me make you a plate. You'll love the albondigas."

"I've got it. But could you turn off that music? It's giving me a headache."

Eliza left Vera to go find the sound system.

CHAPTER 60

NICK

When Nick got into the Innovation Lab, the art supplies were already out. Normally, multiple classes were held on weekends for anyone who was interested, from children to seasoned painters. They tried to have a little something for everyone, but more often than not, the classes were based on replicating a painting or technique or approach. On the walls were two Dalí quotes, supporting that theory: "*Those who do not imitate anything produce nothing*," and "*Begin by learning to draw and paint like the old masters. After that, you can do as you like; everyone will respect you.*"

Miquel was already in the corner, painting. Lucky guy, Nick thought, to have a little downtime amidst the chaos. Nick directed the college students to find seats. While he didn't usually teach the expert classes, he'd been called in a pinch to help out with younger artists and had a few go-tos for those occasions, usually animals on impossibly tall stilt-like legs, sometimes drawn and sometimes made out of modeling clay and toothpicks or chopsticks. Melting clocks were cliché, but also incredibly popular.

Once most of the students were occupied, Meredith approached him, running her hand down his outstretched arm.

"Do you want to paint me?" she asked. "I've always wanted to be a nude model. Maybe there's a private place we could go?"

"I need to stay here and keep an eye on your friends," he said, shrugging her away.

"They'll be fine."

"No, Meredith."

"OJ's watching them, I think."

Nick pointed to OJ, on her phone in the hallway.

"I could model for everyone?"

He shook his head.

"Why not? You used to be fun."

"You know how that turned out."

"Come on? For old time's sake?"

"This isn't the movie *Titanic*. This storm is real. What's wrong with you?"

"Pu-lease?"

"No Meredith. We're done, Meredith."

"It's that kid from Kentucky."

"Tennessee and it's not about her. It's about you, Meredith. You can't keep using people when you need them and turning on them when you don't. It's not right."

"Since when did you become the morality police?"

"I'm not…"

"I'm done with this place." Meredith glared at him, whisked out her phone, and stormed to the back corner of the room where Miquel was still painting.

"Daddy," he overheard her whine. "I'm trapped…"

With the hurricane, Nick figured Meredith leaving would be unlikely, but if anyone had those kinds of connections, it was her. At least he could hope.

Officer Jiménez came back to check on Nick and the students. "No one else showed up. It's almost midnight. Let's move everyone to where they are sleeping. I'll be useless tomorrow if we don't get some sleep."

"I'll have them clean brushes and close the paint first. They can leave their art where it is and finish it up tomorrow. Any word from the outside?"

"There are a few more idiots that didn't leave. Unfortunately, I don't think there's any way to get them out."

"You should check with Meredith," Nick said, pointing to the girl on the phone who was now making eyes with Miquel. "She was looking for a way off this island."

"I'll do that, and then take them upstairs."

CHAPTER 62
ELIZA

After Eliza finally figured out how to get the music to stop playing, she went to apologize to Vera. However, Lucia had beaten her to it. As she walked back into the aftermath of the party with glow sticks discarded in otherwise dark corners of the room, she saw Lucia sitting beside Vera on the bench, rubbing her back. Neither of them was facing her. As Eliza got closer, she could hear Lucia talking.

"Vera," Lucia began, "I'm your biological mom. Miquel is your father. We had you on another continent, a lifetime ago."

Not waiting to see or hear Vera's reaction, Eliza confronted Lucia. "What are you doing? How could you tell her?"

Lucia and Vera both turned toward Eliza, and Lucia stood. "Eliza, she—"

"—Without me? What gave you that right?"

Lucia stopped talking.

"I thought if we told her, we would do it together. But you've been making all the decisions by yourself the whole time. You chose to sleep with the man you knew I loved. You chose to have his baby. You chose to abandon her to the nuns, but I couldn't let you. I just pick up your pieces."

"Eliza…"

"You do not get to speak. Not yet. After what you just did, you gave up that right, just like you gave up your rights to Vera eighteen years ago."

Eliza found a firmness she had never known. She was done cowering to this woman who had defined Eliza's identity in her absence. But Eliza couldn't hate Lucia for it, because if she truly asked herself, she knew Lucia also gave her the one thing she had always wanted, the one thing she could never independently have: a child.

"But I want to hear her, Mom."

"I can explain," said Eliza.

"No, you can't. You had 18 years to explain and you never did. That's why I had to ask her. That's why she told me," Vera said, in a voice almost too small to be heard under the rising roar of the hurricane winds.

"I could never love anyone more than you. But this woman, she carried me. She birthed me. And this may be my one chance to get to know her. Please don't take that from me. That's what I want for my birthday. Not some big party. A chance to get to know my birth parents."

Eliza, taken aback by Vera's honesty and directness, worried most how this would change things. If she denied Vera this, Eliza would push her further away. But if they talked, Lucia might start to take Eliza's place in Vera's life. However, this went, it wasn't good for Eliza. Not sure of what to do next, she did the one thing that she had done over and over again: she backed the fuck off. She continued to jellyfish through life, letting other people's needs and wants that were somehow more pressing than her own and other people's interests in who and what she should be, dictate her actions, life, and choices. What is a life but a sum of our choices, intentional or otherwise? Perhaps, more accurately, a sum of our lack of choices, a sum of choices others have thrust upon us in our moment of indecision?

Eliza took a step back. "Vera, you grew inside Lucia's belly, but I have loved you every single step of the way. If the world had been different, Lucia might have kept you and her education and her career, but at the time… Impossible. But if she had kept you, I wouldn't have..." Eliza couldn't finish the thought. Instead, she offered their secret sign.

Somewhat reluctantly, Vera made the sign back.

Eliza turned to leave them, which was what she thought Vera wanted.

"Don't go," Vera and Lucia said simultaneously. Despite what Vera had said, Eliza was a comfort, a known quantity to them both as they navigated this new normal, something next to normal. But Eliza wasn't entirely sure she wanted to stay.

OCTOBER 14TH

VERA'S 18TH BIRTHDAY

CHAPTER 61

VERA

"Happy Birthday!" Nick interrupted, surprising Vera. "It is after midnight. I set an alarm."

"Thanks," she said, still miffed about Meredith.

Lucia and Eliza joined in the well-wishes.

We're pretending everything's fine, Vera thought. Too much was happening at once, and she didn't know who to trust anymore. Everything she thought she knew had shifted so suddenly. Unsettled, she needed a distraction from the thoughts reeling in her head.

"Where's Miquel?" Lucia asked Nick.

"He went to bed. Said something about jet lag."

"Not with the students?"

"I took him to a private office, don't worry."

"And the students?" Eliza asked.

"Bed too," Nick said.

"Maybe we should head—" Eliza started to suggest.

"I'm not tired, Mom. There's no way I could sleep with this storm and everything else."

The storm was on them, now, getting stronger by the second. Even with the eye approaching, in this fortress of solitude, time stood still. They were oblivious to the raging toddler-tantrum Hurricane Phoenix was having on St. Pete.

"She could stay up with me," Lucia suggested. "Nick or I need to keep watch in case any of the systems glitch."

"I'm not tired either," Eliza said. "What do you want to do, Vee? It's your birthday."

Vera knew it was pointless to suggest having alone time with Nick, even if Eliza and Lucia both liked him. She looked at the three of them and got an idea. "Do you have any cards here?" she asked Nick.

"Playing cards?"

"If we don't, I'm sure the gift store does."

"What'd you have in mind?" Eliza asked her.

"I was thinking about Nana and Pops. How we used to play Spades on my birthday."

"Why not?" Lucia agreed. "We've got nothing but time, waiting for the storm to pass. I'll go get some." She went towards the gift store when she paused and turned, "Nick? You're in?"

"I'm more of a Setback guy. I don't think I've played Spades before..."

"We'd need a fourth," Lucia said.

"If you can play a trick game with trumps, you're fine," Eliza said. "Spades is easier, all things considered. All the cards are in play. It's a finite set problem, much easier to count cards."

"I hate Setback," Lucia said. "Too many unknown variables in the pile of cards not used. You have to read people more."

Vera nodded in silent agreement, knowing just what Lucia meant.

"Can you give us a minute?" Nick asked them.

They both looked at Vera, who nodded.

"We'll be back soon," Eliza said. Lucia left to get cards, and Eliza went to get snacks.

Nick turned to Vera. "It's been a crazy day…"

"You have no idea," Vera agreed.

"I have no interest in that girl. I want to start over. Or at least go back to this afternoon. When we were eating ice pops and riding bulls. I kept this," he said, pulling out his popsicle stick. "I hear you can recycle them."

Vera smiled, pulling out hers, too.

"I'm Nick," he said, holding out his hand, "And you must be…"

"Vera." She went in for a hug, and he wrapped his arms around her. Grateful for his presence, Vera relaxed for the first time since they'd last been alone.

"So, do you want to play cards with me and my moms for my birthday?"

He looked at her quizzically.

"Long story," she said.

"I'll give it a shot," Nick said, "But if we are stuck here for a while, we are learning Setback, and my rules will be house rules."

She nodded, leaning in for a kiss. She hoped it took Lucia and Eliza a while to return.

CHAPTER 64

ELIZA

Eliza had been tired, but didn't want to miss this. She made a cup of coffee, grateful for the caffeine, and gathered the remains of the birthday tapas.

When she returned with snacks, Vera and Nick both started giggling. Vera suddenly started explaining the rules to Nick. She must have interrupted something. Eliza pretended not to notice and joined in to explaining the game, adding things Vera left out and vice versa.

By the time Lucia returned with cards, cava, and a way to keep score, everyone was ready to start playing. Holding up the cava, Lucia said, "Just in case we need it."

"I'm sober now," Eliza said. She surprised herself, sharing that with Lucia. Given their many late nights and drunken adventures in Barcelona, she wasn't sure if Lucia would judge her. Every new person she told and every new milestone she faced were new hurdles to overcome.

"Since when?"

"Since Vera's diagnosis."

They drew cards for teams, his and lows, and Lucia and Eliza were paired up against Vera and Nick. Eliza hesitated for half a second before remembering what a good team they once made, how good Lucia was at counting cards. Nick and Vera didn't stand a chance.

In the end, they played cards for almost three hours, and collectively consumed the same number of bottles of cava. Even Vera had a small glass, after Eliza okayed it. It might have been her first taste of alcohol, at least to Eliza's knowledge, but Vera was eighteen now, and had already survived brain surgery, met her birth mom, and was in love. And then there was the hurricane. Yes, she would let her daughter who was old enough to vote to have a small glass of champagne.

First, they played Spades, then Setback, and finally, when the cava started to kick in, switched to Pitch, as it was less nuanced and quicker. Eliza and Lucia beat Nick and Vera twice to 500 before they broke up the teams, reorganizing in every possible combination. Between hands, Eliza and Lucia shared stories from their Barcelona days, including their day trips to Tibidabo, an old-school amusement park on the top of a nearby mountain, and their lazy afternoons at the Plaça del Nord. Eliza shared funny and borderline embarrassing stories from Vera's childhood. Vera laughed more than protested, blushing when Eliza mentioned a boy who used to write Vera love letters and leave them in their mailbox.

Eliza couldn't help but notice what a good team Lucia and Vera made, or how intuitive Nick was as her partner, reading the cards she laid as well as her expressions, her not-always-subtle subtext. They laughed hard when Nick and Eliza Shot the Moon and came out ahead when Vera pulled out a true low after everyone thought the low had been played. They forgave Lucia and let her have a do-over when even Lucia, the queen of perfection and protocol, forgot to follow suit. It was Vera who called her on it, much to Eliza's pleasure.

CHAPTER 65

LUCIA

It was Nick's idea post-card games to go on a flashlight-led tour of the museum. Eliza bowed out to finally go rest, noting she would be needed to help feed the students in the morning. Perhaps Nick was hoping for a few quiet moments alone with Vera. Viewing masterpieces in this way, heightened by a multitude of hyper-focused beams of light and the shadows their absences created, not to mention the other-worldly outlines the structure itself created—this was the best Dalí experience Lucia herself had ever had.

After the storm, perhaps in the new wing when the funding came through, Lucia thought she would launch an exhibit entitled Dalí v. the Phoenix. She could tout the integrity of the building's structure, the work of the architects, and set up a mini-collection of Dalí's works that guests could tour under emergency conditions using only a flashlight. She could play up the fine line between dreams and nightmares, between seeing and not. Dalí, a whore for publicity, would have approved.

That is, unless the town suffered catastrophic damages. If it did, it might be seen as garish, quite possibly a publicity nightmare. She would do a public poll first. Perhaps she could convince up and coming artists to do renderings of the hurricane's impact, perhaps on found materials from the aftermath of it all. Her ingenuity led to the virtual art exhibit, *The Lazarus Project,* and the plan for the expansion. No one knew this place better than her, and no one could see into the Dalítorium's future.

In protecting, preserving, and promoting his art, in increasingly avant-garde ways that Dalí would have approved of, she was simultaneously promoting her career and deepening her dependence on Dalí himself. For now, she would have to wait to see the aftermath and the extent of damage in the light of day. It was a good idea or the beginning of an idea, and she knew it.

Andre would approve. Or at least she could use him, and hopefully some of his more reliable constituents to give feedback on the plan before she pitched it. It was only then, after hours into waiting out the storm, she realized she didn't know where Andre was. They had had the falling out earlier over using the Dalítorium as back up shelter, but he was her person. She had a sudden urge to know where he was. If he was okay. She forgave herself for not wondering, for not wanting to know before just this minute, after hours of unknown. Nick. Nick would know.

Interrupting the flashlight tag game of would-be lovers, without the supervision of two overbearing mothers, Lucia stopped Nick. "Have you heard from your dad? Is he okay?" she asked.

"Aside from overflowing shelters, I think so," Nick said.

"Good." Lucia breathed a sigh of relief.

"When I talked to him, when I first got here, he was at the largest facility, trying to find enough beds, enough space for all the pets people brought. He called it a fucking menagerie, not having anticipated the pet population equaling or exceeding the people."

"But he's okay?" Lucia asked.

"Yes, or at least he was. You haven't talked to him?" Nick asked.

"No. I know, I know… My only thought was the collection, and then, with Eliza and Vera showing up… I should have called him earlier," Lucia realized.

"He knows you are okay," Nick said.

"How do you know?" Lucia asked.

"I told him. I told him we were safe at the Dalítorium," Nick said.

"We?" Lucia whispered, deflating like a popped balloon.

"We. I told him you and I and some others had hunkered down in the Dalítorium. That we're together and safe," Nick reassured her. "Don't worry. He knows how indestructible this place is. He's got enough on his hands without worrying about us."

"You told him other people are here?"

"I wanted him to know we were safe."

Lucia crumpled. She saw everything she had been working for all those years, not just with Andre, but at the museum, melting away, just like Dalí's clocks. She couldn't blame Nick. How could he have known the fight she and Andre had just before the hurricane hit was about opening up the Dalítorium as an emergency shelter if needed. Here he was, manning overcrowded, underprepared facilities while she was hosting a curated cocktail party in the museum after hours? Something she could have marketed as a reprieve from the storm to top end donors, but didn't. Something she could have opened up to the community for humanitarian reasons, but didn't. She hadn't planned to have anyone here. She had planned to prioritize the safety of the collection above all else. She might be tried for this, but the jury would be the board, not her peers.

The color drained from Lucia's face, her shoulders falling, head toward the sky, neck longer than a swan. In a reverse Schrodinger's cat exhibit, she preferred to be in that box alone, unaware of the fate of those outside. If she opened the door to any of them, she would have to face the truth. She preferred the door locked.

"What's wrong?" Nick asked. "Should I not have told him?"

Lucia took her time to find the right words. With everything to lose, she realized she didn't need to hide anything from him. "We had a fight, your dad and I, right before the storm hit. When he asked me to open the museum for refugees, I told him I couldn't promise that because it would compromise the collection and possibly my job."

"That seems reasonable."

"I might have also mentioned that his lack of preparation wasn't my fault. We had the same information. I can't sacrifice everything I worked for because of his lack of preparation."

"I can imagine how he took that," Nick chuckled to himself.

"Right. Exactly," Lucia said. "I wasn't even sure if we were together after he left to help at one of the shelters. But you can see my point: if we opened the museum to the masses, the likelihood of a piece of art being damaged, being destroyed... I know other places have converted to safe havens, hospitals, and evacuation centers in moments of necessity, but I can't make that call without the board's full support. The city's not prepared. We're overdue for a Cat. 5, and with climate change, building structures rated for lesser storms just to save a dime is foolish, gluttonous even. You want cheap houses on the beach, and when the hurricane destroys them, you want insurance companies to rebuild them. Why support backing shoddy construction here in the first place? I want to protect those who come across hard times after making educated decisions. Why should I compromise everything I have sacrificed, have worked for, for people—and their leaders—who continue to make stupid decisions? At what point is their fate my responsibility?"

Yes, Lucia was socially liberal, but fiscally conservative. Why should those who prepare bear the burden of those who don't?

Nick didn't know what to say. "I'm so sorry, Lu. I messed up. I didn't think it would be a big deal to tell him. I thought he'd want to know."

This was the fundamental difference between men and women: how they dealt with failure and setbacks. Women internalized and overburdened themselves with their responsibility in endings. Most things end. Women just took it harder. Nick could move on—a luxury afforded to well-meaning, young men who compartmentalize mistakes. A similar mistake might render a woman paralyzed with guilt for years to come.

She needed to get in touch with Andre to do damage control before it was too late. She realized she had two missed calls from him, and another from the president of the board. No messages, though. She didn't have any bars, and despite her multiple attempts, she couldn't get a call to go through. Perhaps if she waited till the eye of the storm. Or, everything she cared about may disappear in one gust of wind.

CHAPTER 66
VERA

When Nick and Lucia started talking about Nick's dad, Vera took the opportunity to try and find her own. Emboldened by her card game with Lucia, she didn't want to waste the chance to get to know Miquel as well. She took her threadbare Senyor Conill and stuffed him in her pocket for luck.

When she got to the second-floor offices, she found heaps of sleeping students, many in pairs. But no sign of Miquel.

After exploring multiple galleries, Vera finally found signs of life. Three figures were climbing the ladder towards the escape hatch out of the third-floor gallery. "Miquel?" she called, unsure if it was his shadow cast in the blue emergency-light din. The third body stopped climbing and turned toward her. She wanted to say "Dad" but changed her mind.

"Where are you going?" she asked. She'd finally met him and barely got to know him and here he was, sneaking out and leaving her all over again.

It was OJ who responded. "Some other people need help. Meredith's dad got a 'copter to come get us. We're going to help them."

"Speak for yourself," said Meredith. "I just want to get off of this island."

"But the storm?" Vera asked.

"There's a break in the eye." OJ cracked the hatch, peering out in search of the helicopter. Through that portal of sky, Vera could see stars. "Let the students know where I've gone, so they don't worry. I left a note on Lucia's desk and another with the students, but in case they don't see it right away. No need for them to send out a search party."

"Miquel. Dad. You're leaving me?"

Hearing her voice, he froze. "Oh, Vera."

"Dad?" she said, the words feeling foreign in her mouth.

"It's time," he said.

"I've waited my whole life to meet you and... Why now? Can't you wait?" She realized her pleas were in vain.

Instead of answering her questions, he left her with the only child support he would ever give, his mantra on life: "*L'ocasió s'ha d'agafar pels péls.*"

"What's that supposed to mean? I studied French."

"Grab opportunity by the hair," he said.

If that was his advice, she might as well start now. "Then why are you leaving?" she asked.

"People need help."

"Are they more important than me?" She didn't believe him for a second. What would he be able to do? He was running away from her all over again.

"When are you coming back?" She noticed the overly-stuffed shoulder bag he was lugging. If he was planning on coming back, he would have left it, right?

He just shrugged.

Even to Vera, it was obvious he was leaving for good. "Please don't. Don't go. Don't do this," Vera realized she was begging. She hated begging.

"Miquel, come on," OJ called down. "'Copter's landing." OJ and Meredith disappeared through the hole in the sky.

And with that, Miquel turned to climb.

"*Salut i forcą al canut!*[7]" he called out before crawling out of sight.

She realized how little she had in common with this man, how little respect she had for him, and how she was lucky he hadn't been around when she was growing up. She didn't wait to watch him leave.

"You make me sad," she said, dropping Senyor Conill—and any hope of a relationship with this sperm donor—to the ground. She needed to find Lucia.

---

7 Catalan saying: Health and strength to your purse.

CHAPTER 67

LUCIA

In the calm of the eye of the storm, some limited reception had been restored, at least enough for Lucia to get in touch with Andre.

"How are you?" Lucia started.

"You don't get to ask that. You told me you couldn't let anyone into the museum because it would compromise the collection," Andre accused.

He was right, but how could she ever explain? There was too much history she hadn't yet shared with him.

"The shelters are a mess. No casualties in St. Pete at least."

"Thank goodness," Lucia said.

"I need you to trust me, Andre. It was just extended family, including your son, and it was a true emergency. Nick came to help me secure the collection."

"So, that's it?"

Lucia sighed. "Some other people showed up."

"So now you get to decide who should be admitted to your private bunker of safety?"

"They turned up when it was too late to go elsewhere. I couldn't just turn them away."

"Then why didn't you let me pitch it as an alternative shelter? You basically told the world how safe it was."

"That's not fair, Andre. We're surrounded by water and the building has never been tested before," Lucia said.

"Whatever this was, it's over, Lucia," Andre said, confirming what she already knew. Perhaps the first casualty of the storm. Her first worry was how it might impact her getting the role at the Dalítorium or the expansion plans for the museum, as she knew how petty and vindictive Andre could be.

"I didn't plan on letting anyone in, Andre. I swear. It was an emergency. It was my family."

"Tell Nick to come to me as soon as he can, after the water level recedes," Andre said. He hung up, not waiting for her reply.

Lucia hated it when he did that: just assumed his order would be followed.

CHAPTER 68

VERA

Vera found Lucia right where she'd seen her last. Lucia looked at her phone, dazed.

"Lucia, OJ left," Vera said.

"What do you mean she left?" Lucia asked.

"She wanted me to tell you."

Lucia stared at Vera, eyebrows raised.

Vera went on, filling the silence, not sure where to start or how to explain. "OJ said she left a note on your desk."

"But how?" Lucia asked, frown lines crumpling between her eyes.

"A helicopter, I think. I didn't see it, but that's what they said."

Lucia shook her head in disbelief. "But wouldn't that be impossible? I don't understand."

"OJ got a call about survivors in the area, and somehow Meredith's dad got a helicopter. He said they were going to help people."

"He? They?"

"Miquel and Meredith went with OJ." She was glad Meredith was gone, but that paled in comparison to her heartbreak of losing the father she just met all over again.

"But Miquel? Why?"

"I don't know," Vera confessed. Maybe he didn't like me that much, she thought. "But I don't think he's coming back."

"Why not?"

"He had his bag with him. Who takes all their stuff if they are coming back? I was surprised he could carry it up the ladder, it looked so bulky."

"What?" Lucia said, almost dropping her phone. "You didn't try to stop him?"

"I tried, Lucia. Believe me, I did. I wanted to get to know him, and he's leaving me all over again." Seeing Lucia's reaction, Vera knew this wasn't enough. She hadn't done anything wrong. So why did it feel that way? Vera was disappointing everyone today.

Lucia didn't respond, so Vera tried again. "I'm sorry, but I don't know what you wanted me to do! Should I have grabbed his leg and pulled him off the ladder? Restrained him to keep him from going? Tried to out-scream the hurricane and get someone to help me convince him to stay? If I'm such a disappointment to him that he'll leave in the middle of a hurricane just to get away from me..."

"It's not you, Vera. It's about what he took, or may have taken." Unfrozen, Lucia started spinning into action. "Where was he exactly?" she asked Vera.

"He was climbing the ladder to the escape hatch on the third floor," Vera said.

As Lucia headed in that direction, Vera's gut lurched. Should she follow Lucia? She was clearly upset, but why did Lucia care so much? He was leaving Vera, not Lucia.

Why had she trusted her father, this stranger? Both Eliza and Lucia had known him for much longer. Lucia had borne his child and Eliza had married him. Trusting him was not her decision to make. Being hurt by him was.

Nick. She wanted to find Nick. He would be able to help. He would know what to do.

CHAPTER 69

LUCIA

Lucia forgot about abruptly ending the phone call with Andre.

Miquel must have had another reason for leaving. Vera's description of his bag troubled her the most. Given his history, she was almost entirely sure he had taken something. Saving the collection, at any cost, had to be the priority. She knew this building better than anyone. She sprinted to where he ought to be, given Vera's intel, but she worried she was too late.

With her first move now clear, she climbed up the same ladder he must have used and opened the escape hatch. As she shimmied through the hole in the sky, she gasped. Surrounded by a cylinder of thick, swirling clouds, in the belly of the beast, she looked up through that tunnel toward a sea of stars. The waxing moon, directly overhead, seemed bigger than she'd remembered, and she could make out a number of constellations she'd never seen in St. Petersburg before, thanks to the light pollution.

She looked down across her abandoned city, the part she could see. Much of it was boarded up. Water filled the streets, and cars, illuminated by moonlight, bobbed up and down like toy boats. An eerie emptiness enveloped everything.

There was no sign of the helicopter—of life. If they actually took a helicopter, like Vera said, by now it was long gone. She couldn't tell how deep the storm surge was from this vantage point, but the palm trees by the water looked more like bushes. She stood on top of the museum in the eye of the hurricane, humbled by nature: so calm, so clear, so quiet. Surreal.

She had heard that the second wave, after the eye of the storm, could be more damaging than the first part. Perhaps that's why he had left now. As she scoured everything in her field of vision, looking for some sign of him, she was almost certain Miquel had left with part of her collection and—likely—her career.

The normal security measures were on stand-by, with cameras down. Even if they were on, security guards who monitored them were at home, or a long way from here. When Lucia turned the building over to hurricane mode, all energy and resources went to protect the collection from external threats, like water seepage, winds up to 200 mph, and humidity. In no way did the plan have mechanisms to prevent threats from within. It's why they weren't going to let people into the building. If Miquel had taken something on display, it should be easy enough to identify—just look for what was missing off the wall. Few pieces were even small enough to be portable by a single individual. She would track down the piece, track him down, and convince him to give it back. She'd pay him off if necessary, anything to bring it to an end before the board knew or before the decision about the promotion was finalized. She hoped to handle the entire thing quietly.

At least the vault was secure. Without a code, it was impenetrable. But the vault also had the most variables. If he'd gotten into the vault, it would take days to figure out what was missing, especially if she was doing it without her staff. How they'd gotten a helicopter on the roof with the hurricane was beyond her, but his opportunistic skill set never ceased to amaze her.

In the eerie dusk, not trusting her eyesight alone, she used a flashlight to meticulously scour every room. If he were to take something small—and it would have to be small for him to carry it out—what would he take? *The Disintegration of the Persistence of Memory*—the famous melting clocks and perhaps the most valuable small work?

She scanned the flashlight along the wall, relieved to find the melting clocks, wondering how much time she had left. So was *Autumn Sonata*, with the pallid yellow sky so much like the one she'd seen earlier that afternoon, before the storm. So were the smaller photographs capturing Gala and Dalí's intimate moments. Everything on the third floor was in place.

She descended further into the depths of her own personal hell, checking the collection still on display on lower floors. Both the phallic *Catalan Bread* and *Atmospheric Skull Sodomizing a Grand Piano*, two Miquel may have been drawn to were still there. So was the one she couldn't shake, the one that reminded her of exactly how she felt when her milk kept coming in, the *Fountain of Milk Spreading Itself Uselessly on Three Shoes*. Everything on the second floor was also secure. Her mind started to spin with hope that Miquel had simply overreacted to the pressures of this awkward family reunion and seized the opportunity to leave.

She went to the first floor, taking that last lap in vain. Everything was in place, exactly as it should be. Nothing was missing, no obvious empty rectangle. Could Vera have been imagining something? Could he have taken whatever he was painting earlier during Vera's party?

But the creeping fear she had missed something was too much. The vault. But that was impossible. He had no way of accessing it without the code.

Lucia raced up the helix-spiral staircase, towards the vault on the third floor. It had been housed there above the worst-case-scenario storm surge line, like every mechanical system critical to building function.

She knew what she would find before she even got there. The vault door was cracked. Even though she knew every inch of this building, she hated that she wouldn't be able to easily determine what he had taken from the vault without exposing this Trojan Horse. How could she defend not opening the building to the public in order to protect the collection when she then hand-selected those that came in? And then to have someone she trusted steal masterpieces? She'd be labeled a hypocrite or worse.

She had to think. How could he have gotten into the vault? How could he have gotten the code? She tried to remember everything since Miquel had shown up, both the first time he came to the Dalítorium, and again, when he came here seeking shelter from the storm. It wasn't like the code was a number he knew, like her birthday, or even Vera's.

Had the situation been less drastic, and if she had been foolish enough to make the security one of their birthdays, she might have been amused that he knew those dates. Who was the last one in the vault?

And then it hit her. When she was with Eliza and Vera, Nick and Miquel had been securing the collection. Had Nick not locked the vault? That wasn't like him. Had Miquel seen Nick enter the code? Or had Nick revealed a clue about what the code was inadvertently? It had to have been Nick. How else would Miquel have gotten access, or even known where the vault was? The blueprints were online. He must have studied them. What if he hadn't come for Vera at all? What if he was just using her to get to the art? Why had she ever trusted him?

Should she try to run after him? Probably too late, but looking wouldn't hurt, would it? She couldn't put the police on watch for Miquel Garcia. The likelihood she would even get through to the police was slim, and they had bigger things to worry about. She would have to tell them what happened, but what would she say? That he may or may not have stolen some paintings, and which ones, she couldn't be sure? That she had no physical proof? Her current case was speculative, at best. She needed more information, especially which pieces were missing, in order to file a report. But she knew that when she reported something had been taken, the press would be all over it, the board all over her.

As of now, she only had time on her side. Her first priority was to determine which artwork, if any, was missing from the museum. Getting in touch with the police, the board, or her boss, would be pointless unless she knew what was missing. If something had been stolen, she could blame Nick. He was the one who had either left the vault open, or had sacrificed the security of the code, and thereby the collection. But again, the only reason Miquel was even here was because of her. Nick had taken Miquel because she told him to let Miquel help. Nick had trusted Miquel because Nick trusted her, and she trusted Miquel. But Miquel was not one to be trusted with space and autonomy. How foolish she had been.

CHAPTER 70

VERA

"Oh, Nick," Vera said, crumbling into his arms. "I've ruined everything. I let him escape and now she hates me."

He pulled her in close, nuzzling the top of her head. "Slow down, Vera. It's going to be okay."

"Nothing is okay," she cried.

"Tell me. What's going on?"

"Miquel left, and Lucia hates me for letting him leave. But I didn't…" Everything about her birthday was going horribly wrong and both of her parents had left her all over again.

"Wait. What are you talking about?"

"Miquel left on a helicopter with that girl you knew. Lucia thinks he took something important."

"We'll figure it out. I'm on your team," Nick said, wiping the tear off her cheek and then pulling her tightly to his chest, calming her trembling.

Vera took a few deep breaths, using the same breathing pattern she did for long runs. In in in, out. In in in, out. When the panic attack subsided, Vera wanted to find her mother too.

They walked toward the make-shift bunk room, careful not to wake the still-dozing students. How could they sleep through this storm? She left Nick outside Lucia's office, where her mom was sleeping on the same sofa where she'd napped seemingly ages ago.

Vera tapped her hand on Eliza's shoulder. "Mom?" Vera said, shaking her mom awake. "Mom?"

"Oh, Vera, let me sleep. Just five more minutes."

"It's important. Please."

"Okay, okay," Eliza said, stirring and sitting up.

Vera sat beside her, confiding in her. "It's Miquel. He left, possibly with something important. And Lucia's mad at me. I need your help."

"Oh honey. Whatever it is, it's not your fault. I'm sure she's not mad at you."

"You didn't see her face, Mom."

"We will figure this out. No one knows her like I do. And if I know anything, I know she loves you."

"It didn't look like it. And if she loved me, then why did she leave me?" Vera asked, confused.

"She didn't leave you," Eliza confessed. "I took you. I'm so sorry, Vera."

"What do you mean, Mom? You lied to me about being my mom? And then you stole me?"

"It wasn't like that. I promise. Lucia couldn't keep you, but I didn't want you to grow up in some Catholic orphanage in Spain. So, we decided I would raise you in Barcelona while she and Miquel worked."

"What happened? Why didn't you?"

"They were both so busy. They were almost always gone. I couldn't raise you by myself in that run-down flat. I reached my breaking point. I needed help and felt totally alone. That's why we went back to Nana and Pops. So, I wouldn't lose my mind. And so you could have the childhood you deserved."

"Who would let you fly with a baby that wasn't yours?"

"My name is on your birth certificate."

Vera was speechless, unsure of what to believe. Of what was real. Vera had so many questions, but figured there would be time later for them. So, this was what being an adult was like? Facing difficult choices. Trying to survive. After everything she'd been through, she now mourned her shattered illusions of family. Of childhood. Of happiness.

"Let's go see if we can help Lucia, if you're up for it?"

Vera nodded, and they left Lucia's office.

"Nick?" Vera asked. "Where do you think Lucia is?"

Nick took her by the hand, fingers interlaced, and guided her toward the stairs.

Eliza stopped to quickly grab a cup of coffee before following Nick and Vera to go find Lucia.

CHAPTER 71
ELIZA

As they headed towards the vault to find Lucia, Eliza wasn't sure how Vera took the news. At least now, there were no more secrets. The weight of Vera's reaction, whatever it may be, was much lighter than carrying the burden of the past single-handedly.

Lucia looked more helpless than Eliza had ever seen her, spiraling and darting from one part of the vault to another.

"Lucia," Nick said. "I am so, so sorry. I don't know how he got the code. The vault was locked when I left, but I probably didn't cover the key pad enough. I'm not used to having someone without clearance with me when I lock it. I entered it the way I always do, out of habit. I am so sorry, Lucia."

"It's not your fault," Lucia said, but Eliza didn't believe that she meant it.

Eliza went up to her and put hands on her shoulder, grounding her. "Lucia. Let me help."

"What can you do?" Lucia asked.

"Please? You don't have to do this alone."

"We need to figure out what he took. Nothing's missing from the galleries, but… something's not right. The vault… So many variables with things moving in and out, loans to other places and exhibits on rotation."

"Let's check the catalog," Nick suggested, grabbing the backup binder used to track such things.

"I know my Dalí, remember? I was the one who introduced you to him in the first place." Eliza's love of Dalí—not Lucia's—led them to take the train from Barcelona to Figueres all those years ago to see his art in person and explore his stomping grounds. "Let me help."

And yet, had Lucia not convinced Eliza to cut class and go to Figueres, Lucia would not have fallen in love with Dalí or chosen this career. She definitely would not have hunkered down in the museum, much like Gala must have hunkered down in her castle. Unlike Gala, where Dalí would need an invitation from her to visit, Miquel just came and went as he pleased, uninvited. In any event, Eliza knew Dalí's works and could help assess what was there and what might be missing.

"We need to check every piece that should be here against what actually is. We need to know what he took," Lucia said, "If he took anything."

"I can't believe this is happening all over again," Eliza said. "What a jerk."

"Could we not just check for the small ones? The dimensions are in the catalog. Based on what I saw it couldn't have been bigger than a foot and a half in any direction." Vera suggested. Eliza was proud of her daughter's critical thinking skills.

"But what if we miss something?" Lucia asked.

If they approached it as a finite set problem, like Spades, they would know for sure what was there, and what was missing. But if, instead, they worked with a subset of works of art, like in Setback or Pitch, there were more variables, increasing the likelihood something could be missed.

At the end of the day, Eliza preferred Setback and Lucia preferred Spades. They divided and conquered: Eliza and Nick tried to narrow in on what might be missing, based on size and relative value, prioritizing locating the smallest and most expensive pieces first, while Lucia and Vera started from the top of the list, making sure everything was there.

It took them most of the rest of the storm to carefully find and document each piece, making sure everything was accounted for. Even then, after hours of work, unwrapping and rewrapping, moving and storing, they could not figure out what was missing. But something must be. They all knew it.

CHAPTER 72
LUCIA

Morning was likely breaking, but since the eye had passed, the storm was raging once again. From that second-floor balcony, the same place Lucia had stood during *The Lazarus Project* gala, the view had completely transformed. How many days ago had that been? Now, water completely surrounded the building, with a torrent of waves sloshing ever-higher, almost reaching her second-floor perch. Even though she knew the building was solid, she found herself rocking back and forth, mesmerized by wind and water. She fancied herself captain of this now-sinking ship.

Lucia needed to think. Something still didn't add up. Food would help. She climbed the double helix towards where the food had been set out, glad the students were still sleeping.

The tapas spread was still out from the night before. Lucia was surprised Eliza hadn't cleaned it up. She remembered that they never went to bed with dishes in the sink, without wiping down the counter. She picked at what seemed safer to eat, preserved meats, dried fruit, finding her energy slowly returning.

Lucia realized despite the time she had spent with her daughter during this storm, she'd been laser-focused on her career and Dalí's collection. What had she learned about Vera?

As Eliza joined her, taking a piece of Jamon, Lucia asked, "What are we missing?"

"What if we're asking the wrong question?" Vera asked.

"What do you mean?"

"Didn't he forge my birth certificate?"

Eliza and Lucia looked at each other and then back at Vera.

"What if it's not 'What are we missing?' but instead 'What did he replace?'" Her eyes lit up, electrified.

Eliza added on. "He's an artist. And a magician. A master of both bait and switch and sleight of hand. What if he didn't just take some small, valuable piece of artwork, but replaced it with a replica of his own creation?"

"I know it sounds crazy, but..." Vera trailed off.

"But what if you're right?" Lucia asked. "Then we're not looking for missing small, valuable works. We're looking for replicas of those pieces that have replaced the original," Lucia added. "He's cocky enough to think his works will pass as Dalí's, undetected."

"But how do we even begin to do this? How can we check every small work for its authenticity?" Eliza asked.

"We're not experts, but we have to try," Nick agreed. He then lost the color from his face, braced himself on a chair, and sat back down. "The miniatures..."

"What about them?" Lucia asked.

"He asked about them specifically. He knew they were here, even if they weren't on display," Nick said. "I didn't think much of it, just him trying to show his interest in Dalí. But those would be the easiest to take, and they're the ones we were least familiar with."

"But they already shipped, right?"

Nick's face fell. He shook his head. "Something came up."

"What are you talking about?" Lucia asked.

"The director asked me to do something..." Nick trailed off.

It wasn't like him to be this dodgy. "To do what?"

"After Stu's interview, he wanted me to show him around St. Pete and then take him to the airport."

"Stu? From the MOMA?" Lucia didn't know if she was more upset about Nick not shipping the artwork or not telling her about Stu. Now it all made sense. That's who she'd seen Nick and Harold with.

But what should she do? They could, and did, unwrap all of the miniatures again, trying to determine which one—or which ones—might have been swapped out, but it was almost impossible to tell. He was that good, and she'd given him the supplies to make the replicas.

More than that, these were works she didn't know as well as the ones the museum owned. Should she send them all back to the museums and private owners? Knowing she was possibly sending back a fake to someone who lent them the original? Or should she come clean to the board, sharing her suspicions that one or more of the borrowed miniatures may have been forged and replaced? By someone she trusted and let into the museum during the hurricane? That in order to do proper damage control, they would have to foot the bill to verify the authenticity of all of the miniatures in addition to numerous other small works?

And even if they did identify the missing artwork what then? Miquel, long gone. The art, sold on the black market. A Dalí with questionable authenticity was hardly new. After signing thousands of blank pages in his final years of life, the market was flooded with fakes.

But the time, cost, and public fall-out verifying the authenticity of all pieces would cost her everything. To go to the board, she would have to admit her own shortcomings, her own failure. And they were already facing a media nightmare, at least if any single St. Pete resident who was turned away from an overcrowded shelter or was in walking distance to the Dalítorium, died. To add this on would be career suicide.

"We don't know if he took anything. We can't prove it, not easily. We don't have video footage, or even character witnesses to say they saw him taking the art or which art," Lucia said.

"But I saw him," Vera said. "He had something in his bag."

"It could have been any number of things, including food or supplies or what he painted at your party," Lucia reasoned.

"But what if they ask me?"

"Tell them you're just out of surgery and still on pain meds." Not to mention Vera could have a grudge against her absent father. Lucia could bring that up if she needed to, but she hoped it wouldn't come to that.

Lucia made a decision. "We're going to stay here until the storm passes, and then, we are going to make the Dalítorium the leader in the restoration and revitalization of St. Pete. We are going to lead the rebuilding charge. And we are going to send the miniatures back to their homes."

"We can't just send back possibly forged works," Nick protested.

"Hello?" a voice came from the office area. The students must be waking up.

"You three take care of them. I'll figure the miniature part out," Lucia said. Yes, one or more of them may be Miquel's work, but figuring it out would cost too much. If she couldn't tell, and they had no actual evidence, what other choice did she have?

CHAPTER 73

In the end, their suspicions were right. Miquel had replaced at least three of the original miniatures. One private collector and two separate museums claimed they had sent the Dalí an original, but were returned a fake. They hired lawyers who were suing the Dalítorium, for both the return of the original and additional money for the damages it had cost those entities. Unfortunately for Lucia, they didn't have the originals or any idea where they might be. Miquel was long gone, possibly using another alias, and they didn't have a way to find him. They also didn't know how many other paintings he had taken.

The public hated this press, and attendance began to drop, despite *The Lazarus Project*. What was worse, with the swift change in public sentiment, the town—controlled at least in part by Andre—denied the Dalítorium the right to expand, reneging on their former deal. They claimed that in the aftermath of the Phoenix, rebuilding the city and not expanding a museum was their first priority. Who—except Lucia—could argue?

To Lucia's relief, loss of life had been minimal. Only three deaths were blamed on the hurricane: two from a car accident during the evacuation and one elderly gentleman who'd fallen off a ladder while trying to board up his second-floor windows. Lucia originally got some credit for harboring the students, one of whom was the niece of a board member.

When the board began questioning Lucia about what had happened to the art, however, it was Nick who cracked and shared their collective speculation. Lucia lost her job almost immediately. They first grilled her on everything she knew about Miquel, and everything that happened during the storm. And then, they fired her. Of all she missed most, it was not the art, or the thrill of standing at the helm of her fortress-ship. She missed the ultrasound picture of Vera that she'd forgotten to take with her. It was the only one she had, still hidden in the second-to-last file in the left-hand side of her desk drawer.

Even though Lucia had watched one dream dissipate before her eyes, she had gained something she didn't even know she wanted: a relationship with her biological daughter. After their sequestered inventory of every piece in the Dalítorium's vault, after their numerous card games, both Lucia and Vera knew they had more in common than height and coloring.

The bitter irony, Lucia thought: the epitome of surrealism in its truest form.

PART III: DISSIPATION

ONE YEAR LATER

OCTOBER 14TH

THE ANDRE PARKER COMMUNITY ART SPACE

CHAPTER 74

VERA

"Happy birthday, babe," Nick said as he wrapped his arms around Vera's waist. She loved finally being closer to him—and without supervision—having started at Eckerd College that fall. She'd told Eliza she chose it for the Division II soccer but had decided not to try out after all. Perhaps intramurals in the spring.

He kissed her survivor ribbon tattooed on the back of her neck. A year with no relapse was something worth getting a tattoo for, she'd told Eliza only after Lucia had gone with her to get it done. Thanks to both her moms' reborn friendship and what the tattoo symbolized for Vera, Eliza didn't mind too much.

Lucia texted both Nick and Eliza to wish them good luck. Lucia had left town, working with the technology company that built the Deepfake Dalís, traveling from museum to museum and helping others bring muses and historical figures to life. And Nick had taken the lead reimagining the purpose of the Weymouth building.

"You should get down there. It's about to start," Vera said, watching Nick turn and go. After the fallout from the storm, the mayor resigned. Andre, as interim mayor, redirected all funds tagged for special projects, including the Dalítorium expansion, into rebuilding St. Pete. He would be speaking soon, praising the people of St. Pete for their resilience, hoping it would help in his election next month.

Even though the original purpose of the Weymouth structure shifted significantly, the almost-but-not-quite decimated Wish Tree in the

Avant-Garden, and the fortress itself, still remained. It was no longer the Dalítorium officially. Nothing lasts forever. The structure had been repurposed as a community art space, with Dalí's works taking a much smaller role. After the college students spread the word about viewing the Dalí collection with flashlights, Nick set up a similar exhibit with the remaining Dalís. This scavenger hunt, complete with emergency light conditions, enhanced the surreal experience. The exhibits opening tonight were a memorial to the destruction caused by Hurricane Phoenix. Moving forward, thanks to Andre, the building would serve as a first line of defense for when the next strong storm came.

Vera grasped the cool metal railing and looked out the tessellated triangles toward the glowing streaks of pinks and oranges illuminating the evening sky. Through the windows, she could see people gathering outside with sheets of spray-painted plywood, inflatable palm trees and flamingos, and shopping carts full of toilet paper. She wondered if this is what Nick had in mind when he asked the people of St. Pete to bring their own artifacts of the hurricane to add to the community exhibit. She'd helped him set out the Sharpies for them to write their own stories of the storm.

Vera had been Nick's sounding board as he envisioned a museum-of-the-people and now she got to see it come to life. The state-of-the-art climate resilient architecture exhibit, where children could build structures and see how they fared against gale-force winds. The space for the community to bring their own artifacts of the storm and share their own stories. The *Book of Wishes*, a curated collection of wristbands from the past decade of visitors. The wreckage from Phoenix, transformed into beautiful sculptures by local artists.

A significant portion of the exhibit was dedicated to the banyans: to the role they'd played for those seeking refuge from hurricanes and cyclones historically; and more recently, in regenerating ecosystems devastated by human choice or natural catastrophe. Vera knew that, of course. She was studying environmental studies at Eckerd, a passion sparked in St. Pete when she first saw that banyan.

When the death count for a typhoon in Vanuatu was much less than predicted, scientists realized people sought shelter in the root infrastructure of the banyans. Not only did the trees provide a strong defense against ordinary objects transformed into deadly projectiles, but the skyroots kept people, even children, from being swept away. Who needed a hurricane-proof structure when Mother Nature had provided one already?

Today, scientists and re-foresters relied heavily on banyans and other fig species when rebuilding ecosystems, planting at least two banyans for every three other trees in areas they wanted to recultivate. St. Pete had partnered with Eckerd's environmental studies program to plant numerous more along the coast. Vera couldn't wait to show Eliza at Family Weekend. Lucia wasn't coming but not because of Vera or Eliza. It was too soon, Lucia had said. Vera understood.

Vera's gaze passed over to the Wishing Tree. One day, its aerial roots would conceal playing children, nurture budding romances, and shelter innocents from ravaging wind and water. The roots sent deep below the surface were water-seekers, navigating around the flotsam and jetsam of modern creation. These trees, Vera thought, like her mothers and like her, were survivors, destinies intertwined.

With that, she descended the double-helix toward the crowd, looking for her roommate.

DISCUSSION QUESTIONS

1. In *Catastrophe Theory*, the main characters each face losing something central to their identity: Vera's soccer, Eliza's role as a mother, and Lucia's career are all in jeopardy. What does defining themselves in one way cost them? When faced with the possibility of losing those things what new opportunities emerge?
2. One major theme in *Catastrophe Theory* is the tension between art and life. This is debated by Andre and Lucia in Chapter 33. How do the characters grapple with these priceless things? Which do you think is more important to preserve? Why?
3. From Hurricane Phoenix to *The Lazarus Project* to Miquel showing up, the idea of rebirth and reinvention appears throughout the novel. Where else do you see this? How does rebirth interact with other literary elements (e.g. plot, theme, characters, setting) in the book?
4. Hurricane Phoenix is a force of nature against which the characters are essentially powerless. How does its arrival parallel other forces which render the characters powerless?
5. Settings, including the banyan trees, the Dalítorium, the Avant Garden, and the labyrinth, play a central role in *Catastrophe Theory.* Find a passage vividly describing one of these settings. What is the significance of this setting? How does the setting parallel the internal and external conflicts the characters face?
6. How does Vera—and her relationship with the other characters—change over the course of the novel? Select three pivotal moments of Vera's. What do these moments reveal about her?

7. Many characters in *Catastrophe Theory* make choices to deceive others. This dishonesty may be intended either to help or hurt. Characters may make these choices for their own physical or emotional safety, to spare someone's feelings, or to carry out a crime. Think about these moments of deception: what motivates these deceptions? How do these moments contribute to the novel overall?

8. Eliza has sacrificed so much to be a perfect mother for Vera, while Lucia has sacrificed so much for her career. "So, neither of them had led a full life." Is Vera more similar to her birth parents (nature) or the mother who raised her (nurture)? What would it mean for Vera to live a 'full life'? What does it mean for anyone to lead a 'full life'?

9. The title *Catastrophe Theory*, based on Rene Thom's theory that a seemingly small shift can trigger something much bigger, disproportionate, is filled with symbolism. How does this title apply to different characters and their personal catastrophes? To St. Petersburg?

10. Eliza reflects that, "She continued to jellyfish through life, letting other people's needs and wants… dictate her actions, life, and choices. What is a life but a sum of our choices, intentional or otherwise? Perhaps, more accurately, a sum of our lack of choices, a sum of choices others have thrust upon us in our moment of indecision?" Do you think this is true? To what extent is it true of the characters in the book?

11. In what ways did the ending offer a sense of satisfaction and closure for the characters? What emotions did you feel when reading the final chapter?

12. Catastrophe Theory asks what it means to leave a legacy. What legacies are the characters in this book leaving? For you, what does it mean to leave a legacy? What do you want your legacy to be?

ACKNOWLEDGMENTS

Thank you to Salvador Dalí and his museums in Figueres and St. Petersburg, Yann Weymouth's delightful design, Mike Shanahan's brilliant banyan book, *Gods, Wasps, and Stranglers* and the Tampa Bay Regional Planning Council for their Project Phoenix.

Thank you to my New York roommates, Ali Ayala, Stephanie Hill, and Cambra Overend, who have been champions of this book since it was just a fledgling idea. To everything that helped me write the first draft for NaNoWriMo in 2019, including Karen Prager's texts, the Pomodoro method, and Counting Crows and Explosions in the Sky albums on repeat.

To my book club, Emily Banks, Erika Dunham, Peggy O'Neill, Lauren Kiely Skardal, Brenna Kehew Skulley, and Christen Snyder, for reading the very first draft (It's come a long way since then, I promise!) and meeting over Zoom to discuss in those early pandemic days.

To my West Hartford Fiction Writer's Club, and especially to my beta readers, Chris Blake, Elizabeth Brown, Mark Derks, Amy Finch, Tara Moore, Andre' Snellings, Paige Witkin, and Zack Vose. To my fellow writing community, including Rhonda Douglas, Molly MacDermot and the Girls Write Now editorial committee, and my 22Debut group.

To my fellow Demon Deacons who made me feel like an insider, from Alyssa Colman's glimpse into publishing, Alison Delaney and Paul Bright's perspectives on the art world, Jane Bianchi and Mary Beth Lowry's marketing advice, Ben Whiting's magician knowledge, Chris Meazell's contract knowledge, and all my theatre professors, especially Sharon Andrews, Brook Davis, Cindy Gendrich, and Leah Roy for their continued support.

To Sydney Shepherd, Glen Phillips, and Bandits on the Run! The muses were speaking to us at the same time, and I'm so grateful to be able to share your "Hurricane" music video! To Kinetic Media for creating a spectacular book trailer. To Shana Sureck for taking fabulous headshots.

To Rosemary and John for taking the kids so I could write, consulting on everything from film crew accuracy to comma placement, and gracing Sunday mornings with donuts and coffee. To Tony and Chris for hosting holidays, sharing books, and always asking for the latest update.

To Emma Irving, Asha Hossain, Amber Griffith, Athen Desautels, and Peggy Moran, *Catastrophe Theory*'s early advocates and midwives. To Ben Tanzer and Marilyn Atlas for helping me strengthen my own story and marketing plan. To Peter and Susan MacLaren for creating a sacred space at West Hill House Bed and Breakfast. To Amy Blue, Julie Cadman, Shawn Samuelson Henry, and Alison McBain, my fellow Phoenixes. To Barb Newman for inspiring us to saddle our own horses but blazing the path first. To Steve Eisner for reimagining debut author development, creating a sacred space and process to nurture new voices through When Words Count.

To Colin Hosten, David LeGere, Christopher Madden, Matthew Winkle, and everyone at Woodhall Press for reinventing publishing for modern times.

This is for my students and fellow teachers, past, present, and future. Thank you to the entire Latimer Lane community for sending me to Pitch Week with blessings and snacks, voting on favorite covers, and even staying after a faculty meeting to let me practice my readings.

For the Lucias, Elizas and Veras in my life.

To Don for his adventurous spirit and love of a good story. To Fred for being my *4-Hour Workweek* accountability partner in the early days of *Catastrophe Theory* when it was still a play. To my dad Fred for getting me a book on *Homeopathic Psychology* so many years ago to help me make my characters more realistic (I bet you can spot the Lycopodium!), reading my book even though he doesn't read fiction, and hosting his family for my practice barn reading. To my twin Amanda for reading the whole book aloud with me, making sure all the medical parts were accurate, and helping me make the romance spicier. To my mom Theresa, thank you for the roots and wings.

And to Drew, for holding down the fort and protecting my sacred writing time, getting me coffee in the morning, trekking to Figueres and all over Barcelona, and being my thought partner any time I asked. Thank you for Spain and everything.

ABOUT THE AUTHOR

Rebecca Lowry Warchut brings characters and stories to life. For almost two decades, she's done this in the classroom and on the stage, and now she does it again in her debut novel *Catastrophe Theory*, inspired by the Dali museums in Florida and Spain. An alumni of Wake Forest University, Teach for America, and Bank Street College of Education, she currently teaches writing and social studies in Simsbury, Connecticut. She nurtures young voices by serving on the 2022 Girls Write Now Anthology Editorial Committee and running a NaNoWriMo Club. Rebecca lives in West Hartford, Connecticut with her husband and two daughters, Lowry and Athena. You can visit Rebecca Lowry Warchut online at rebeccalowrywarchut.com or follow her on TikTok and Instagram at @rebeccalowrywarchut.